Praise for the authors of

A NASCAR Holiday 3

"The writing team of Liz Allison and Wendy Etherington has produced an excellent novel in *No Holding Back.* Between the roar of engines and the cheering crowd, two people discover that nothing should stand in the way when love is the prize."
—*A Romance Review*

"Jackson's trademark ability to weave multiple characters and side stories together makes shocking...truths all the more exciting."
—*Publishers Weekly*

"[Marisa Carroll's] *Forbidden Attraction* is accurate on the race details. These ladies know their racing and seem to know their romance as well."
—*Stock Car Gazette*

"Jean Brashear's unique writing style gifts readers with marvelous love stories filled to the brim with high drama, full-bodied characters and heated sensuality."
—*Romantic Times BOOKreviews*

Liz Allison &
Wendy Etherington

Brenda Jackson
Marisa Carroll
Jean Brashear

A NASCAR Holiday 3

HQN™

ISBN-13: 978-0-373-77337-4
ISBN-10: 0-373-77337-4

A NASCAR HOLIDAY 3

This edition published by arrangement with Harlequin Books S.A.

www.HQNBooks.com

Printed in U.S.A.

CONTENTS

LIZ ALLISON

married into NASCAR in 1989 when the second-generation driver Davey Allison stole her heart. Though Liz's life took a tragic turn in 1993 when Davey was killed in a helicopter accident at the Talladega Superspeedway, she has continued to share her love and passion for racing by hosting numerous TV and radio shows, as well as authoring seven books about America's fastest-growing sport. Liz's book *The Girl's Guide to NASCAR* helped draw more attention to the ever-growing female fan base of the sport, which is now nearly 45% of NASCAR's fan base. Liz lives in Nashville with her husband, Ryan, and three children, Robbie, Krista and Bella.

WENDY ETHERINGTON

was born and raised in the deep South—and she has the fried chicken recipes and NASCAR ticket stubs to prove it. She has nearly twenty published novels to her credit and has been a finalist for many awards—including the Booksellers' Best Award and several *Romantic Times BOOKreviews* awards. In 2006, she was honored by Georgia Romance Writers as the winner of the Maggie Award. She writes full-time (when she's not watching races) from her home in South Carolina, where she lives with her husband and two daughters.

HAVE A BEACHY LITTLE CHRISTMAS

Liz Allison and Wendy Etherington

This story is dedicated to the Our Kids Center, a real-life Hope House, where help, hope and healing begin for the most vulnerable children in Tennessee.

CHAPTER ONE

THE DOORS TO THE EDEN Resort opened with a quiet whoosh as Jesse Harwood stepped into luxury.

Even after all the things he'd seen and done over the years with McMillan Motorsports, he wasn't prepared for the staggering extravagance of the lobby. The ultrahigh ceilings were painted with pastel beach scenes and trimmed in gold. Giant, leafy palms speared out of decorative urns. Vases boasting wildly colorful tropical flowers rested on thick glass tables, sitting on tiled floors of soft coral. And, because it was nearly Christmas, potted poinsettias, wreaths and a tree that had to be twenty-five feet decorated the room, giving it a holiday feel—even if it was seventy-five degrees outside.

He was equally unprepared for the stunning, curvy blonde standing, right where she belonged, in the middle of the opulence.

"Oh, good," Tiffany McMillan said, striding briskly—but still somehow sensually—toward them. "You're finally here."

But he didn't belong here. And moments like now baffled him as to just how he'd managed to drag himself from outcast to respectable, responsible engineer.

"Lady Tiffany," Greg Foster, the crew chief of the No. 56 team they all serviced, stepped forward and lightly brushed her cheek with his lips.

Jesse said nothing. Former outcasts didn't talk much around the boss's silver-spoon-fed daughter.

But then none of the other guys did more than nod at Tiffany. She was the kind of woman who turned confident men speechless and made the rest fight the urge to fall at her feet.

She smiled warmly at Greg, a teasing light in her sea-blue eyes, her long, straight, platinum-blond hair flowing down her back. "I've told you guys a dozen times not to call me that."

She wasn't simply beautiful and rich. She was nice. And seemed not to notice that every man in the room was staring at her with longing, while most of the women watched with envy.

Of course it hadn't always been that way. Well, the money and staring had always been there, but the niceness had come along more recently. Back in high school—the private and privileged school he'd attended only due to a financial scholarship—she'd been the stuck-up head cheerleader, homecoming queen and prom queen who'd dated the perfect, Ken-doll quarterback, while Jesse was the motorcycle-riding rebel pariah in torn, hand-me-down jeans.

As much as it was a cliché, that was their past.

Ten years later, the present was entirely different. Ken the Quarterback had gotten some other girl pregnant in college, gotten tackled too hard his junior year and lost his scholarship, and now supported their five kids with the liquor store they owned, though the rumor was he drank more than he sold.

And while Jesse had gotten his degree in mechanical engineering, thanks to a full scholarship, Tiffany had moved on to another loser guy, then another, and yet another. The last disastrous relationship had ended with Mr. McMillan driving down to the local police department to pick up the family silver that the guy had lifted on his most recent visit to the McMillan lakeside mansion.

Tiffany, after taking the lumps of her misfortune, had apparently come to the conclusion that so many wise people had before her—money doesn't buy happiness.

Tiffany Phase Two was nice. Everyone from the janitor at the shop to the CEO of Parsons Motor Oil, whose company sponsored their team, earned a sweet, welcoming smile from the boss's daughter. She knew the names of everyone's spouses, kids and mothers.

For Jesse, though, she still managed to reserve a special, hard place in her heart.

"You need to address her as *Your Highness,* Greg." Jesse smirked at her. "She is Daddy's Little Princess, after all."

Her gaze flicked to him, her eyes icing over.

Since he'd earned the hard place, he took no offense and instead smiled back sweetly.

Darrell, one of his oldest friends and a fellow engineer on the team, nudged him. "Cut it out," he whispered.

He wished he could, but he resented her being the one weakness in his life he hadn't overcome, cut out or simply ignored. Still, it wasn't her fault he'd fallen head over heels for her in high school and had never managed to completely let go of those feelings.

She walked—really more like *slinked*—toward him, her green-and-white halter-top sundress hugging that amazing body, her smile firmly in place, though the steely gleam in her eyes remained. She drew her pink-painted fingernail down the center of his chest. "I'm especially glad to see you, Jesse Harwood," she said in a sweet-as-sugar, exaggerated Southern drawl.

Though all the spit had dried in his mouth, he cocked his head insolently. "Is that so?"

She licked her lips, painted the same glossy shade as her nails. "Oh, yeah."

Every molecule in his body had stopped moving. Heat and longing spread through him like a fever.

How many times had he fantasized about her walking up to him one day, throwing herself into his arms, declaring she'd had a wild crush on him for years, and she just couldn't hold back her feelings any longer?

While he was tempted to punch himself to see if he was dreaming, she pulled out a stack of paper and envelopes from the designer briefcase slung over her shoulder. "For you," she said, handing him a sheet and an envelope.

As she turned away, handing the same items to the rest of the assembled group of shop employees and pit crew, it took him several moments to realize she'd dismissed him. The haze of desire began to lift. He glanced down at the paper. *Schedule of Obligations.*

What the hell was this?

As if she'd heard his thoughts, Tiffany faced the group and said, "My father and I are pleased you've all come to enjoy the weekend at the Eden Resort here on the beautiful Grand Bahama Island." She waved her hand to encompass the opulent lobby around them.

Like a damn spokesmodel, Jesse thought bad-temperedly.

"Together, McMillan Motor and Parsons Motor Oil," she went on, "are funding your entire trip. Our only request is that you fulfill the obligations to Hope House, the shelter for abused women and their children in the Charlotte area, which our company and Parson's have selected as our holiday charity project.

"There are two main events. The bachelor auction and fashion show will be held tonight by the pool, then the team dinner tomorrow night. Most of you will simply have to volunteer a bit of time tonight as service staff." She turned toward Greg. "Though you and Danny will be the stars of our bachelor auction."

Obviously unsurprised, Greg grinned. "Looking forward to it."

Jesse exchanged a relieved look with Darrell. At least they didn't have to strut around onstage like cattle. Their obligations were the same—assisting the resort's bartenders at the auction fund-raiser. Greg and their driver, Danny Walker, could have the embarrassing, high-profile jobs all to themselves.

"Where *is* Danny?" Greg asked.

"He arrived a few hours ago," Tiffany said.

As one of the top drivers in the NASCAR Sprint Cup Series, Danny, like many drivers, could afford his own jet for traveling. Not that the rest of them had suffered on their journey. The McMillan Motorsports plane was lush and fast. Jesse still couldn't help shaking his head in amazement every time he stepped on board.

"He was by the pool last time I saw him," Tiffany continued. "Your rooms are all ready, and your luggage is being transported to them now. Inside the envelope are your room key, which also serves as your resort charge card, a map of the resort and information about Hope House. All your purchases will be taken care of with the exception of souvenirs. The concierge desk will be glad to organize any golf or shopping outings. My room number is listed on your schedule, and I can be reached by walkie-talkie at any time during the weekend if you just ask a member of the resort staff to contact me. Any questions?"

"When does the bar open?" one guy asked.

Tiffany glanced at her diamond-encrusted watch. "It opened ten minutes ago. I hear the drink of the day is Santa's Special Bahamian Delight. It packs quite a punch, so be careful. Anybody else?"

Darrell poked Jesse with his elbow, a clear warning to keep silent.

Since Jesse's only question was wondering what color—and how small—her bikini was, he decided to keep that to himself.

"Thanks for coming," Tiffany said cheerfully when no one else spoke up. "Enjoy your weekend."

The group broke apart, couples heading off together, while the single guys remained in a gathered knot. Unfortunately, this gathering of employees from McMillan didn't have any single women, except for Tiffany—and she was off-limits.

Since the business had grown so much over the past several years, the trips had been broken into two groups. The office staff, flight crews, maintenance, research and development and interns had come down the beginning of the week. Now, for the weekend, they had the shop employees, pit crew and hauler drivers.

The beach, though, was sure to provide plenty of curvy distraction for Jesse and his buddies.

As he and Darrell started to head toward their rooms, he overheard Tiffany say to Greg, "Please make sure Danny doesn't overindulge today and gets to the auction on time."

He bowed. "Your wish is my command, Lady McMillan."

She smiled slightly, then caught Jesse's gaze and all but snarled. With one last, fulminating look at him, she turned and walked away.

"Why are you always such a jerk to her?" Greg wanted to know.

Shoulders hunched, Jesse jammed his hands in the pockets of his jeans. "Damned if I know."

"He's got a thing for her," Darrell said.

"I do *not*." The fact that he'd once worn a black leather jacket to school, while Darrell had cherished his pocket protector, but they'd become like brothers in the years since, was one of the great mysteries of growing up. "She's too prissy for me."

"Prissy?" Greg echoed. "You're crazy, man. She's smokin' hot."

"And way out of our league," Darrell added with a sigh.

And always will be, Jesse thought, watching her go with no small pang of regret.

Jesse Harwood. What a jerk.

Why he had to be a dangerously gorgeous, rebellious, successful and smart-as-the-devil jerk was a topic she and God needed to have a serious discussion about.

Even though her temper was bubbling, Tiffany forced herself to walk down the hotel hallway as calmly as if she were attending a board meeting in a downtown Charlotte high-rise office building.

No telling what sort of debauchery he and his buddies would get into this weekend.

Debauchery *she* certainly wouldn't be invited to.

Nobody ever invited the boss's daughter, whose sole job was running the family charitable foundation, which, like everything else in her life, had been handed over without request.

No mother. A father who ignored her. But plenty of cash and a trust fund to weep glorious tears over.

Poor, pitiful Tiffany.

She turned her nose up in the air. Didn't everyone whisper behind her back that was her best, if expected, pose?

Why should she care what everyone thought of her? As long as Jesse and his gang didn't ruin her auction, she didn't care what they did. Though it did annoy her that Jesse didn't seem to notice her like other men did.

But then who knew what thoughts lurked behind his dark brown eyes? Who knew how many women had brushed their fingers across the jet black waves that fell over his forehead?

The way she'd always longed to do.

No.

She stopped, watching absently as a group of tourists clad in brightly colored Bermuda shorts walked by her. One wore a red velvet Santa's hat trimmed in white fur.

It was Christmas. She was supposed to feel positive and charitable toward her fellow man.

Still, she wondered why he wasn't a loser, as she continued down the hall. If the world were spinning on its axis in the *correct* direction, Jesse Harwood would have been a major loser.

But he wasn't.

It was long past time she came to terms with that reality, she told herself, even as her mind drifted into the past. Her junior year in high school, her quarterback boyfriend had given her a gorgeous diamond bracelet that had turned her wrist green a couple of months later. Ultra-Nerd Darrell had given her a sappy poem written on notebook paper. Motorcycle rebel and charity case Jesse had either ignored her or said something cutting and sarcastic. Now Jesse and Darrell were successful engineers and devoted members of a first-class race team.

"Girl, you really ought to bottle that judge of character and sell it," she muttered as she rounded the corner and headed toward the activities director's office.

Though, unlike sweet Darrell, she was sure Jesse was trouble anyway. And she was done with men. They were *all* trouble. Cheating, lying, stealing. Trouble.

Jesse's character, their past and his lack of attention were the last things she needed to worry about. She had a fund-raiser to plan. She'd been on the island for nearly two weeks, meeting with the hotel manager and his staff, seeing to every detail of the parties and events held earlier in the week.

To see that this weekend went off as planned, she needed to meet with the food and beverage manager to go over the final details about the buffet and the untrained, volunteer assistant bartenders she was foisting upon the woman. Tiffany also had to consult with security, guest services and accounting.

After entering the reception area guarding the staff offices, she waved and walked by the receptionist, then moved down the hall, knocking on the activities director's office door.

"Come in," Sarah Lester called. "Oh, Tiffany, it's you," she added with a smile. "I just printed out today's revised schedule of events."

As Tiffany sat in the chair in front of Sarah's desk, she accepted the printout and glanced at it. "The pink poinsettias came," she said, and some of the knots in her stomach loosened.

Sarah nodded. "Receiving got them in less than an hour ago."

"You're a miracle worker."

"I also have a friend who works in shipping at the airport."

The last Christmas her mother had been alive, she'd let Tiffany decorate the fireplace. Since she'd only been three, she'd chosen pink, white and silver, after she and her mother had seen a beautiful collection of pink poinsettias at the florist's. It was the earliest memory Tiffany had.

Her mother, pale and fragile, had smiled at the flowers as she sat by the fire, the silver tinsel lighting her face.

Since then Christmas had not been the same. After his wife's death, her father retreated into work, while Tiffany suffered in grief and anger alone. She'd been surrounded by nannies, gifts and pretty clothes. Later, she had cars, designer clothes, credit cards and boys who complimented her. Now, she had a luxury lakeside condo, her work at the McMillan Foundation, a few true friends.

And still she was alone.

"...so, we need to— Are you okay?"

Tiffany jerked her attention back to Sarah. She swallowed. "Fine. Sorry. I was visualizing."

Sarah's warm brown eyes sparkled. "I've got the crews building the runway now. Wait till you see your fantasy in real life."

For some ridiculous reason, Jesse Harwood, shirtless, sandy and tanned flashed through her mind.

And lingered.

Scowling, she snapped the paper in her hands and forced herself to study the details. "Are you sure we don't need two chocolate fountains?"

"No. The one we have is big and a crowd around it is a good thing. Plus, being at the beach, there'll be a bunch of people who are so into their bodies they'll stand around drinking mineral water and eating celery all night."

"Good point." She worked out and worried about excess inches like everybody else, but giving up chocolate? *Not* an option. "But my guys are going to want meat and beer."

"We have that. Page two."

Tiffany saw the updated list of proteins, from lobster to mini cheeseburgers to smoked Italian sausage, and figured Sarah had that aspect well under control.

Truthfully, Sarah had everything well under control. They'd worked closely together to plan these retreats for the past six months, and Tiffany knew she could count on her to come through with a terrific event.

At a knock on the door, Tiffany turned to see Paula, the supervisor of the women's shelter the fund-raiser was going to benefit. "Am I interrupting?"

"No." Sarah stood. "Come in. We were just going over some final details about tonight."

Paula slipped inside, and they all discussed the mechanics of catering for the party, then moved on to the orchestration of the bachelor auction.

"I've had some second thoughts about the auction," Tiffany said to Paula.

A couple of the women and their kids from the shelter were enjoying a complimentary trip to the resort as well, though their identities had been kept a secret to prevent them from feeling embarrassed or intimidated.

Island fun? Romance? Auctioned dating? To benefit women who've been victims of abuse.

It's one of your more brilliant moments, Tiff.

"Are you sure your residents won't be insulted by the presentation?" Tiffany bit her lip. "It's just for fun, of course, but…well, silly, considering all they've been through."

"On the contrary," Paula said, her speech proper and calm, which was probably why she had the job she did. "I think it's wonderful for them to see that relationships and dating can be fun—and silly. Their lives have been about anger and despair. It's good for them to realize that not all men are interested in controlling and harming them."

Tiffany felt her face turn red. "I know they have bigger concerns than sunscreen, but I didn't think through the concept of the cute bachelor auction thing."

Paula inclined her head. "They *certainly* have bigger concerns than sunscreen or cute bachelors. But normality is important. They need to realize violence *isn't* normal."

"Okay." Tiffany smiled. The women of the shelter and the race team—even she—could certainly use some fun. "So, we'll have fun."

And she would make sure the auction was a success, getting her noticed by the one man whose attention and approval she wanted above all others. Her father.

As a secondary benefit, she'd get to give orders to Jesse Harwood, and there wasn't one dang thing he could do about it.

CHAPTER TWO

THE WARM SUN STREAMING down from the sky as he lounged in a poolside chair with a plastic beer bottle in his hand, Jesse watched a trio of bikini-clad blondes stroll in front of him.

The off-season was nothing short of *amazing*.

Greg propped himself up on his elbows to watch the girls walk by. "I hear Tiffany is wearing a Santa's elf costume to this deal tonight." He waggled his eyebrows suggestively. "Should be a sight to get us through the long, cold winter."

Reminders of that particular blonde, the one Jesse *wasn't* supposed to think about, should have annoyed him, but he was too relaxed and lazy to worry about rules and consequences.

It was hard to believe he'd left Charlotte that morning under a cold, drizzling sky, and a few hours later he was lounging in the sun, staring at the Caribbean Sea.

Wayne McMillan had more than money…he had style.

"How'd you find out about the costume?" Darrell asked.

"The activities director—who's pretty hot herself—told me." The crew chief grinned. "They're both wearing them. You know, I sort of thought this bachelor auction thing was going to be a drag, but not anymore."

Leaning back, Greg sipped from his bright pink plastic cup containing the special of the day, Santa's Special Bahamian Delight, made with a little fruit juice and a whole lot of rum.

Jesse had tried one, but found it tooth-achingly sweet, so he'd stuck with beer. The other guys, though, had been sucking them down pretty steadily all afternoon. He wasn't sure if any of them would be able to walk later, if they even managed to stand, but then the weekend was supposed to be a reward for their hard work all season.

Breaks at the shop involved a soda and sandwich in the kitchen. Breaks at the track were practically nonexistent. They ran nonstop from Daytona to Homestead.

Still, Jesse couldn't follow in his teammates' hedonism. He never let himself go completely. He didn't offer his trust that freely.

More than likely he'd always hold back on some level, since there was part of him still amazed that he was even here, that he'd earned his place as a vital member of the engineering crew of a big-time NASCAR Sprint Cup Series racing team.

People who'd known him as a kid would have said he was destined to never rise above chief fryer at the local fast food joint.

Or a nice, long stint in jail.

But they'd only judged him on his appearance. They hadn't realized he was much smarted than he looked.

"I'm surprised *you* didn't know all the details, Jess," Greg said, nudging his shoulder.

"Why would I?"

Greg and Darrell exchanged a look, then Darrell shook his head. "Because Tiffany has a thing for you," Greg said, his eyes bright with humor. "Doesn't she?"

Jesse fought to remind his suddenly racing heart that he was the only reasonably sober person around him. "No way."

Was there a way?

Greg shrugged. "She seemed pretty interested in you earlier, when we got to the hotel."

Jesse tried not to relive—for probably the twentieth time—the feel of Tiffany's elegant hand on his chest as she'd handed him his schedule. She'd been mocking him, not flirting with him, though the guys seemed to have missed that important detail. "Trust me," he said, and with a good amount of lingering resentment, "I don't have a pedigree to suit her."

"After the boss wound up prosecuting the last boyfriend, I'd think even you'd be a step up," one of the other guys said.

Jesse squashed the hope that the envious smiles around him sparked. How many years had he wanted her? How many years had he gone ignored, unnoticed or downright dismissed?

"You guys are crazy." He sipped his beer and directed his attention to the rippling turquoise waves to their left. The ones that matched the color of Tiffany's eyes to perfection. "And drunk."

So why did a kernel of hope linger?

But then it was the season for hopes, wishes and dreams. Was it any wonder he looked at the bright light emanating from Tiffany McMillan and longed for something beyond what he had, something he might never have, even though the long odds didn't lessen his desire.

As a kid, he'd wanted a few impractical things—a jet being at the top—but mostly regular stuff. A red bike, the latest videogame console, jeans without worn knees…his parents not to struggle to support them. As a man, he wanted a couple of days off, peace on earth, a smile from Tiffany—any or all of those would do.

Maybe a NASCAR Sprint Cup Series Championship…

"Don't look now…well, actually you really *do*

need to look now," Darrell said, inclining his head toward the other side of the pool.

Beyond the waterfall and slide full of excited kids, as if they'd conjured her by simply talking about her, Tiffany walked purposefully toward them.

Still wearing her green-and-white sundress and high-heeled sandals, she managed, as always, to look sexy and ethereal at the same time. Was she aware that every man within two miles had stopped what he was doing to stare at her? If so, did she care?

Amused by himself and the rest of his gender, he sat up, hoping like crazy to find his hard-won cool.

"Having fun, guys?" she asked, then smiled brightly.

Since Jesse wasn't usually the first one—or sometimes even the last one—to speak, he said nothing. But when the silence lingered, he glanced at his friends and colleagues, noting their vacant, vaguely lustful expressions, and was grateful for his dark sunglasses as he managed to find his voice. "We're great." He stood and extended his hand to his lounge chair. "Wanna join us?"

Her eyes registered brief surprise, then she clutched her clipboard to her chest. "Uh, no…thanks. I've got—" she gestured vaguely toward the hotel "—work."

"It's Christmas. Don't you deserve a break?"

She angled her head. No doubt she was confused

about why he wasn't teasing, bugging or outright annoying her.

He was a little confused himself. Over the years, they'd somehow fallen into the rhythm of him aggravating her before she could insult him. He blamed the change on that damned and blessed Christmas spirit. It made some men kinder. And made fools out of even more.

"Come on," he said, and actually tried out a charming smile. "We'll order you a Santa's Special Bahamian Delight." He widened his grin. "The guys love 'em."

She glanced at the guys, who encouragingly raised their plastic pink glasses. A paper Santa wearing martini-glass-decorated boxers clung to the neon-green straws.

Grown men drinking that stuff. It was embarrassing.

But if the silliness would get Tiffany to stay...

"Thanks." She backed up. "But I really have things to do."

Surprised by her apprehension, but driven by the strong urge to persuade her not to leave, he reached out and grabbed her hand. "Stay."

She met his gaze for a moment—he could have sworn he saw longing—but then she blinked and the emotion was gone. She pulled her hand back. "You'd have more fun..." She turned away. "I've got to go," she said, as she walked back the way she'd come.

Jesse glanced at the guys. Darrell shrugged. Greg waved his hands, encouraging him to go after her.

Setting his beer on the table by his chair, Jesse followed her. He caught up to her near the waterslide stairs. He dodged a trio of boys bumping each other in their efforts to get in line first, then laid his hand on Tiffany's shoulder. "Why don't you—"

"Look," she said, spinning and jerking her shoulder from his grasp, "you guys don't really want me around. It's fine. Boss's daughter. *I get it.* I don't need your pity invitation."

The fact that the fire in her eyes turned him on was probably something he should be embarrassed by.

Or at least worried about.

He held up his hands. "Damn, girl, you're prickly. Calm down. We offered you a drink and a chair. We were trying to be *nice.*"

"Since when are you nice to *me?*" she asked, her blue-green eyes blazing.

So maybe he deserved that. Their past—and his defensiveness over it all—had drained him of the charm he would normally show to a woman he was attracted to.

And was he really going to let things that happened in high school, nearly a decade ago, influence him? He could at least be decent, if not charming.

Sighing, he crossed his arms over his chest. "Since now."

"Why?" she asked, looking suspicious.

"Because high school's been over a long time."

"And you've decided to stop being a jerk?"

"I—" He wanted to remind her that if he'd been a jerk it was only because she'd been a snob, and she'd been mean to him first, so—

He forced himself to halt his petty, juvenile thoughts. It was time to let them go. "Yeah," he said finally. "I'm done being a jerk. It's, well…it's Christmas. Time for peace on Earth and all that jazz."

A hint of a smile hovered on her lips. "Is it really?"

"Come have a drink with us."

"Well, I—"

The walkie-talkie clipped to her board crackled. "Tiffany? It's Sarah."

"Sorry." She punched a button on the side of the walkie-talkie. "I'm here."

"We have some questions about the runway. Could you stop by ASAP?"

"Sure. Be right there." She glanced at Jesse. "I have to go. Duty calls."

"Can't the hotel handle those details?"

"It's my event, my responsibility." She smiled and moved off, though after a few steps, she turned back. "Maybe we'll have that drink after the auction."

Jesse watched her walk away, and not only for the pleasure of seeing her hips sway and to think about the possibility of seeing her later.

She'd surprised him.

He knew she worked for her father's foundation, but he'd always imagined her with a team of assistants fluttering around, bowing and begging to do her bidding. He'd assumed Daddy's Little Princess wouldn't care about responsibilities. She was rich and privileged. What duties could she possibly have?

He frowned. Stereotyping wasn't like him.

Hadn't he always resented people who assumed he was a loser because he didn't have money or a high-class address? He was embarrassed to realize he'd done that to someone else. And all because he was attracted to her but didn't want to be.

As he headed back to the guys, he promised himself he would continue to make peace with Tiffany. First, because he should. And second, because if he got to know her better, maybe he'd see her as a person instead of the Ice Princess.

Would he find more ice? Or was there a blazing heart beating there? One that would make him wonder about the true hope of Christmas.

"MS. MCMILLAN, I...I think we have a problem."

Tiffany turned toward the valet and fought the urge not to panic. The party was due to start in less than an hour. Every detail from catering to logistics to security had been checked off at least three times.

The runway and stage were lit to perfection. The

food and beverage manager and her staff were even now preparing to transport the hors d'oeuvres and set up the champagne and chocolate fountain. The weather was a perfect seventy-two with a light ocean breeze. She was wearing a red velvet elf costume in anticipation of escorting their bachelors, Greg and Danny, through the pink, red and white poinsettia and holly archway, making sure she smiled with the joy of the season, assuring that their guests would feel the lighthearted spirit of the night.

This event would finally get her father's attention. The next few hours would make him proud.

And nobody was going to screw it up.

"I'm sure it's something I can handle," she said, and forced a smile at the valet, whose name tag read *Peter* and who looked like an American college student.

Peter cleared his throat. "Okay. Sure. Yes, ma'am."

"Did we run out of candles for the tables?"

"No. I mean, I don't think so." He glanced around the garden nervously, where the tuxedoed waitstaff were inserting votives inside golden glass hurricanes. "I'm not really in charge of that."

"What *are* you in charge of?" Tiffany asked, calmly, *sweetly,* desperate not to betray her racing heart and determined not to shake Peter senseless.

"The bachelors."

Oh, no. No way.

Tiffany closed her eyes. It couldn't be anything serious. It just couldn't. Greg and Danny worked for her father. He and their sponsor had given them this luxury trip in appreciation of their hard work during the long racing season and he'd—*she'd*—asked for one, tiny, minuscule favor in return. Like most within the NASCAR community, everyone at McMillan Motorsports was incredibly generous with charities that needed their assistance. There was no way—

"It's Greg," Peter continued. "The, ah, crew chief, I think he is…. He's, well…indisposed."

Tiffany forced herself to open her eyes. "*Indisposed?* How? Is he hurt? Sick? Do I need to call the doctor?"

"Well…um, I guess not. Though an IV probably wouldn't be a bad idea."

"Spit it out, Peter. I've got seventy-five percent of the staff running around at my direction, and a major event I've been planning for half the year is due to start in—" she glanced at her watch "—fifty-five minutes."

Peter looked everywhere but at Tiffany's face. "He's, well…passed out in his room. The guys sort of revived him, but he can't really, well…stand."

"Santa's Special Bahamian Delight," Tiffany said slowly, with growing dread.

"Yes, ma'am. I'm afraid so."

She was going to strangle the idiot.

But later.

For now, she had no choice but to deal with the problem and somehow save her event. "Let's go, Peter," she said, marching toward the hotel.

"We warn guests about their potency," Peter said, hovering behind her as they walked inside and headed to the elevators. "But sometimes, with VIPs, the bartenders feel uncomfortable cutting them off."

"It's fine," she said, forcing herself to remember her anger and disappointment wasn't his doing. "The staff isn't responsible for stupid decisions. You've all been amazing."

"You think?" Peter jogged up beside her and sent her a hopeful smile. "If, you know, we get out of this without bloodshed, you think you could get me Danny Walker's autograph?"

"If we get out of this without bloodshed, Peter, I'll get Danny to sign autographs for you, your entire family, plus give you and any ten people you designate race tickets and personal tours of the pit road of your choice next season."

"Does that mean I'll have to keep you from hurting somebody, ma'am?"

"Probably. Stay available."

"I'm here for you, Ms. McMillan," Peter said firmly.

Somehow, amid the worry and disappointment, Tiffany smiled. As they turned the corner onto the hallway where Greg's room was located, she considered the appeal of Peter's dimples and wondered if he'd mind strutting his stuff on stage. "Are you a bachelor?" she asked him.

His face flushed. "Well, sort of. I've got a girlfriend back at school."

"Is she the possessive type?"

"I'm not sure. We've only been dating for two weeks."

"I'd hate to cause trouble for young love," she muttered, almost to herself, her mind racing with options for getting herself out of this mess.

She reached Greg's door, glaring at it and burning with the knowledge of the issues that lay beyond.

"Maybe I should knock," Peter said, boldly stepping forward.

"You do that."

He rapped gently on the door, and Tiffany admired his control. She would certainly have pounded.

The door was opened moments later—by Jesse, of all people. "Ah, Peter," he said, shaking his head, "I told you to go get help, not tattle."

"I'm sorry, sir," Peter said with sincere regret. "You're a valued guest, and I know I'm supposed to give you everything you need."

Tiffany jabbed her index finger into Jesse's chest. "You're not dealing with an impressionable kid now. You're dealing with *me*."

He smirked at her. "Nice outfit. If I play Santa, will you sit on my knee and tell me everything you want?"

She raked him with her gaze from head to toe, noting he looked as tough, leanly muscled and gorgeous as ever in jeans and a white T-shirt. She forced herself to glare at him. "How many Santa's Special Bahamian Delights did *you* have?"

"I had two sips and decided to stick with beer, which is probably why I'm the only one still standing."

"The *only* one!" Her heart jumped as she pushed past him and strode into the suite, finding the rest of her father's race team in varying degrees of drunkenness.

Two guys were slouched on the sofa, dazed and bleary-eyed, trying to work the buttons on the remote control. One of the mechanics was passed out, sitting at the dining room table, his hand still wrapped around a bright pink plastic drink glass. Darrell was trying to get a boxer-clad Greg, who was laughing like a loon, to put on a pair of navy-blue pants.

"Lady Tiffany!" he shouted, and tried to bow, but fell over in a heap on the floor.

One bachelor down…

Literally.

She looked frantically around the room for the other star of the show. "Where's Danny?"

"He's on his way to the party," Jesse said from behind her. "He came in a few minutes ago, took one look at all of them—" he gestured vaguely to the others "—shook his head and headed back out."

At least their driver had some sense. She watched Greg attempt to stumble to his feet. And find his dignity.

She turned to face Jesse. "Are you at all sober?"

"I could probably walk a straight line, but I shouldn't be driving anything faster than a golf cart."

"Fortunately for you—and every inhabitant of this island—driving will not be required." She shifted her attention to Peter. "Take Mr. Harwood back to his room and make sure he gets showered and dressed in something decent, buy something if you have to, then meet me on the left side of the stage." She glanced at her watch. "You've got twenty minutes."

"I'm just a bartender," Jesse said. "What do I have to dress up for?"

"Happily, O Sober One, you've been promoted. You're taking Greg's place in the bachelor auction."

"*Aww,*" Greg said, collapsing into a chair.

"No, I'm not," Jesse said.

"You most certainly are. No one besides the eight of us will ever see an employee of McMillan Motorsports looking like *that,*" she said, pointing at Greg.

"Lady Tiffany," Greg said, laying his hand over his heart, "you wound me with your barbs."

Tiffany and Jesse ignored him.

"You can't be serious," Jesse said to her.

"I'm an *elf,* Jesse Harwood! Of course I'm serious."

"Well, you don't really look—"

She grabbed the front of his T-shirt in her fist. "I'm at a luxury *beach* resort wearing red velvet and white ermine, plus little booties with white balls of cotton hanging off the back. I'm not wearing this costume because I think I look cute or because I can't find my bikini. I'm doing my part to make sure this event goes off flawlessly. *Flawlessly,* do you hear me?"

"Ah...I think so."

"I think you look cute, Lady Tiffany!" Greg shouted.

Releasing Jesse, she had the ridiculous urge to laugh. Maybe someday, when her professional reputation and her father's respect weren't hanging in the balance, she'd manage to find humor in the disaster.

"Please, Jesse," she pleaded, looking up at him. "I need help."

He sighed, then made a perfect courtly bow. "I'm at your service, Lady Tiffany."

As he and Peter left, Tiffany turned her attention to the rest of the guys. "Darrell, are you still with us?"

"I'm not focusing too well." He squinted at her. "Your booties are a little blurry, and I might have to throw up, but I think I can walk."

"Terrific. You're in charge of these guys until you have to report for your bartending duties. Get him—" she pointed at Greg "—back in bed." She pointed at the mechanic at the table. "Put a pillow under his head and leave him there. And try, try really hard, to get those two—" she indicated the guys on the sofa "—to stand. Make them take an aspirin and drink some water, then meet me at the stage in thirty minutes."

Looking suddenly alert, Darrell walked toward her—wobbling only slightly. "Yes, ma'am. You can count on me." He paused, angling his head. "What stage?"

CHAPTER THREE

IT WASN'T NEARLY AS humiliating as he'd anticipated.

Jesse walked off the stage, amid shouts and whistles, surprised and pleased to have raised two thousand dollars by offering himself as a lunch date to an elderly resort guest.

Not to mention he now had Tiffany indebted to him.

He watched her take the stage and launch the bidding for Danny. *Cute* didn't even begin to describe her as an elf. Those lush curves of hers seemed out of place as part of a child's Christmas dreams, but white ermine was fast replacing Tiffany in a bikini as the star of his very adult fantasies.

He headed toward Darrell, who was manning one of several bars scattered around the garden. His buddy handed him a bottle of beer. "You've earned it."

Jesse took a grateful sip. "How's the bartending gig?"

"It's been an adventure, with Tim and Chad as assistants."

Jesse glanced at Tim and Chad, who were trying to put ice in a cocktail glass. Since the grass around them was littered with cubes, he figured it wasn't going well. "At least they'll be spared Tiffany's wrath. I wouldn't want to be Greg tomorrow."

"He'll charm his way back into her good graces."

"Eventually. But I'd like to see her glare at somebody besides me for once," Jesse said.

"She doesn't always glare at you."

"Yeah." He watched her move across the stage. "Only when she notices me."

Three people approached, requesting drinks, so Jesse helped Darrell serve them. When the guests moved off, he turned to Tim and Chad. "Why don't you guys go back to your room? I'll help Darrell."

"Nah. We're meeting Greg in the bar later," Tim said.

"He's awake?"

Chad nodded. "He threw up, so he feels much better. He's nearly sober."

The bar seemed like a bad place for Greg to spend any more time, but now that their duties for the party were complete—and they didn't have to be anywhere until the team dinner the following night—he guessed they could stay toasted till then.

"So go meet him."

"You're sure?" Chad asked, already setting his half-full glass of ice aside.

"Yeah." They weren't doing anybody any good here.

"You guys are coming, right?" Tim asked as he backed away.

Darrell shrugged.

"Later," Jesse said.

Darrell watched them walk away. "We're going to supervise, aren't we?"

"Somebody's got to make sure they don't end up passed out on the beach."

They served several more guests before Darrell brought up the subject of Tiffany again. "You'd get further with her if you wouldn't try to rile her all the time."

"I don't rile her."

"There's no way you've already forgotten that *Your Highness* crack." He opened a bottle of merlot, then served it to a customer. "But then maybe you're annoying her so she *will* notice you?" He shook his head sadly. "That went out in the fourth grade, buddy. Try inviting her to dinner or sending her flowers. Compliment the elf costume instead of laughing at it."

"Surely a guy who still wears a pocket protector isn't giving *me* advice on women."

"I keep my pocket protector in my laptop case," Darrell said with dignity. "I'm just saying—ask her out already. You'd be a hero to the common man."

Jesse snorted. "Like she'd go out with me."

"She would." Darrell smiled. "*If* you'd stop annoying her."

Having his friend play into his hopes was too tempting. With that kind of encouragement, he'd be sure to make an idiot of himself by making a move on the boss's daughter.

Jesse grabbed his beer. "I see McMillan. I need to talk to him. Can you handle this on your own a minute?"

"Sure, but I wouldn't advertise that you have the hots for his little girl."

Jesse shook his head as he walked away. He might be tempted, but he wasn't stupid. The boss had prosecuted her last date.

He weaved his way through the crowded garden area, but as he got closer to McMillan, he realized that his boss was talking to Tiffany. He hung back, not wanting to interrupt.

"Weren't the pink poinsettias beautiful?" he overhead her say, her eyes sparkling with warmth. "Mom would have loved them."

Wayne McMillan looked distracted. "I suppose so."

"I special-ordered the pink ones to remind us of Mom."

"The event went off as planned, darling. The color of the flowers doesn't matter."

Still plainly not giving his daughter his full attention, McMillan waved at a group of men a few feet away, so he didn't see Tiffany's face turn white with shock.

Jesse was caught between the urge to back away or pop his boss on the back of the head.

He must have made some sound or movement, though, because Tiffany suddenly stiffened. "Jesse, I didn't see you standing there."

"Just walked up," he said easily, not wanting her to know he'd overheard. "Nice party." He shook his boss's hand. "I didn't mean to interrupt, sir. I wanted to thank you for the trip. Everybody needed a break, and this is a first-class one."

"You're welcome, Jesse. Got to keep the team sharp and recharged for next season."

"We'll be ready, sir," Jesse said, thanking all the stars and Christmas angels that Tiffany, and not her father, had been the one to discover everyone's over-indulgence that afternoon.

"You did a nice job earlier." McMillan raised his eyebrows. "I never would have figured you for the bachelor-auction type."

Jesse cast a glance at Tiffany. "Your daughter is very persuasive."

"Yes, she is. Excellent job as always, darling," he added to Tiffany, brushing his lips across her cheek. "I'll see you later. I need to talk to the Parsons Oil people." He walked away without a backward glance.

The warmth she'd displayed for her father cooled a bit once she was faced with only Jesse. Undaunted, he raised his beer to her. "Pretty flawless, don't you think?"

"I guess." She glanced over at her father. "Not that *some people* notice."

Confused, Jesse frowned. "Of course he notices. You're Daddy's—"

"If you say *little princess,* I'm pouring that beer over your head."

He'd annoyed her again. And, for once, he hadn't even been trying.

"Peace on Earth and all that jazz?" she reminded him, planting her hands on her hips.

"Yeah, yeah. I remember. You're just so easily riled. Darrell thinks I do it on purpose because I have the hots for you."

Her eyes widened. "Because you...you do *not.*"

Now he was an annoying liar? Was he doomed to always be the loser with her? "Yeah. I really do. I'm not sure I'm happy about it, but...there it is anyway."

"You're attracted to me, but you don't want to be?"

"Pretty much."

She crossed her arms over her chest. "How flattering."

He'd never been much for fancy words, but he was bungling this in a unbelievably huge way. He sipped his beer and desperately searched his normally quick brain for something clever to say. He settled on honesty.

"I just mean we don't seem compatible. We're very different. Different backgrounds. You're designer gowns. I'm jeans and a T-shirt." He glanced at the ground, not knowing what else was different about them, because he'd never taken the time to actually get to know her. "You're organized," he added, having learned that today. "And good at keeping a lot of things going at once. I'm more single-minded."

"You're honest and straightforward," she said quietly, bringing his gaze back to hers, "and I'm quick with a smooth lie."

"Is that your way of telling me I'm making an idiot of myself by admitting my attraction to you?"

"Not at all. It's my way of telling you that you're not alone, though I've been covering my feelings pretty well. I have the hots for you, too."

All the moisture in Jesse's mouth dried up. "Oh. Well. Great."

"It's probably just a physical thing, right?" she asked, seemingly looking for reassurance. "We don't really know each other, after all. It's chemistry."

Jesse managed a nod. "Yeah, probably."

"We could talk about it."

Talk about *chemistry?* He hadn't done that since college. He was actually hoping for a practical demonstration. "We could do that," he said neutrally, not wanting to say anything to screw this up now.

"But later, I—"

The walkie-talkie clipped to her waist beeped, and Jesse would have cheerfully flung it into the ocean if he had a Cy Young–worthy arm.

"Sorry. Tiffany here," she said into the speaker.

"We can't find the gift bags for the auction winners," a voice said.

"They're in my room. Send—" She waved her hand. "Never mind. Everybody's busy. I'll get them."

"Thanks."

"I've got to go," Tiffany said to him, clipping the walkie-talkie back to her waist.

He nearly sighed in relief. He needed to gather his thoughts and come to terms with the fact that his long-held attraction wasn't one-sided. He needed to make his world stop spinning.

And, most importantly, he needed to figure out how to talk her out of talking and into *acting.*

"I need to get back, too," he said, trying to act cool, as if drop-dead gorgeous blondes he'd had a crush on for a decade admitted they had the hots for him all the time. "The team's meeting in the bar later. You said you'd have a drink with us after the auction. You want to join us? We could…talk."

She hesitated a second, then nodded. "Sure. See you there."

As she backed away, the anticipation of getting his hands on her lush curves nearly sent him to his knees in gratitude.

Then he thought of something important.

"Leave that thing—" he pointed to her walkie-talkie "—in your room."

"ARE YOU GOING IN or just hovering in the doorway?"

Tiffany turned her head to see Jesse standing behind her. Close enough to touch.

Even if he hadn't spoken, she would have known he was there. The scent of his cologne. The way the air shifted. The imperceptible *something* that was Jesse—and made all the nerves in her body tingle with awareness.

"Going in," she said, swallowing her nerves.

With the tips of his fingers pressed into the lower part of her back, they made their way across the crowded, oceanfront bar, which, despite the rest of the hotel's elegant appearance, had a tacky, Tiki-themed decor—complete with grass umbrellas, plastic glasses shaped like coconuts, tube-shaped necklaces that lit up in neon colors when snapped and fake-flower leis hanging from fishing lines strung up near the ceiling.

Mardi Gras beads, tropical-style.

Tiffany wondered what had been done by the resort guests to leave—and collect—them.

And the McMillan gang seemed more than willing to participate. Most of the team was assembled, toasting each other and laughing.

Including Greg, who sat at the bar. He pointed at his plastic cup and mouthed the words *soda* and *sorry.*

Tiffany was so edgy from being in the midst of the entire team, she simply nodded. Greg was the least of her concerns. Several people looked surprised and uncomfortable by her appearance. The conversation died, with some turning to their drinks and others clearing their throats and looking at their friends to make the first move.

Tiffany tried to act unaffected by the snubs. "I realize the boss's daughter dropping in on your little get-together is a bit unusual, but it does have its advantages."

She slid onto a bar stool and flipped her hair over her shoulder.

All three bartenders rushed toward her.

"Ms. McMillan," one began in a musical Jamaican accent, "we are so honored to have you in our island paradise. What may we bring you to drink?"

Tiffany sent a knowing look toward the crowd around her, then smiled at the bartender. "What do you recommend?"

"Today's special is the delicious and potent Santa's Special Bahamian Delight."

She started to refuse, then shrugged. *When in Rome…* "Love one."

While the bartenders fought over who would make her drink, Jesse slid onto the stool next to her. "You do have a way with people."

"Sure," she said, knowing she could let her guard down a little with him. "Great piles of money I didn't earn speak volumes."

He slid his hand over hers. "I don't think it's only the money."

"Yeah? Why did you help me tonight?"

"You threatened me."

"I—" She considered whether he was angry about that, but his eyes were lit with humor. "I suppose I did."

"But I would have helped anyway." He leaned close. "Something about a smokin' hot blonde always puts me in an agreeable mood."

"Men are easily pleased," she said, though her belly fluttered in response to his compliment.

"We certainly are."

When they realized they could get their drinks in a split second, the rest of the team warmed up quickly. Several of the new people asked about the beginnings of McMillan Motorsports. Others wanted information about the foundation and the money raised for Hope House.

Still others wanted to know if it was true that her last boyfriend had run off with the family silver.

It was a start at least.

And by the time she was through a quarter of her drink, she'd become philosophical about plastic leis, snubs, daughters and even larcenous boyfriends.

"You guys are all right," she said to Jesse a while later as they sat next to each other at the end of the bar.

"I'm glad we passed the coolness test for you, Miss McMillan."

"That's sarcasm, isn't it?" Bleary-eyed, she studied him. "You're very good at it. I used to mistake it for meanness."

He raised his eyebrows. *"Meanness?"*

"Yeah. Like in high school, when you were too cool to talk to me."

"*Me?* You were the one who strutted around with your rich friends like you were better than everybody else, swinging your key ring to your brand-new-every-year sports car and attached at the hip with that dense, self-absorbed quarterback."

She said nothing for a long moment. "Been holding that in awhile?" she commented finally, running her finger around the rim of her glass.

He took a gulp of beer. "Apparently."

"You have any other issues with me?"

"I don't think so."

"You feel resentment toward me, yet you still have the hots for me. That's kind of deep." She angled her head. "Or possibly disturbing."

He leaned back. "I'm over it. My resentment," he added.

His face had taken on a familiar sullen expression—the bad-boy attitude he had in school. "Uh-huh."

"High school's over."

"And yet we're still on opposite sides of the social spectrum."

His gaze drilled into hers. "How do you figure that?"

"You're part of the team. I'm not. I know you guys, and the girls, have parties together all the time. You go out to the lake on your off days, hang out at the track. I always hoped somebody would invite me, too. But nobody ever did." She sighed, then frowned. "That was a little self-pitying, wasn't it?"

"I'm glad you said it, not me."

She stared down into her drink, which was mostly gone now. "I think this thing is affecting me weirdly."

"I was hoping it would encourage you to take off your clothes and dance on the bar. I even bet Darrell you would." His brooding apparently over, he grinned and leaned toward her. "Wanna help me win the bet?"

"You bet on my becoming a stripper under the influence of alcohol?"

"Sure. You don't get that kind of excitement at your country club cotillions, now do you?"

"No, actually I don't."

Not that that was necessarily a *bad* thing. Still, she was oddly flattered by the bet.

"It's sweet of you to, well…think of me." She narrowed her eyes. "But there will be no table dancing, lap dancing or pole dancing at any time. Clear?"

"Absolutely. And—" he trailed a finger down her cheek "—for the record…we didn't invite you to parties because we figured you weren't interested in hanging out with us."

"Well, I am."

"So consider yourself invited to the New Year's Eve party."

"Then, about high school…I know I was a brat. I was a teenager. You get to be self-involved and make mistakes. It's practically a job requirement."

"Sure it is."

"As for my quarterback, we all know how that turned out."

"High school's over, remember?"

"Right. Though I have to say, you haven't changed much."

He sipped his beer. "How's that?"

"You were sexy and dangerous back then, you're sexy and dangerous now."

He choked.

She clamped her hand over her mouth. "I can't believe I just said that."

Laughing, he pried her hand away. "Oh, no, let's hear more."

"This is why my relationships with guys are always a disaster," she said, wishing she could hide under the bar.

"Maybe you're just picking the wrong guys."

That was true, too. But she didn't want to dwell on it. She rolled her shoulders and looked at him directly. "You were so cool on that motorcycle."

"I was so without funds for a car," he corrected.

"You looked born to ride it." She sighed lustily and cast her mind back to the image, still fresh after all these years. "Very James Dean."

"Go on."

"The football players might have been the popular guys during the day, but you were the fantasy of every girl at night."

"Including you?"

Especially me. "Maybe a few times," she said, knowing she needed to back off. She'd probably scared him off by the fantasy stuff.

"Would the lovely Ms. McMillan like another drink?" the bartender asked, hope shining in his dark eyes.

Jesse nodded at her empty glass. "If you drink another one of those, you're going to pass out."

"Or say something else idiotic. Thank you, but no," she added to the bartender, who scooped up her glass and moved off.

"Let's go to my room instead," Jesse said.

CHAPTER FOUR

STANDING AWKWARDLY in the living room of Jesse's suite, Tiffany wasn't sure exactly how she'd gotten there.

She was torn between running out and running into his arms.

But she always made lousy choices when it came to getting involved with men. Did she really want to make another one? Throwing herself at a guy who worked for her father? A guy who'd insulted her more times than he'd flirted with her? At least until this weekend.

Come to think of it, what had prompted—

He snagged her hand and led her to the sofa, pulling her down beside him. "So I was the object of a *few* of your fantasies?"

She struggled between honesty and not humiliating herself further over that fantasy confession. She also fought to ignore the spicy, seductive scent emanating from his body, the desire that rolled through her body when he looked at her.

"Well, I—" She cleared her throat. "Sort of. Nothing too interesting. I was only seventeen, after all."

He slid his hand down her thigh, left mostly bare from her miniskirt. "I had some pretty good fantasies at seventeen." His voice lowered; he turned her face toward his. "And you were the star of almost each and every one."

She swallowed hard. "I was?"

He leaned close, his lips a breath away from hers. "Oh, yeah."

Then his mouth was on hers, igniting the fire that had been smoldering for ten, long years.

The reality was better than the fantasy, which was odd, since she'd been attracted to a lot of guys over the years and *none* of them ever lived up to her wishes and hopes.

Even the ones who hadn't run off with the family silver.

She gave herself over to the moment, to Jesse and the feelings he aroused. She'd admitted her attraction reluctantly—given her luck with men, who could blame her? But now that she'd let her inhibitions go she couldn't believe she'd allowed so much time to pass without taking a chance, to trusting a man with whom she could share so much, trusting him to take care—

Heart pounding, she jerked back.

Realizing she'd practically crawled on top of him, she sat up, her face burning. "I—" She took a bracing breath, keeping her gaze on the sofa instead of him. "I can't. We have to stop."

"Okay," he said, his breathing labored, but his tone mild.

She leaped to her feet, smoothing down her skirt and wondering how fast she could run to the door in her high-heeled sandals. "I'm sorry. I shouldn't have come."

He stood next to her, laying his fingers beneath her chin and raising her face to meet his gaze. "What's wrong?"

"I just need to go. This is moving too fast."

"It was a kiss, Tiffany. No big deal."

She blinked. "It felt like a big deal."

He said nothing for a long moment, his eyes searching hers for something she couldn't explain. "We like each other. We have great chemistry. We're together on a tropical island." He smiled. "This has all the makings of a great island fling."

Wary, still shaken up by the idea that she'd been on the verge of trusting him with her emotions, she stared at him. "An island fling?"

"You know…sun, sand, surf, making out under a cabana, moonlit walks on the beach." He stroked her cheek with his thumb. "We'll have fun."

"Fun."

"That thing you're supposed to do when you're not running around with your clipboard and walkie-talkie, giving orders and scowling at me."

"I'm good at giving orders."

"So I've seen."

She bit her lip.

He groaned. "Don't do that. It makes me want to, too."

Her flush spread. He had a way of making her long for something beyond her lousy romantic past, making her hope for the future in a way she hadn't for a long, long time. "You're very tempting."

"My personal specialty. Why don't you think about it? If you want to spend the day with me tomorrow, meet me at ten at the poolside bar. If not, I'll hang out with the guys."

"It's that simple?"

"It can be."

"Okay. Tomorrow at ten."

Smiling, he linked hands with her, then kissed her softly. "You'll be an expert at island romance in no time."

Though she tingled all the way to her toes, she lifted her chin proudly. "It's not me I'm worried about. My last boyfriend got arrested, you know."

"I'll make sure I have a lawyer on standby." He squeezed her hand and led her toward the door. "Come on, I'll walk you to your room."

AT NINE-FORTY-FIVE the next morning, Jesse sat on a bar stool at the resort's poolside hut and wished he wasn't such an idiot.

Island fling.

He shook his head. What a bunch of bull.

Now that he and Tiffany had broken down the wall of resentment between them, he could fully open himself to those crazy fantasies he'd had in high school. The simple ones that involved her smiling at him, her blue-eyed gaze locked on his, with no one else anywhere in the picture. The sexy ones he hoped to eventually share with her. The impossible ones, where they linked hands and walked off into the sunset.

And beyond her feisty personality and eye-popping figure, he realized what an intelligent, kind and strong woman she was. He knew how dedicated she was to the team. The foundation she ran wasn't a time-passing hobby. It was a passion, and the organizations it benefited were clearly helping people.

Hope House, in particular, gave women and their children protection from their lives of turmoil and violence, provided them a chance for a new start. Because of Tiffany and her staff, there would be a merry Christmas for some who might never have seen hope.

"Jesse," Danny said as he approached with his girlfriend—this week's, anyway. "After those Santa's

Specials, I had to drag Greg out of the bed this morning with gallons of coffee. Surely you're not going that route so early?"

"No way. Those things are lethal." Obviously, Greg hadn't stuck with his soda drinking for long. He probably shouldn't mention that to Tiffany. "I'm just hanging here, thinking about going for a walk."

The driver grinned. "Waiting for Tiffany McMillan to stroll with you?"

Jesse shook his head and muttered, "You can't keep anything quiet around here."

"Not on a race team, man. You ought to know that by now."

"Yeah, well. That's what I'm asking for this Christmas."

"Her? Or privacy?"

"Both."

Danny patted his shoulder. "I've got faith in you, man. Didn't your genius get us on the right track to all those wins last summer?"

"It was a team effort," he said, though he felt a renewed sense of pride in their successful season.

Wayne McMillan had given him more than an education, he'd given him a sense of accomplishment and team spirit. Was he really crazy enough to pursue Tiffany and risk his relationship with his boss and mentor?

"You think McMillan will approve of your chasing after his princess?" Danny asked, as if reading his thoughts.

"Sure," he said without much confidence.

"Uh-huh." Danny chuckled and started off. "Good luck."

The *you're going to need it* was implied.

Over the next ten minutes he looked at his watch at least ten times. Would she really show?

When he finally saw her strolling out of the back door of the hotel, wearing a big straw hat and a flower-print cover-up—under which he could only pray was a skimpy bikini—he allowed himself to relax.

At least until she was ten feet away, and he realized something important.

He wasn't having an island fling. He was falling for her in a big way.

"Hi," she said when she reached him.

Hoping he didn't look as nervous as he felt, he kissed her, lingering for just a second longer than he should. "Hi."

Her eyes were hidden behind big, dark sunglasses, so he couldn't tell what she was thinking, but at least she didn't smack him.

"Is there a lot of kissing during an island fling?" she asked after a moment.

"Definitely."

She smiled. "Good." Linking her hand with his, she asked, "Beach or pool?"

"Beach." He led her toward the path to the sugary white sand. "I reserved chairs and an umbrella."

"Great. I love the sun, but it doesn't love me."

"You look pretty tan."

"Spray tanning. It's a miracle product."

"Like one of those booth things that shoots misty stuff at you?"

"Yep. I own one, actually. It's in the spare bedroom in my condo. Year-round sun-kissed skin, no aging or risk of skin cancer." She glanced at him as they reached the lounge chairs. "You're probably one of those people who're brown after four minutes in the sun."

"Don't hate me because I'm bronzed," he said as he stripped off his T-shirt and flopped on the chair, laying his head back into his linked hands.

She waggled her finger at him. "You still need sunscreen."

She stepped outside the neon-green beach umbrella and waved her arm in the air. A moment later, a deeply tanned, muscle-bound guy with really white teeth appeared beside their chairs.

"We both need some serious SPF twenty-five," she said, sitting on her chair and sliding off her shoes.

"We're under an umbrella," Jesse pointed out.

"Not for long. We'll get in the water and walk on the beach." She turned her head toward him. "You wouldn't want that hot bod of yours blistered, would you?"

Before Jesse could come to grips with the idea that she thought his body was hot, she gripped the edge of her flowered cover-up and pulled it over her head.

Those impressive curves of hers, just hinted at beneath sundresses and fitted jeans, were only a bubble in the lava pot. There was so much toned muscle and sleek, smooth skin, his eyes were watering in an effort to absorb it all.

Grinning, Tan Guy held up a tube of sunscreen. "It will be my pleasure to serve you, madam."

Jesse sat up in a flash and snatched the bottle from his hands. "I got this."

"He's the tanning butler," Tiffany said. "It's his job."

Jesse pulled off his sunglasses and exchanged a hard glare with the *butler,* who walked away, obviously disappointed.

Then Jesse shifted his gaze to Tiffany. His heart kicked at his ribs. *Oh, wow.* "Where should I start?" he managed to ask.

And why the hell didn't I know about jobs like tanning butler when I was struggling to pay attention in Geometry?

She turned and flipped her hair forward, exposing her shoulders and back. “Here.”

Swallowing hard, he squirted lotion into his palm, then spread it slowly across her skin. She was warm, and his hand grew hot. His fingers tingled. And suddenly he wondered whether this was such a good idea.

Not that he didn’t want to touch her. He did. He *definitely* did.

But the attraction between them seemed to be leaping forward weeks in the space of a few minutes. The sense of intimacy was strong and powerful. Desire was on fast-forward.

Normally, he didn’t mind a relationship with a woman moving ahead at warp speed. So, why the caution? Why the questions? Why was Tiffany so different? Special? Why did he want to pummel the crap out of the tanning butler who wanted to touch her?

He didn’t think of women in a possessive, ownership—and definitely archaic—way.

“Are you sure you’re qualified to do this?” she asked, turning her head, a sexy little half smile on her lips.

He shifted his focus from her eyes to her bare shoulder. He couldn’t quite remember what he was supposed to be doing. “How hard can it be?”

She grabbed the bottle from his hand. “Pretty difficult apparently.”

Watching her apply the lotion was almost as torturous as doing it himself. He lay back on his chair and closed his eyes, trying to concentrate on the warm breeze and the salty tang of the sea.

This was what he’d come on the trip for—relaxation, no pressure of an upcoming race. Looking at bikini-clad babes was just a side benefit. An *uncomplicated* side benefit. And Tiffany was complicated in a whole bunch of ways.

“Are you finished?” he asked after a couple of minutes.

“Nearly. Why?”

“Because I’m not opening my eyes until you are.”

“O-kay,” she said, sounding confused.

Moments later, without any warning, her warm hands were rubbing lotion on his chest.

His eyes flew open.

“What are you—”

Leaning over him, she held up lotion-covered palms. “Sunscreen. Just because you’re already tanned doesn’t mean you shouldn’t have protection.” She tilted her head, studying him. “Are you sure you’re okay? You’re kind of jumpy.”

“I’m fine.” He snagged her hand. It was barely ten o’clock in the morning and the thoughts he was having about her rubbing his chest had nothing to do with sunscreen. "Let's go for a walk on the beach," he said, sitting up.

"But I have to do your back first."

"Fine. Make it fast."

She sat next to him on the lounge chair, but she didn't spread sunscreen on his back. She wiped her hands on a towel. "What's up?"

"Up?"

"You've said *fine* twice. When a guy does that, everything is most definitely *not* fine."

His chest contracted at her wounded expression. He slid his thumb along her jaw. "Tiffany McMillan is perceptive? Now all my teenage clichés are dead."

"This date isn't going very well, is it?"

"I think it's been an amazing thirty minutes. And my being jumpy has nothing to do with you." He paused, shaking his head. "Actually, it has *everything* to do with you."

She raised her hand, waving it. "Not feeling better over here."

"The thing is…I need to touch you—and have you touch me—in small doses. It's a little, ah… intense for me."

Her eyes widened with realization. "Oh."

He rose, tunneling his hand through his hair in frustration. "This isn't normal for me on a first date. On *any* date. For one thing, my control is usually better." As he looked down at her, the instinct of protection and possession rose again, like a monster raging inside his chest. "You seem to be a special case."

"That's very sweet, but are you sure that's it?" Her eyes were shadowed with doubt. "Maybe you're regretting—"

"I'm trying to be a gentleman here, Tiffany."

Raising her eyebrows, she stood, sliding her fingertip down the center of his chest. "Jesse Harwood a *gentleman?* Now all of *my* teenage clichés are ruined forever."

It's going to be all right. He slid his hand into hers and tugged her toward the surf. "It's just that kind of day."

They walked through the sand to the edge of the water and let the ripples of the ever-moving turquoise sea splash over their feet. Jesse thought that if he was the fanciful type, he might be reflecting that the water swelling over the sand, dragging out the old and leaving a clean, shining surface behind was indicative of his and Tiffany's relationship.

But he was an engineer, often accused of having a computer for a brain, so that thought passed him by quickly.

Just as they started to walk along the shoreline, she pulled him to a stop. "Oh, and since that seriously hunky, leanly muscled body of yours clearly demonstrates that you don't spend *all* day running dynos and communing with your laptop, my control isn't the strongest either." She smiled sweetly. "Please do your best to hold on for both of us."

His stomach dropped. *His* control? They were completely doomed.

CHAPTER FIVE

"CAN I ASK YOU A PERSONAL question?"

Tiffany glanced at Jesse across the small dinette table where they were having a post-lunch drink by the pool. Frankly, after being forced to leave him earlier so he could eat lunch with the auction winner—who had to be somebody's grandma—she was more than ready for personal questions.

"How personal?" she asked with a small smile.

"Very."

Under normal circumstances, she'd have said no, but there was a reason the word for their relationship was *fling.* It was like tossing yourself off a cliff and hoping the water beneath was cool, rock free and deep. "Sure."

He grinned. "Do you have tan lines?"

She threw her napkin at him. "You're crazy."

"It's a legitimate, scientific question. Plus, I'm trying to picture you in the tanning spray booth." He leaned forward. "What, exactly, do you wear?"

"Do guys think of nothing else besides naked women?"

"Racing cars."

She rolled her eyes, but her happiness at being included with all the other women the guys teased was gratifying. She wasn't the Ice Queen or Daddy's Little Princess anymore. She was becoming one of them.

Jesse and the rest of the staff now saw her as somebody to joke with, but also as a business professional. She wished her dad viewed her the same way. If only *he* noticed how hard she worked at the foundation, how meticulously she'd coordinated the last week for the team, how much time she'd spent preparing the fund-raisers and organizing the dinners.

"What?" Jesse asked, sliding his leg against hers under the table.

All day, those casual touches and probing questions had set off wild fireworks and comforted her at the same time. No matter how unlikely it seemed a few days ago, she and Jesse had bonded.

They wouldn't walk away from this weekend the same as when they arrived.

At least *she* wouldn't.

"I was thinking about my dad," she admitted, meeting Jesse's gaze with an honesty and vulnerability she would have shown very few. "The way he views me as a daughter, but not a friend. I really wish—"

"Tiffany, I'm so sorry to interrupt."

Looking up, Tiffany smiled at Sarah. She had to force the politeness—this was supposed to be her day to relax, after all—but she knew Sarah was working just as hard. "No problem. Did you need something?"

"Actually…" Sarah cast a nervous glance at Jesse.

"It's fine," Tiffany said, understanding Sarah's need to keep the less-than-pretty demands of the hospitality business from the resort's guests. "Jesse's fairly sturdy. He can bear the occasional crisis."

Sarah nodded. "It's the menu. Chef Andre apologizes, but he can't serve the artic char. His shipment didn't come in this morning. He suggests salmon or sturgeon, but will either of those change the wine pairings? Do you have a minute to come to the kitchen?" She cast another nervous glance at Jesse. "We'll get it all worked out in a few minutes, I'm sure. But we need a decision now."

Tiffany glanced at her watch. *Two-fifteen.* The team dinner was supposed to be at seven-thirty, so Sarah's request of a decision now wasn't a stretch. "I'll meet you in the kitchen in ten minutes."

Sarah backed away. "Terrific."

Tiffany shifted her gaze to Jesse. "I've got to handle this, which will involve a detailed discussion and delicate negotiation of wine and sauces with an eccentric chef. The team is probably—again—knee-deep in Santa's Specials by now. You want to hang with them or me?"

Jesse rose. "I'm with you."

"Brace yourself."

As she signed the check, he said, "When we get back home, I'm going to take you out for an actual date, where I make reservations and pay."

She stopped, staring at him, her heart pounding. "I thought we were having an island fling. At home, we won't be on an island anymore."

He was quiet for a moment. "Right," he said finally.

Was he thinking about seeing her beyond this vacation? If so, how did she feel about that? This was supposed to be no-commitment fun. Back home, if they dated, people would talk. She would be in a *relationship.* Which she was uniquely bad at having.

Jesse cleared his throat, interrupting her troubled thoughts. "Are we having fish eggs for dinner?"

"No," she said as they headed into the hotel.

"What else do you do with a sturgeon?"

"You eat it. Though we're not. And I'm sure I'm not the only person sick to death of salmon."

"Oh, I definitely am," he said in a way that made her wonder if he'd ever even eaten salmon. "What kind of wine do you have with cheeseburgers? That's my vote."

She bumped her shoulder teasingly against his.

"You guys have cheeseburgers all the time. I was hoping for something a little more elegant. I also wanted one darker, richer fish and one light white. Then I could pair them with the same kinds of wine. Arctic char and Bahamian mahimahi. Arctic for the Christmas theme and the mahimahi for the islands."

"You thought that deeply into dinner?"

"Goofy, I know. My dad says I have my mother's neurotic attention to detail."

"You're not neurotic, just particular."

"I bet you didn't think that last night when I was ranting at you in my elf costume."

"No, then you were adorable."

She stumbled, and he grasped her arm to steady her. He'd been saying things like that all day. Unexpected compliments that made her realize his admission to liking her wasn't simply a ploy to get her into bed or get in good with her father. There was something incredibly simple and honest about Jesse, even as she sensed complexity beneath his I'm-just-one-of-the-guys attitude.

"So how are you solving the fish problem?" he asked, bringing her back to the issue at hand.

"We're only going to have the mahimahi."

"Sounds like a simple fix. Less for the chefs to cook. And I actually like mahimahi. Why is there going to be a delicate negotiation?"

"Because we're still having both red and white

wine—each guest can choose what he or she wants—and Chef Andre is French, with traditional views about wine pairings. He'll want to eliminate the red."

"Why does he care?"

She glanced at him out of the corner of her eye as they walked down the hallway leading to the working areas of the hotel. "What brand of spark plug do you prefer?"

"Cannade," he said instantly. "Why? What does that have to do with fish and wine?"

"How about…the next time Suzy orders spark plugs, I convince her to order from Patton?"

"I'll never speak to you again."

"I rest my case about fish and wine."

They dodged employees in various states of panic, and as they drew closer to the kitchen, Tiffany could hear shouting, then several long streams of French that included a number of colorful curses.

"Glad we caught him in a good mood," Jesse said wryly.

"You speak French?"

"No, but curses are universal."

She smiled. "I guess they are." She rolled her shoulders as they approached the door. At least her cover-up looked decently enough like a sundress. Having this meeting in a bikini wasn't her idea of professional.

She started to push open the door, Jesse caught her hand, turning her to face him. "I don't know anything about wine pairings or fancy fish."

"So?" she said, though she could feel the tension in his body.

"You're silver spoons. I'm grease-under-the-fingernails."

Huh? Surely brilliant and cool Jesse couldn't care less about superficial differences like that.

On the other hand…she'd let tags like "Daddy's Little Princess" intimidate her so much, she couldn't even bring herself to try harder to be part of the race-shop clique.

Casualness seemed the best way to defuse the moment.

She kissed him lightly. "That's okay. I don't know anything about spark plugs." She cocked her head. "What do they *do* exactly?"

He squeezed her hand, and the tension left his face. "After we deal with Chef Snooty, I'll tell you all about them."

"Fine," she said, though she thought *bor-ring.* "As long as you fit that in between making out under the cabana and a moonlit walk on the beach."

He coughed. "The what and the what?"

"That's what you promised on your list of Stuff To Do During An Island Fling."

"I did, didn't I?" He wrapped his arm around her

waist and tugged her against him. "I think I'm starting to like these neurotic lists of yours."

"Hey, you told me I'm not neurotic."

He wiped the scowl away by kissing her.

JESSE COULDN'T HAVE found a more romantic beach stroll if he'd ordered one from Islandgetaways.com.

Linking hands, they walked barefoot through the rippling edges of the surf. The moon hung like a bright, white globe above them. She was wearing a pale pink dress with a jagged edge that floated over her body like a cloud, and he still had on his khaki pants, white shirt and navy jacket from dinner.

A postcard of perfection.

Tiffany's tendency toward neurotic detail had to approve.

But a ball of anxiety had settled in his stomach. The moment he'd mentioned—even accidentally—something beyond the weekend, she'd backed away. He was trying to build a relationship on a partial foundation and was nearly sure everything would crumble at his feet.

And yet he couldn't help but continue the pretense. He wouldn't spoil the peace they'd found.

At its core, Christmas was about hope. He chose to believe that spirit was a beginning for him and Tiffany. When they got home, he'd find a way to convince her to take a chance on something beyond a vacation romance.

He could still believe in dreams.

And he sensed she needed hopes and dreams, too. The single-minded determination she had toward perfection, the past relationships she saw as failures on her part, the conversation he'd accidentally overheard between her and her father last night…they led somewhere. He wanted to follow that road.

He glanced from her to the moon, then back again. "Earlier, after lunch, you said you wished for something. What was it?"

Her hand twitched, then she shrugged. "I don't remember. What were we talking about?"

"We were talking about naked women and racing cars, but I don't think that's what you wished for."

"Probably not."

"Then you mentioned the way your dad doesn't see you as a friend."

She said nothing, and they continued to walk, but a tension had risen in the air. Palpable. Real as the stars glistening above them, just as hot and elusive.

Maybe the pretense will collapse after all…

"Pink poinsettias," he said quietly.

She stopped and faced him. Even in the moonlight, he could see her eyes were flashing with anger. "You *did* overhear us last night."

"I didn't mean to, but, yes, I did."

Her eyes searched his for a moment or two, then—to his shock—she wrapped her arms around his waist and laid her cheek against his chest. "He doesn't even remember her," she said in a choked voice.

He held her against him. "I think it's more likely he doesn't *want* to remember."

"Like you don't want to be attracted to me?"

Good going, Harwood.

"It's much deeper than that. My not wanting to be attracted to you was more about my worrying you'd reject me."

"Why would I—"

He laid his finger over her lips. "It's nothing. We're way past that." Knowing she'd never accept the vague answer, he added, "Leftover high school stuff. We've settled the past."

"Silver spoon versus grease."

She was incredibly perceptive. Was that something only the two of them shared with each other? He hoped so.

"Exactly," he said. "But for your dad…his feelings for your mom…" He searched for the words that would comfort Tiffany and still be honest. He wasn't even sure his instincts were accurate, but he thought they might be.

His parents had the bond everybody longed for, the one he suspected Tiffany's parents had also shared. The one he wanted someday. Was Tiffany the woman he'd find that connection with?

He hoped so.

He brushed the hair the wind had stirred off her forehead. "He misses her *too* much. She was the love of his life, and she's gone, so he fills his life with racing because that's what gets him through the day. And you remind him of her." He brushed his thumb across her cheek, wet with tears. "You look like her."

She looked startled. "How do you know that?"

"There's a picture of the three of you on the cabinets behind his desk. It sits between his two championship trophies." He paused, staring at her. "The loves of his life."

She cupped his face in her hands, then kissed him with a tenderness and watery emotion that couldn't possibly be on the Island Fling list. "You're okay, Jesse Harwood," she said when she lifted her face. "You're really okay."

Incredibly moved by the tears shimmering in her beautiful eyes, he said, "I'm so glad I've passed the coolness test of the princess."

"I think I should be promoted to goddess."

"I'd vote for that."

She hugged him, then stepped back, joining their hands and continuing the walk down the beach. "My mother loved pink poinsettias…."

"YOUR BACK IS RED." Tiffany said, dropping Jesse's shirt on the floor of her room and sliding her lips over his reddish-brown skin. “You should have let me put on the sunscreen.”

“Next time,” he said, breathless by her touch. “I promise.”

Their breathing heated the air around them as desire took over and the magic of Christmas, the lure of the island moon and hunger surged through their blood.

Jesse lifted her high, then laid her gently on the bed.

“You really don’t have tan lines, do you?” he said after a moment.

She wrapped her hand around the back of his neck and drew him close. “Maybe you’d better check, just to be sure I didn’t miss a spot.”

CHAPTER SIX

SHE STILL HAD HIS SHIRT.

Somehow, it smelled like an enticing mix of him, his cologne, the sea, the sand and a hint of the Santa's Special Bahamian Delight she'd drunk sitting next to him at the bar. A lifetime ago.

Or so it seemed.

She'd been back home in North Carolina for barely a day; she'd stayed behind at the resort for an extra day after the team had left to wrap up the trip's details with the staff. It was Tuesday, and Christmas was two days away. Normally, she ushered in the holiday with cookie baking, parties, shopping and a candlelight service at church.

This year, it seemed she'd welcome it with nerves and anxiety.

As she paced her lakeside condo, she—again—ran through Jesse's possible motives for leaving behind his shirt, then guessed at his feelings and wondered about her own.

Wouldn't it be a complete humiliation if he'd left it by accident?

But then Jesse was a pretty observant, thorough guy, so she seriously doubted he'd left her room Sunday morning and failed to notice he wasn't wearing a shirt beneath his jacket.

So it was deliberate. Should she call him and tell him? Should she return it? Was that why he'd left it? In order for her to have an excuse to see him and give it back?

The shop was closed all week; there was no chance of them seeing each other unless they made an effort. Plus, she'd agreed to an island fling, and she wasn't on an island now. She was back to ice warnings and bogged down traffic, a cold, unwelcoming reality.

And yet there were signs of hope everywhere.

Cheery smiles from neighbors, bright lights, homey decorations. The families in NASCAR were together, instead of preparing for the next race. The new season would roll off soon enough, and life would be crazy again. But, for now, the spirit of the holidays was alive with anticipation.

She'd gone to the islands to spend time with her father, to get his approval on her hard work. Instead, she'd captured the attention of a sexy engineer and landed herself in yet another complicated relationship.

Maybe she should call him, hopefully leaving a

message, tell him she had his shirt and ask him over to Christmas dinner.

No, no, that was a bad idea. One, because he was probably already going to his parents' house for dinner, and two, because her father would be coming to *her* dinner, and Jesse showing up to collect his shirt probably wasn't the way to tell her father she was involved with one of his employees.

But *was* she involved?

She stared out the window in her sunroom, looking at the deep blue lake, the sun glimmering across its choppy surface and wondered. Did a beach date and a sleepover count as a relationship? She'd never had a one-night stand in her life, so she had no basis for comparison.

The doorbell rang, and her heart leaped ridiculously.

Had Jesse come to her? What did that mean? What would she say? What would *he* say?

She crossed to the door and discovered an even bigger surprise on her welcome mat. Her father.

"Hi, honey," he said, kissing her cheek as he walked inside. He headed toward the kitchen. "Where are the cookies?"

She'd forgotten all about them. The dough was probably a dry, cracked mess in the fridge by now. "I haven't made them yet."

"But you always make cookies two days before Christmas."

She shrugged and slid onto one of the stools pushed up to the bar separating the kitchen from the sunroom. "I've been too busy."

"Uh-huh." His blue eyes that matched her own narrowed. Then he walked around the corner, no doubt seeing the abandoned mugs of tea she'd left in various places around her living room. She hoped he wouldn't go into her bedroom and see the luggage she'd yet to unpack.

The only thing she'd been able to bring herself to remove was Jesse's shirt.

"What's wrong?" he said the moment he returned.

"Nothing. I'm just…tired," she finished lamely.

"Are you sick?"

Probably. But with what, she didn't know. "I don't think so."

He laid his hand on her forehead, like he had when she was a child.

The gesture brought tears to her eyes. She wondered, if he found her too warm, if he'd call their family doctor and drag him over here so close to Christmas.

"You don't have fever."

"Oh, goody."

He angled his head, staring at her. Whether it was the sarcasm or the listlessness in her voice, she wasn't sure, but he said with certainty, "Something's wrong. Does this have anything to do with Jesse Harwood?"

Her jaw literally dropped.

"You two seemed pretty cozy Saturday night," he continued. "Did you have a fight?"

"H-How do you…?" she began in a sputtering voice.

"I've got eyes, don't I?"

"You saw us?" *But you never notice me,* she almost added.

"Walking on the beach."

At least he hadn't seen Jesse, shirtless, leaving her room the next morning. And how odd that he'd spotted them, when they were probably talking about him at that very moment.

"How long have you two been seeing each other?" he asked.

"Ah, well…recently."

"How do you feel about him?"

"How do I—" She shook her head, trying to clear it. She and her father *never* had conversations about guys. His *secretary* had told her about the birds and the bees. She stood, pacing beside her chair. "Don't you have a meeting to go to?"

"The shop's closed."

"Since when has that stopped you from working?"

"It's Christmas."

"Since when—"

He held up his hand. "I know I work a lot. I still want to know what's happening in my princess's life."

She wanted to snap, *Since when,* again, but she didn't want to provoke him. She desperately wanted to know why he'd started this conversation. "Why are you suddenly interested in who I'm dating? Unless the police are involved, anyway."

"Okay, okay, you caught me." He sighed, then stood. He led her back to her stool, then took up the pacing himself. "When I saw you and Jesse, I realized how little I know about your *life*. I know about your work. I know who your friends are. I know you run the foundation better than anybody could. But I see you and Jesse nearly every day, and I had no idea you were dating. Actually, I always thought you two didn't get along."

Tiffany nearly smiled. Maybe her dad did notice *some* things.

"It's just—" He lifted his hands, then let them fall, clearly frustrated. "These are the talks you're supposed to have with…with your mother."

Tiffany sucked in a breath and held it. The talks they'd had about her mother were more rare than the ones they'd had about guys.

"I know she'd handle this stuff better. I don't know what to say, or how to say it." Reluctantly, he met her gaze. "So I don't say anything."

"There's no right or wrong way, Daddy," she said slowly. "You only have to try."

"I am. Is it too late?"

Tears clogging her throat, she walked toward him. "Of course not." She hugged him tight, laying her head against his chest, feeling all the hurt and doubt drain away. "She'd be proud of you."

He kissed the top of her head. "You, too, princess."

They held each other for several minutes, each lost in their own memories, relishing the new bond and beginning. Then Tiffany leaned back, knowing it was her turn to share. "He makes me feel special."

"You like him a lot, huh?"

"Yeah." In fact, given a little time, there might be more than *like*. There might be a great deal more.

He scowled. "You remember you're my little princess."

"How could I forget? You remind me every five minutes."

"At least I don't have to worry about him running off with the silver."

Laughing, Tiffany headed into the kitchen. Suddenly she felt like making cookies. Especially the ones shaped like poinsettias. Maybe she could convince her dad to help her decorate them with pink icing.

Nope, that was probably pushing it.

JESSE JANGLED HIS KEYS in his palm and stared up at the third floor of Tiffany's building.

He'd made a deal for fun in the sun, an island fling with none of the anxiety and problems of a relationship.

He was breaking that deal.

Would she slam the door in his face? Would she laugh? Was he crazy to think their weekend together had meant something more than they'd promised it would?

He used to ask for silly things for Christmas. He was a grown-up now, but he still believed dreams came true.

Maybe there *was* magic in Christmas. Maybe Santa and all the wishes he could grant with a rosy-cheeked wink could really happen.

He strode quickly across the parking lot and up the stairs to her door. He didn't want to give himself time to change his mind. *Again.*

She probably wanted to spend Christmas with her father and her friends, not some guy she'd hung out with on vacation. She might not even be home. He wouldn't know. He'd been too chicken to call and find out.

Swallowing his nerves, he glanced over the balcony railing and scanned the parking lot. Her bright red sports car was parked at the end.

Okay, well, that little cop-out is now unavailable.

He wrapped his hands around the iron railing and stared at the starry sky, then back at the car. He couldn't picture himself riding in it. He now made great money as an engineer, but he didn't belong there. Who was he kidding, dreaming that they could be together?

Just get it over with. At least you'll know.

He turned, prepared to make the ultimate sacrifice of bravery and knock on her door—only to find her standing in the open doorway.

"Jesse?" she asked in surprise.

After taking in the mouth-drying, curvy length of her in jeans and a fuzzy red sweater, he noted her purse slung over her shoulder, her keys in her hand. "Ah, hi. I guess you're going out."

"Yeah." She smiled, then she laughed.

His stomach dropped like a stone. He could have done without the laughing.

She moved toward him, close enough that their chests nearly touched. "I was coming to see you, actually."

"You were?" he said stupidly, desperately searching her face for some kind of positive sign.

She reached into her bag and pulled out a piece of cloth. As she held it up, he realized it was his shirt. "You left this in my room."

He'd wondered what had happened to that thing. "I did?"

Her smile fell away. "You didn't know?"

"I was a little...distracted when I left your room."

"Oh."

Silence fell. A car door slammed. Jesse's thoughts raced.

She was coming to him. Did that mean she was interested in more than a weekend, too? She could have mailed his shirt back. Hell, she could have thrown it in the trash.

"Could we talk about this inside?" he asked, feeling the anticipation of following through on his plan return.

"Sure." She turned and headed through the doorway.

His heart pounding, he followed, shut the door behind him, then let his gaze zip around the high-ceilinged entryway and plush living room, decorated in moss-green and gold, her lit Christmas tree and fireplace in the corner. "Where's the kitchen?"

"What is it with men and my kitchen today?" she asked.

His gaze jerked to hers. "You had a man in your kitchen?"

"My father."

Relief rushed through him, along with the scent of sugar. "You have cookies?"

She looked annoyed, but dropped her keys and purse on the foyer table then extended her arm toward the doorway beyond the sofa. "Help yourself."

He knew he was being vague and irritating, but he hoped she'd understand—and be glad—in a minute. If only…

"You have one," he said with wild joy as he nearly ran into the kitchen.

"One what?" she asked from behind him. "Jesse, you're—"

"Confusing you," he said, grabbing her hand. "I know." He braced his hands on either side of her waist and lifted her onto the marble-tiled island in the center of the kitchen. "Try to imagine you're back on the *island*," he said, cupping her face.

"I'm on—" She glanced beneath her, the confusion clearing. When she lifted her gaze to his, her eyes were sparkling. "You're very clever, Jesse Harwood."

"I have my moments." He'd planned a fancy speech, which had left his brain the moment he'd touched her. "I don't want us to be over," he blurted out.

"Is there an us?"

"There is for me."

He lowered his head, kissing her softly. When he would have pulled back, she laid her hands on his chest, curling her fingers into his shirt and urging him closer. The kiss deepened, the blood roaring in his head, desire humming through his body. It seemed a month since he'd touched her.

"I've missed you," she said breathlessly when

they finally parted. “I thought you’d left your shirt in my room so that I’d have to return it.”

“Now *that* would have been clever.” He grinned, sliding his fingers through her silky hair. “Unfortunately, I wasn’t thinking that clearly Sunday morning. I was trying to figure out how to convince you to break our deal to have only a weekend fling.”

“I’ve been trying to figure out how to do that ever since I got back. My dad finally convinced me to go see you.”

Gulp. “Your *dad?* As in, *my boss.*”

She toyed with the buttons on his shirt. “Uh-huh. He wants to see you in his office promptly at seven on Monday morning.”

“Tiffany, maybe you shouldn’t have told him yet. He has a serious temper sometimes, and—” He stopped when he saw the expression on her face. “You’re messing with me.”

“Oh, yeah.”

“I didn’t know you were such a comedian,” he said as his heart settled back in his chest. He’d hate to be dating a woman with Tiffany’s financial means and be unemployed.

She wrapped her arms and legs around him. “You want to find out more?” She kissed the side of his neck. “I have many talents besides comedy and being neurotic.”

“I want to find out all of them,” he said, suddenly

serious. "I guess if you and your dad talked about me, you talked about a lot of things."

"We did. He's off to find more pink poinsettias to take to the church tomorrow. Knowing him, he'll wind up owning a florist. And he's happy about us." She angled her head. "Or maybe he's just happy he'll have somebody to watch football with on Christmas. You *can* come over on Thursday, can't you?" she added.

"I'm not leaving this condo without you for at least a week." He stroked her back and imagined making love to her beside her tree and fireplace. "Maybe a month."

"We're going from barely friends to roommates pretty quickly," she commented, though she didn't seem worried about it.

"I like to go fast," he said. As he held her and looked into her stunning eyes, he knew that, however they'd gotten there, he was sure it was the right place to be. "I have no idea what the future holds. I only know I'm crazy about you, I have been forever, and I can't spend Christmas—or any other day—without you."

"Merry Christmas, Jesse," she said, her lips nearly touching his. "You're the first, and last, thing on my heart's list of holiday dreams."

BRENDA JACKSON

is a die "heart" romantic who married her childhood sweetheart and still proudly wears the "going steady" ring he gave her when she was fifteen. Because she believes in the power of love, Brenda's stories always have happy endings. In her real-life love story, Brenda and Gerald, her husband of thirty-six years, live in Jacksonville, Florida, and have two sons. A *USA TODAY* bestselling author of more than fifty romance titles, Brenda is a recent retiree who worked thirty-seven years in management at a major insurance company. She divides her time between family, writing and traveling with Gerald. You may write Brenda at P.O. Box 28267, Jacksonville, Florida 32226; at her e-mail address, WriterBJackson@aol.com, or visit her Web site at www.brendajackson.net.

WINNING THE RACE

Brenda Jackson

To the love of my life, Gerald Jackson, Sr.

What does a man get for all the toil and anxious striving with which he labors under the sun?
—*Ecclesiastes* 2:22

CHAPTER ONE

LISA ST. CLAIRE TOOK a deep breath as she closed her car door, and glanced toward the lit entrance to the church where the wedding rehearsal was being held.

She couldn't help asking herself yet again if she was ready for this. Could she look Myles Joseph in the face and pretend nothing had happened? Ignore the fact that he had broken her heart five years ago when instead of giving her the engagement ring she had expected, he had delivered the news that he was leaving town to pursue his dream of becoming a race-car driver? Now he was fast becoming one of the most popular drivers in the NASCAR Sprint Cup Series.

Yes, I can do this, she convinced herself as she began walking, feeling the cool breeze penetrate the light cotton blouse she was wearing. *Myles means nothing to me anymore. He's a part of my past and I don't begrudge him his success.* Like everyone else in the small town of Chiefland, Florida, she was glad he had made it big. She wished him the best.

But then another part of her wished he hadn't returned at all.

That same part of her didn't care one iota that his best friend, Ronald Harris, was getting married and Myles was here to be Ronald's best man. As far as she was concerned it didn't matter. Nor did it matter that the woman Ronald was marrying was none other than her best friend, Sheila Townsend, and she was Sheila's maid of honor.

As Lisa got closer and closer to the church's entrance, she thought the only thing that mattered was that she would have to go through the evening pretending that she had gotten over Myles. And the sad thing about it was that up until she had driven into the church's parking lot she was convinced that she had.

Now she was thinking differently because on the other side of that door was the man she had loved since discovering what love was about; the man who had been her first in everything, even heartbreak. Everyone in her family, especially her three older sisters, had tried to warn her that Myles would one day break her heart. But she had ignored all the warnings. She had seen something in Myles they hadn't seen and she had believed in him when no one else had.

And she had loved him with all her heart.

The only thing she could take comfort in was

knowing that Myles had proved everyone wrong. He had made something of himself just as she'd known that he would one day.

She opened the door and walked inside the vestibule, where a huge decorated Christmas tree sat, reminding everyone of the holiday season. Sheila and Ronald wanted a Christmas wedding and would be getting married on Christmas Day after all of the church services had ended. They had promised to have a short rehearsal so everyone could enjoy dinner and be home early. After all, tonight was Christmas Eve. Plus the church was having a night service starting soon.

She opened the doors and felt a stirring sensation in the pit of her stomach when her gaze crossed the room to the man standing on the sidelines talking to Ronald and a few other men. A few years ago, except for Ronald, the others would not have been caught in Myles's company even if they had been paid a million dollars. And now it seemed they were hanging on his every word.

The crowed shifted and she got a better view of Myles. He stood tall, almost six-two, and was dressed totally different than he would have been years ago when a pair of tight jeans, a T-shirt and a black leather bomber jacket would have been his usual attire. Tonight he was wearing a pair of pleated trousers and a dress shirt that emphasized broad shoulders and a tight abdomen. His face was as handsome as she remembered, with dark eyes, sharp cheekbones, full lips and dark hair that was cut short and neatly trimmed around a face that was the color of rich cocoa.

And he still had that friendly dimpled smile, the one that came to life whenever he spoke. She could vividly recall the times when he'd had very little to smile about and when he did, his smile had been reserved for her.

She stepped into the sanctuary and, as if her feet were made of lead and had made some sort of loud noise, Myles stopped talking in mid-sentence and glanced over at her. Breath rushed out of her lungs the instant their eyes connected. She felt it all the way to the bones. She knew he recognized it as well, the seductive chemistry that had always flowed between them, even when they had been too young to understand it.

It was strange how, although they hadn't seen each other in five years, he could still look at her and his gaze could touch her in a way no other man could. She tensed, noticing that when he had stopped talking all eyes had gone to her. Everyone knew that at one time she had been Myles Joseph's girl.

Just like everyone knew how he had dumped her.

But she had sorted out her life and moved on. Upon graduating from the University of Florida, she had decided to open a gift shop near the campus. The shop was doing well, and she didn't mind making the forty-five-minute drive each morning from Chiefland to Gainesville. She even had an apartment in both places and on those days when she worked late into the night and was too tired to drive home, she stayed in the small apartment she had above her shop. She had started dating again although she hadn't gotten serious about any one guy.

Her attention was pulled back to the present when she noticed that Myles had moved away from the crowd surrounding him and was walking toward her. She braced herself, fought to control the way her pulse was racing. There was no way she could avoid the attention the two of them were getting. Everyone was waiting to see what would happen after all this time.

She knew these days he was a very wealthy man due to numerous endorsements. And if she could believe what she read in those tabloids, he was a sought-after bachelor, living the life of a playboy when he wasn't on the race tracks. Just last week his name had been linked to some actress's.

Over the years Lisa had never imagined Myles returning to Chiefland; however, as soon as Ronald and Sheila had announced their wedding plans, she had heard he would attend. When it came to those he considered friends, he was as loyal as any man could get.

It seemed that becoming a big star in NASCAR hadn't changed that about him. He still valued true friendships.

This made her wonder where she would fit. There was a time when she had been more than a friend to him...or so she had thought. The five years that had passed made her uncertain of everything, other than what her true feelings were for him. Even with the way things had ended, she didn't regret the impact he'd had on her life. Both good and bad. The good because she had enjoyed the time they had shared together; the bad, because he had shown her there was no such thing as true love. Not really.

Before she could ponder that further, she saw that he was there, right in front of her, and more handsome than ever before. "Lisa, it's good seeing you again."

She noticed the huskiness in his voice and couldn't deny that hearing it brought back memories she would rather not recall. Deciding to be as cordial as possible, she responded in kind. "It's good seeing you as well, Myles."

"Liar."

His whispered comeback had been so quick and unexpected—and so like old times—that she could feel her face soften with amusement. He could joke around her, but only with her. She would see his lighter, less serious side when others didn't. "You think so?" she found herself asking.

He chuckled. "Yes, but only because you could never lie worth a damn." After a few seconds he asked. "Do you know what I think?"

"No. What?"

"I think that we should give the good people of Chiefland something to talk about." And then just as unexpectedly, he leaned over and brushed a kiss across her lips.

Lisa's breath caught, and there was a struggle within her to do something other than just stand there speechless. Doing something as outlandish as kissing him back popped into her usually level-headed and rational mind. But at that moment she was saved from acting on it when the wedding planner claimed everyone's attention.

"I think she wants us," Myles said, offering her his arm. Knowing that eyes were still on them, she placed her hand on his arm and they turned together as if he was leading her toward a dance floor instead of the front of the church. They strolled together down the aisle to where the bride and groom to-be, as well as other members of the wedding party, were standing.

Sheila's blue eyes immediately darted to hers and Lisa registered the concern she saw there. Lisa smiled, trying to assure Sheila all was well, when deep down she wasn't completely sure of that, herself. The only thing she knew for certain was that

Myles still had the ability to stir emotions inside of her in a way she could definitely do without.

Another thing she knew for certain was that he smelled good. Whatever cologne he was wearing was definitely an attention getter. She had picked up on the scent the moment he had walked up to her. It was a manly fragrance, definitely one that had the ability to seduce. She quickly reminded herself that she was beyond getting seduced by Myles and hoped he was well aware of that fact.

MYLES FELT LISA'S eyes on him and was tempted to look at her but refrained from doing so. Instead, he tried to concentrate on the instructions the wedding planner was giving them. It wasn't easy. All he could think about was that the only woman he had ever loved was standing by his side. How many times had he pictured such a scene and wanted to capture such a moment again?

In his opinion she hadn't changed much. At twenty-five she was still as beautiful as she had been at seventeen…and the last time he'd seen her, at twenty. She still had shoulder-length black hair that cascaded around her honey-brown-colored face, and incredible dark eyes that seemed the color of dark chocolate. Dimples would form in her cheeks when she smiled. Her full lips had always been a total turn-on for him, always tempting. She was tall and leggy with a body he remembered well. The blouse she was wearing along with the dark slacks emphasized her curves to perfection.

He had a sinking feeling that she didn't have a clue as to the real reason he had broken things off with her that night. Why he had left Chiefland and not looked back. But that didn't mean he hadn't thought of her, although he'd made it seem that the main reason he'd left was to pursue his dream. She had no idea that she had been his dream and nothing could ever compare to her. True, he'd always wanted to race in the NASCAR Sprint Cup Series, but he'd always figured he would do that with her by his side.

He was certain she had no way of knowing that her parents had paid him a visit that week and pleaded with him to get out of her life after she had told them of her plans to drop out of college and come back home to be with him. It was bad enough that she had refused to go up north to college like they had wanted, and instead had gone to the University of Florida as a way to remain near him. Her parents had been furious about that and he had tried to change Lisa's mind but she hadn't budged. The last straw for her parents had been when she contemplated dropping out of college. That had not been acceptable to them. And it hadn't been acceptable to him, either.

He had already purchased the engagement ring he

intended to give her for Christmas. But when he'd found out she planned to forgo her last year of college, he knew he had to do what her parents had suggested, which was to get out of her life by leaving town. The job offer to be a part of Bronson Scott's racing team had given him an excuse to leave. It had been a lie, of course, but he had loved her too much to let her mess up her life for him. Lisa was highly intelligent. He'd figured that one day she would grow to regret not finishing college and would have ultimately resented him.

"Does anyone have any questions?" Agnes Bonner asked.

The wedding planner's question invaded his thoughts and brought them back to the present. When no one said anything, the older woman's regard landed on him. "Mr. Joseph, if I can get you to step over here for a moment," she said.

He inhaled deeply, hating the idea of leaving Lisa's side even for a moment. He would be gone soon enough at the end of the week.

"Sure," he said, and stepped away without looking at Lisa. Kissing her had been a huge mistake. He knew that now, but he hadn't been able to resist the opportunity. Besides, it would be what got him through another five years without her in his life.

He had asked Ronald about her often and his best friend had grudgingly filled him in. He had never told Ronald the reason he had left, so like everyone else, Ronald thought he had dumped her to chase his dream. More than once he had thought about contacting her after she'd graduated from college to tell her the real reason he'd left. He'd even thought of taking the time while in town to clear things up between them now. But he'd figured it was best to leave well enough alone. He'd done what he felt needed to be done by getting out of her life when he had.

The next hour consisted of a series of rehearsals and the hardest for him was when Lisa, who was Sheila's maid of honor, walked down the aisle. He could imagine her a bride instead of a maid of honor, and wearing a long flowing white wedding gown—walking down that aisle to him.

"That about wraps things up tonight, folks, but please be back here tomorrow, fully dressed no later than noon. And you are all invited to the rehearsal dinner at Victoria's Steak House," Mrs. Bonner announced.

Myles glanced at Lisa, who was standing talking to Sheila's bridesmaids. Ronald leaned over and asked. "You are going to Victoria's with us, right?"

Myles gave his best friend a smile. "Yes, I'm going."

"Good," Ronald said. "I'll ride with you."

Myles lifted a brow. "Aren't you and Sheila going there together?"

Ronald rolled his green eyes and pushed a mass of blond hair that was just as long as Sheila's away from his face. "No. Sheila intends to make our honeymoon special and decided six months ago that I needed to keep my hands to myself until the wedding. I figured with one more day to go, there's no need to test my willpower. If it was left up to me we would never make it to the rehearsal dinner. We would go someplace where the two of us could be alone."

Myles shook his head, grinning. "Then I guess it's a good thing it's not left up to you." His eyes went back to Lisa.

Ronald said, "You still care for her. I can tell. I still don't get why you dumped her in the first place."

Myles turned toward Ronald. "Is that what you think I did?" he asked.

He and Ronald had been best friends since grade school and just like his relationship with Lisa, everyone in town had wondered what had drawn him and Ronald together. The answer was simple enough. Both he and Ronald had had a love for cars. The only difference was that Ronald's family—one of the wealthiest in Chiefland—owned the only car dealership in town. In their early days, the two of them would hang out at Harris Autos and watch the mechanics at work. It wasn't long before he and Ronald were under the hood of some car or other. In fact that was how he had met Lisa.

The Harrises and the St. Claires attended the same church, and Lisa had stopped by the Harris Autos garage, wanting someone to check out a clinking noise she'd been hearing whenever she drove her car. Ronald had introduced them. At the time Lisa had been seventeen and in her last year of high school. He had been twenty-two years old and enrolled in an auto mechanics class at night while working at the garage during the day.

Sheila had come into the picture after Lisa went off to college in Gainesville and Sheila had been her roommate that first year. Sheila would often come home with Lisa on the weekends and it was during one of those weekend visits that Lisa had introduced her to Ronald. The reason it had taken so long for them to tie the knot was because Sheila had been a medical student but was now a resident intern.

"What else was I to think when you weren't talking?" Ronald said, interrupting his thoughts. "It was either thinking that or believing her family had run you off. I of all people know her sisters can be a pain in the rear end, but you always seemed to be able to handle them."

Myles shook his head at the mention of Lisa's sisters—the notorious busybody triplets. George St. Claire had worked at the local television station as the weatherman for years and evidently thought it was cute to name his three daughters Sunnie, Wendy and Noraine. By the time Lisa had come around, evidently Lilly St. Claire had put her foot down and insisted their fourth daughter be named after her mother. The joke was that Lisa had been spared being named Stormy.

Ronald was right. Sunnie, Wendy and Noraine were a handful. There was a five-year age difference between them and Lisa and they had taken their roles of oldest sisters to the max. They hadn't liked him because they felt he hadn't been good enough for their baby sister. The feelings were mutual. He hoped they had lightened up and had found lives of their own instead of constantly being in Lisa's.

He glanced back at Lisa. Now she was talking to Sheila, which made him wonder if she was deliberately avoiding him. "We'll talk about it in the car," he finally said to Ronald. "There are things I think you should know."

"About time," Ronald said, although this time Myles was well aware Ronald's focus was on Sheila.

"Hey, you only have one more night," Myles said, thinking that would ease Ronald's torture somewhat.

Ronald met his eyes and smiled. "Yeah, man, but the wait is killing me."

CHAPTER TWO

"SO, YOU WANT TO TELL me what that kiss was about?" Sheila asked as Lisa eased her car out of the parking lot to follow the one ahead of them. The one that Myles was driving and Ronald was a passenger in.

Lisa shrugged her shoulders. "I have no idea. Myles made the first move."

Sheila laughed as she pushed a few strands of blond hair from her face. "Yes, but I didn't see you resisting."

"In front of everyone? No way."

Now it was Sheila's time to shrug her shoulders. "Why not? There wasn't a soul in church tonight who didn't know your and Myles's history, including the untimely breakup."

Lisa didn't say anything for a moment. "I guess that kiss was Myles's way of saying, in front of everyone, that we're still friends."

"How do you feel about that?"

Again Lisa took a moment to think about Sheila's

questions. And then she responded. "Honestly, I'm trying not to say much of anything, and as far as my feelings, you of all people know what I went through when Myles left the way he did. Right now I'm just trying to handle him being here the best way that I can."

When the car came to a stop at a traffic light, Sheila seized the moment to reach out and touch Lisa's shoulder. When she had her attention, she asked softly, "You still love him, don't you?"

Lisa felt a sensation in her stomach when she recalled the moment of walking into the church and seeing him. And then when he had turned his dark gaze on her… Her heart rate increased just thinking about it now. "A part of me will always care for Myles, Sheila. We have too much history for me not to. But there's love and then there is love. I loved him once but don't know just what I feel now. Besides, I'm not so certain he truly loved me back then."

Sheila frowned. "Now that's where you and I differ in our beliefs. I always thought Myles loved you, just like I've always thought there was more to him leaving town than what he'd said."

"There was no other reason for him to leave, Sheila. He had the opportunity of a lifetime come his way and he seized it."

"Are you still bitter?"

"I tell myself I'm not, but then I have to admit a

part of me *is* bitter. His dreams had become mine and to know he fulfilled them without me still hurts. But then at the same time, I am so proud of what he has achieved in just five years. There hasn't been a race he's participated in that I wasn't cheering him on, all the way. I may not have been there on the sidelines, but I was there."

Sheila nodded. "Now for my final question. You know how your family felt about Myles in the past. They will hear—if they haven't already—that he's back in town for the wedding. And they will see him tomorrow since they're attending the wedding. How will you handle them, especially your sisters?"

Lisa frowned. "My family doesn't have anything to worry about regarding Myles, but even if they did, what goes on in my life is my business and they should know that by now. My sisters can't find husbands of their own because they are too busy trying to run my life. I love them but they can get on my last nerve."

"Well, I think you just need to be prepared. Dorothy Satterwhite was on the piano tonight and you know what a gossip she is. Chances are everyone in Chiefland knows that Myles kissed you today. At least they'll know by tomorrow morning."

"It wasn't that kind of kiss."

"You and I know it wasn't, since I've walked in on you and caught you and Myles kissing before and could actually feel the heat ten feet away. But you know how Dorothy likes to embellish things, so like I said, be prepared."

Lisa knew that, unfortunately, Sheila's warning wasn't anything she could take lightly.

RONALD SAID NOTHING FOR the longest time after listening to what Myles had told him. Then he said, "Gee, man, Lisa's folks used your love for her to get you to do what they wanted. I wonder if Lisa knows the whole story now."

Myles glanced over at Ronald as he turned into the restaurant's parking lot. "I doubt it. I can't see them ever coming clean and admitting to anything."

"You're probably right. Besides, if they had, she would have told Sheila and Sheila would have told me."

Myles nodded. "I'm not finding fault with her parents for what they did. They saw me as a threat to the life they wanted for Lisa and felt they had to do something about it."

"Hmm, I wonder what they think now, with the way your career has gone." Ronald chuckled as the car came to a stop. "Hey, you wouldn't be a bad catch for a son-in-law."

Myles decided not to mention that evidently a number of people felt that way. He didn't want to think of the number of his friends who'd tried playing their hands at matchmaking by introducing him to a number of eager prospects—daughters, sisters, cousins and so on.

"You've been dating a lot."

Ronald's statement intruded into his thoughts and he glanced over at him while unbuckling his seatbelt. "How do you know?"

Ronald smiled. "We still get the tabloids here, Myles. Mr. Jones over at the grocery store always manages to put the papers out front, right next to the vegetables bin, putting you and all the details of your affairs right in plain view. Everyone thought it was kind of cool when you were dating that movie star."

Myles rolled his eyes. "I never actually dated her. It was a promotional gig, nothing more. We're just friends."

Ronald chuckled. "Hey, I wished I could brag about being friends with her."

Before he cut off the engine, Ronald turned to Myles and asked, "So what do you plan to do about Lisa? You'll be in town for almost a week."

Myles knew he needed to have his head examined for agreeing to hang around and stay at Ronald's place while the new furniture Ronald had ordered as a surprise for Sheila was being delivered. Ronald and Sheila were leaving right after the wedding reception to drive to Jacksonville to catch a cruise ship to the Bahamas for four days. They would return before

New Year's, in time for him to leave to attend the New Year's Eve charity race in Daytona. He wouldn't be racing this time around, but wanted to be there to support his good friend and boss, Bronson Scott.

"I know. I'm sure there's something I'll be able to do to stay busy. I might drop in on your dad's dealership and mess around in the garage like the old days."

Ronald laughed. "Hey, the old man will just love that, to be able to boast about having you there. Hell, he might sell tickets. You've become a celebrity in these parts."

That statement should have given Myles a sense of satisfaction but it did not. He didn't want the townspeople to accept him because of his celebrity status; he wanted their acceptance because he was one of them and always had been. He had been born and raised right here in Chiefland, although it had been on the poor side of town. But still, he had roots here. And being the only member of his family still living, they were roots he was proud of.

Although Ronald joked a lot about his dad, it had been Mr. Harris who had opened up his garage and made it possible for Myles to hang around and learn things and work under Joe Spivey, the best mechanic in the South. Myles had known he was a goner when he had changed his first spark plug under Joe's watchful eyes. He had taken all the things Joe had taught him about the best way to get a car to run and had used his skill for NASCAR, first as a mechanic then—after convincing Bronson to let him try out—as a driver for his team, Scott Motorsports.

And as far as Chiefland was concerned, another thing Myles hadn't been able to forget was the woman he had left behind. More than once after racing in Daytona he'd been tempted to get on Interstate 95 and head west toward Interstate 10 to Chiefland and see the one woman he had loved. The only woman who would ever have his heart.

"Ready to go inside?" Ronald asked as he secured his hair in a ponytail before opening the car door.

Myles smiled over at him. "As ready as I'll ever be."

LISA TRIED TO REMAIN calm as Myles sat next to her. But when his thigh brushed against hers, she immediately felt a tingle in the pit of her stomach. And from the way he looked at her, she knew he had experienced it, too. Some things just wouldn't go away.

Lucky for her, Judy Small, who was known to be a chatterbox, sat on the other side of her. Judy was Sheila's cousin and loved talking about just about anything and had kept the conversation going. Every once in a while one of the guys would squeeze in a question for Myles—wanting to know about the upcoming season and how he was preparing for it.

Since it was Christmas Eve, most people had wanted to eat quickly and leave, because they had the morning for opening presents before heading to the church for the wedding. By the time the waitress returned to clear the table the only persons left were Sheila and Ronald and Lisa and Myles. Lisa glanced down the long table and saw that Ronald and Sheila were engaged in tense conversation. From the frown on Sheila's face, Lisa figured Ronald was trying to plead his case as to why it would be okay for her to spend the night with him. A smile touched Lisa's lips knowing Ronald was wasting his time. He of all people should know that when Sheila made her mind up about something, that was it.

"Do you want to take a bet on who's going to win?"

The warmth of Myles's breath when he leaned close to her reminded her he was there. Not that she had really forgotten. His cologne was still getting to her on a level that was totally provocative. In her book he was drop-dead gorgeous and he didn't need to add anything to boost his sexiness.

"No need for us to place bets. You will be taking Ronald home and I'm taking Sheila to my place. However, the big question is when that will happen, since it doesn't appear they'll be leaving anytime soon."

Myles nodded as he glanced down at his watch. "It's almost ten now. I thought most places closed up early on Christmas Eve."

Lisa couldn't help but smile. "Most places do but, like you, Victoria is probably willing to wait it out just to see how the evening will end. She and her husband probably have their own bets going."

Lisa took a sip of her coffee and then said, "Besides, you're here and you're a celebrity. They will probably not wash the plate and utensils you used and put them on display next week."

Myles rolled his eyes. "Aren't you getting a little carried away?"

"No. This is Chiefland, Myles. Remember? The biggest event we host each year is the Watermelon Festival. It's not every day that we get a famous race-car driver to grace our town. And what makes it even more special is knowing that he's one of us."

Her words stuck in his brain. She had always considered him one of them. But it had taken him winning the race at Talladega, one that had gotten national attention, for the townspeople to admit to anything. He was certain there were still a few out there who would rather not claim him. Namely her family. For that reason he decided to bring them up.

"How are your parents?"

He could tell his question surprised her. "Mom and Dad are doing fine. Dad finally retired from being a weatherman and Mom taught her last class at the middle school in May. Now they just hang around the house and get on each other's nerves. My sisters and I are thinking about putting our money together to send them someplace this spring."

Myles lifted a brow. "Someplace like where?"

"We're checking into a seven-day Alaskan cruise."

Myles smiled. "What can happen in a week?"

"For one, being together without any distractions will remind them why they got married in the first place. Over the years, their workaholic lifestyles kind of drove them apart."

Myles decided not to say it hadn't been that way on the night her parents had shown up at his place. George and Lilly St. Claire had presented a united front when it came to their daughter's future and their belief that he would do nothing but ruin it.

"And how are your sisters doing?"

He could tell from her expression that she knew he was asking just to be polite. "They're doing fine. Still single and bossy as ever. Sunnie replaced Dad at the television station earlier this year and is now the Chiefland meteorologist. Wendy is busy with her accounting office, gearing up for tax season. And Noraine, like me, commutes every day into Gainesville where she works as a counselor on campus."

She added, "You'll get to see all of them tomorrow at the wedding."

Myles tried keeping the grimace off his face when he said. "How nice." He then looked down at his watch again before glancing at Ronald and Sheila. Sheila was no longer frowning. There was a softening in her features as if she was considering whatever Ronald was saying.

"Are you sure you don't want to make that bet?" he asked Lisa.

She smiled. "I'm sure. She might be understanding and sympathizing with him, but in the end she won't change her mind."

Myles wasn't so sure about that. "How long do you think it will take for Ronald to get it into his head that she won't?"

Lisa laughed. "He's a typical man. Stubborn and determined. We might be here until midnight."

"I don't think so," Myles said, deciding he would give the couple ten more minutes max. "I drove in from Charlotte this morning and haven't gotten much sleep. It would be most embarrassing for them if I were to fall flat on my face in the middle of tomorrow's service."

Lisa smiled, envisioning that happening. She could just imagine how Reverend Hall would handle it. "So, do you like living in Charlotte? I heard it's a nice place."

Myles thought about her question. He wished he could be honest and tell her the truth—that when he had first arrived he had been so lonely for her, there had been times when he'd been tempted to disregard what her parents wanted for her. He'd thought about returning to Chiefland, asking her to marry him and taking her back to North Carolina with him. But the more time he spent apart from her, the more he knew he had done the right thing. She had encouraged him to pursue his dreams so many times; it was a small sacrifice to make sure she did the same for hers.

"Charlotte is nice. I've met a number of good people there."

"Tell me about them." She shifted in her chair and he picked up the scent of her perfume. From the moment he had approached her at the church he had noticed she still wore the same one and he was glad. It mixed well with her body's chemistry and always made him think of flowers and honey. It was a tantalizing combination and one that always made him want to make love to her. Whenever. Wherever.

"First there is Bronson Scott, he's the owner of the racing team I work for. The man is simply awesome. Bronson hired me on as a mechanic and later took a chance on me as a driver."

"You've won a couple of races," she noted, and he couldn't help but wonder if she kept up with the races because of him.

"Yes, for Scott Motorsports. It was sheer luck that both Bronson and I managed to make the chase for the NASCAR Sprint Cup. We celebrated for days."

And a part of him wished she had been there to

celebrate with him. Several times over the years he had been tempted to call her. But her parents' words had rung in his ears. *"If you love our daughter as much as you claim you do, then you will want what's best for her and let her go."*

"Do you have big sponsors?" she asked him moments later when the other end of the table had gotten quiet.

He glanced in Ronald and Sheila's direction and saw they had sneaked in a kiss. He almost felt sorry for Ronald, especially if he wasn't changing Sheila's mind.

"Yes, the Steele Manufacturing Corporation is one of our biggest sponsors, although there are others. That's one of the reasons why the race car I drive is steel gray. The Steeles send a lot of money our way, and when we win it's a big promotion and good advertising for them. And they are close friends of Bronson's, especially Donovan Steele, the youngest of the four brothers who own the corporation. Bronson and Donovan are best friends."

Myles looked at his watch again, thinking it was time to get the couple home, although he was thoroughly enjoying being here with Lisa. If he had his way, Ronald would go home with Sheila and he would go home with Lisa.

"So where do you live now?" he asked.

"I have an apartment here and one in Gainesville.

The one in Gainesville is right above the shop I own and on busy days when I'm too tired to make the drive back here in the evenings, I spend the night there."

"You own a shop?"

"Yes?"

"What kind?" he asked.

"A gift shop. It's located within a mile from campus and most of the customers are college students. Business is good when they are on campus but this time of the year, when most of the students leave for the holidays, business is slow, which is why I've closed up until school starts back the first of the year."

She owned a gift shop? This was news to him. He'd never asked Ronald, preferring to only know that she was in good health versus knowing anything about her personal life. Therefore, he had always assumed once she had gotten her degree she had done what she always talked about doing, which was to come back to Chiefland and teach school.

"What about becoming a teacher? I thought that's what you really wanted to do."

She shrugged. "I thought so too, but changed my mind after my first week in the classroom."

He studied her expression, and then saw how she quickly diverted her eyes to look down into her coffee. He had a feeling she wasn't being completely up-front with him about something. Becoming a teacher used to be all she talked about. He couldn't help but wonder what had happened to change her mind. He would have to ask Ronald about it later.

"I think it's time to call it a night or I might be falling flat on my face right along with you tomorrow," she said, standing. Then to Ronald and Sheila, she said, "All right, you two, break it up down there. Save all that smooching for tomorrow. Some of us would like to go home and get into bed."

A sly smile touched Ronald's lips. "Hey, I'm feeling you, Lisa. That's what I've been trying to convince Sheila all evening, that we should go home and go to bed."

Lisa rolled her eyes. "Yeah, I bet you have. Sheila, please tell Ronald good-night so I can take you home."

Sheila stood and smiled. "Good night, Ronald." She then looked at Myles. "And I'm depending on you to make sure he stays in when he gets home. I don't want him showing up over at Lisa's place later tonight. Understood?"

Myles laughed. "Do you really think I can stop him if he decides at three a.m. that he can't hold out and wants to see you?"

"Yes, just throw him in the shower and turn on the cold water," Sheila said, as she moved to meet Lisa at the end of the table. "That should work."

"I can't believe you're going to leave me this way," Ronald said, in what actually sounded like a pout.

Myles shook his head and wondered if his best friend would start sobbing any minute now. Just in case, he tossed him a cloth napkin. Ronald glared at him and said. "I don't need a napkin, I need my woman."

"Your woman will give you everything you want after she becomes your wife tomorrow. I promise, sweetheart," Sheila said softly. "Now be good and go home and stay there." She then grabbed hold of Lisa's hand and the two women rushed out of the restaurant.

CHAPTER THREE

LISA WASN'T SURE HOW Myles managed it, but he had kept Ronald from showing up. She wished someone had taken the same notion to her sisters. She heard the loud knock on her door, deciding Sheila needed to sleep for as long as she could this morning, she rushed to open her door to find the three of them standing there. She took one look at their expressions and knew they had already heard the news. Myles Joseph was back in town—and had kissed her.

"Merry Christmas," she said, waving them in. "But isn't it kind of early to be visiting?" Everyone had agreed to meet at her parents' home for breakfast where they would exchange gifts before enjoying their mother's delicious home-cooked meal.

Of course it was Sunnie who spoke first. Being the oldest triplet she appointed herself the spokesperson for the three. "Tell us what we heard is not true."

Lisa closed the door behind them and leaned against it. "Depends on what you heard."

The look they gave her let her know that they weren't amused by her comment. "Someone is spreading a rumor that you let Myles Joseph kiss you," Wendy said, not smiling.

"And right there in church," Noraine tacked on.

Lisa crossed her arms over her chest. She wasn't up to them this morning. This was the season to be jolly, not bossy—and her sisters were the bossiest. They were also very attractive women and more than one man had shown interest, but to no avail. At thirty-one Lisa figured their biological clocks should be ticking, but they were too busy trying to run her life to notice.

"First of all, I didn't let Myles do anything. He has a mind of his own and a brush across my lips was his way of saying hello. Personally, I saw nothing wrong with it."

"Need we remind you that the man dumped you," Sunnie said unceremoniously, without sugarcoating of any kind while raking a frustrated hand down her face. "If I were in your shoes I wouldn't be talking to him, let alone allowing him to get close enough to steal a kiss."

"But you're not in my shoes, Sunnie. None of you are. Myles and I have been friends too long for us to become enemies."

"Even after what he did to you?" Wendy asked.

Lisa didn't say anything for a moment. Then she moved away from the door and crossed the room to sit down on the sofa. "I would be the first to admit that I was hurt by what Myles did, but I've moved on. I suggest the three of you do the same."

They looked surprised. "Us?" Noraine asked.

"Yes, the three of you need lives. If you had your own, then you wouldn't have time to be such busybodies in mine."

There was a moment of silence in the room, and then Sunnie said, "We worry about you, Lisa, because we love you."

Lisa knew they truly did. "And I appreciate your care, concern and love, but you're worrying for no reason. I've gotten over Myles. Besides, he's probably leaving Chiefland as soon as the ceremony is over today."

"No, he's not," Noraine said as she came to sit down next to her on the sofa. "I heard he'll be in town until right before New Year's Eve."

Lisa gave a quick shake of her head. "I'm sure you heard wrong."

"And what if I heard right?"

Lisa was not sure whether she liked the thought of Myles hanging around, but she had no intention of mentioning her apprehensions to her sisters. "Then I'd say this is a free country and Myles can do whatever he wants. I would also say that he and I are friends. I'm happy for his success and don't hold anything against him."

It was Sunnie who came to sit down on the other side of her. "Have you forgotten who you're talking to, honey?" she asked in a soft voice. It was the voice Sunnie would use whenever she wanted Lisa to know that she had thoroughly thought her words through. "We're the ones who helped you pick up the pieces of your heart the morning after Myles left. It was our shoulders that you cried a bucket of tears on, while chanting how much you hated him in one breath and how much you loved him in the other," she reminded her.

Lisa remembered that day. She had to admit that her sisters had been wonderful and had kept her pitiful state from their parents. They had helped her put on a happy front around them, refusing to let George and Lilly have reason to say *We told you so.*

"Okay, I will be the first to admit I was hurt, but it's been five years and like I said, he plans to leave Chiefland. If not today, then eventually."

"But we're worried about what he plans to do while he's here and if he has included you in those plans. We don't know if you've read the tabloids lately but he dates *a lot,* considers himself a playboy," Wendy said.

"He probably enjoys the role," Noraine tacked on.

"And we don't want him to think he can drop into town and make a play for you," Sunnie said, bringing up the rear. "I bet he figures that he can break down your defenses. You're probably nothing more than a country bumpkin to him now since he's sampled the city treats Charlotte has to offer."

Lisa didn't want to hear any more, mainly because her sisters might have a point. The old Myles wouldn't do her that way. But did she know the new Myles? The one who was now a wealthy race-car celebrity?

"We want to know that you'll be able to handle him, Lisa. You're still young and naive when it comes to men. Myles is the only boyfriend you've ever had. For some reason you've refused to get serious about anyone else."

It was on the tip of Lisa's tongue to point out that they weren't knocking down any doors to get serious about any men, either. "Look, I'm a big girl. Thanks for your concern but I can handle my own business. I don't need the three of you telling me how I should handle Myles. I'm not stupid."

Sunnie shook her head sadly. "No, you're not stupid, but you're a woman who's still in love."

"I NOW PRONOUNCE YOU man and wife," Reverend Hall said smiling. "You may kiss your bride."

As soon as Ronald pulled Sheila into his arms, Myles looked at Lisa and mouthed, *This ought to be interesting.*

And it was.

It took several cleared throats and concentrated coughs before Ronald released Sheila from his arms while beaming proudly. He didn't appear the least embarrassed that he'd practically gnawed her lips off in front of a church full of people.

When most of the attendees left for the reception, which was to be held at the Chiefland Civic Center—Sheila's parents were paying top dollar to have it open on Christmas—the wedding party stayed back for pictures. And it seemed the bride and groom had wanted a slew of them.

Lisa found, more often than not, she was paired with Myles or was squeezed close to him for several group shootings. And each time she tried convincing herself that, as she had told her sisters earlier that day, any feelings she once had for him were in the past, and what she was experiencing around him was due to overwrought hormones. Although she was convinced that was the case, her pulse rate still went up whenever he was within five feet of her, which was most of the time.

"Hey, how about taking a picture of me and my wedding partner," Myles surprised Lisa by asking the photographer. "I'll pay for it.

"Certainly, Mr. Joseph," the man said, smiling brightly, and it was easy to tell he was a NASCAR fan.

Before she could recover from Myles's request, he had pulled her into his arms and plastered her to his side while they looked into the camera. She tried ignoring him. It didn't help matters that he looked excruciatingly sexy in his black tux and white shirt.

The photographer wanted several different poses and Myles was happy to oblige the man. She decided not to make a fuss and go along with things, wondering what Myles intended to do with the photos when he received them.

Mrs. Bonner clapped her hands to get everyone's attention. "Listen up, folks. We're about to leave for the reception. There will be more pictures so it would simplify things quite a bit if you remained partnered for a while so I won't have to look for anyone. That means—" Mrs. Bonner said, smiling over at the bride and groom "—you two will remain together, although I doubt anyone would try to pry you apart."

Lisa thought so, too, especially with the real serious look on Ronald's face. He hadn't let Sheila out of his sight since they had been presented as man and wife. If anything, she figured the wedding planner needed to worry about whether Ronald and Sheila would actually make it to the reception.

"Are you ready to leave for the reception?"

Lisa almost jumped. Myles's warm breath was close to her ear. "Yes, but I drove my car, so we can meet up there."

He shook his head as if that suggestion wouldn't work. "You heard Mrs. Bonner. You and I are supposed to stay together. Besides, if we ride over in one car, that will give us a chance to talk."

She glanced up at him. "About what?"

"A number of things, but mainly the hard glares I'm getting from your family."

She raised her eyes to the ceiling. "Really, Myles, when did my family's attitude ever bother you?"

He met her eyes. "I didn't say they bothered me. I said we need to talk about it."

She took a deep breath. First her sisters and now him. Everybody had one thing or another to say. Her parents had tried cornering her before the start of the wedding, but she had dashed off, saying Sheila needed to see her.

"Fine, I figure it's about time anyway," she said, walking ahead of him out of the church. In two long strides he caught up with her and took her hand into his.

"Hey, slow down, will you?"

She didn't say anything. She couldn't. The feel of her small hand encased in his brought back memories of a time when holding hands had been as much a part of their lives as eating. She almost pulled her hand back but rationalized that he was only holding her hand and it was no big deal.

By the time they made it to the parking lot it was

a big deal. It reminded her of all the things she had missed over the past five years; things she had been denied because of him—the companionship of a man who cared about her. What her sisters had said that morning was true. Since Myles had walked out of her life, she hadn't wanted to get involved with anyone else, refusing to share her heart and risk another heartbreak.

Myles had been quick to kick her to the curb when the opportunity came racing his way, no pun intended. For the past five years she had convinced herself that it was okay; that she had loved him enough to want to see him chase after his dream, even if it had meant leaving her behind. But there was one thing that teed her off each time she thought about it…which was the reason she tried not to dwell on it.

Not once had he returned to Chiefland. He had left without looking back. He hadn't called her on her birthday, Christmas, New Year's Day or Valentine's Day. It was as if once he had left town he hadn't felt he'd left behind anything of value.

She pulled her hand from his, no longer wanting to feel the warmth. He looked at her, but her attention had moved to the car they had approached. It was a beautiful steel-gray convertible.

She glanced at him. "Is this your car?"

He opened the car door for her. "Yeah, it's my personal wheels."

"Nice."

"Thanks." He closed the door and walked in front of the car to open the driver's door. He hesitated before starting the engine. He waited until she was buckled in, then said, "Tell me something."

"What?"

"Just now, why did you pull your hand out of mine?"

Lisa frowned as she thought about the answer to his question. She also recalled something else that bothered her. The comment one of her sisters had made about her being a country bumpkin compared to the city treats he'd been sampling.

"Lisa?"

She turned to face him and tilted her chin. "You want to know why I pulled my hand out of yours? Why don't you tell me the reason you were holding my hand in the first place?"

Myles met her gaze and asked softly, "Do you really have to ask me that, Lisa?"

"Yes."

He frowned. "Why?"

"Why not?" she shot back.

"I like touching you, Lisa. I always have."

Lisa's heart began pounding in her chest as she remembered his touch. She inhaled deeply and quickly decided they were memories she could do without. Memories she needed to make off limits around him.

"That was then, Myles. This is now. I'm not your girlfriend anymore, remember? I don't mean anything to you."

Seemingly annoyed with what she had said, he started the engine and replied, "You only got that partly right, Lisa. You aren't my girlfriend, but you do mean something to me. You mean a lot to me, in fact."

"Yeah, right."

His frown deepened and he glanced over at her, giving her an incredulous look. "You don't believe me?"

"Why should I? As I recall, you're the one who broke things off. You wanted a clean break and that's what you got. This is the first time I've seen you in *five* years. You left town and didn't stay in touch. I could have died for all you know."

He stepped on the brakes and brought the car to a screeching halt. "Don't say that."

He was angry. She could tell. The only thing she didn't know was why; especially when everything she had said was true. "Why are you upset? Does the truth hurt, Myles? If so, then good. Now you get to feel my pain."

She quickly looked away from his penetrating stare, wishing she hadn't said that. The one thing she didn't want him to know was how his leaving had affected her. Even when he had said goodbye, she had held back her tears, refusing to let him see her cry. Just like she was fighting to hold them back now as she remembered that night.

"Lisa, I—"

"No," she said, quickly turning back to him. "It's Ronald and Sheila's wedding day. Let's not ruin it for them by bringing up our past when it doesn't matter anymore. You moved on and I survived."

While the car began moving again, she brushed aside the thought that she had been holding her feelings inside for so long that she was beginning to believe what she'd just said about surviving.

He turned into the parking lot of the civic center and moments later brought the car to a stop. Without wasting any time she unbuckled her seatbelt and was about to get out of the car when he touched her arm. She came close to jerking back but didn't. She looked over at him and met his intense eyes.

"We won't talk today, but we *will* talk, Lisa. You can count on it."

CHAPTER FOUR

LATER THAT EVENING Myles entered Ronald's apartment alone. The newlyweds were on their way to Jacksonville where they would spend the night before catching the cruise ship tomorrow for the Bahamas.

Myles couldn't stop the smile that touched his lips when he thought of the intensity of his best friend's desire for the woman he had chosen for his wife. Later tonight, behind closed doors, Sheila would find out whether putting Ronald off for six months had been such a good idea. She had been a beautiful bride and Ronald a hot-and-bothered groom.

Tossing his tuxedo jacket onto a chair, Myles crossed the room with his hands in his pockets and walked over to the window. Ronald's condo was located in one of the exclusive areas of town and the huge home he was having built for Sheila was on ten acres of land close to the Suwannee River.

He stood at the window, gazing out at the

darkness, seeing nothing but feeling everything. Feeling more love for a woman than he had a right to feel. More love than she could possibly know he felt. Five years hadn't destroyed his love for her; it had only intensified it. Seeing her again made him realize that every moment he spent away from her had boosted the emotions he felt. He hadn't needed to see her to know it. But he had needed to see her for his own peace of mind. He could admit that now.

When he had gotten the call from Ronald in the summer asking that he be his best man, he had immediately known he would do so because he would have a chance to see Lisa again without breaking the promise he had made to her parents; a promise that he loved their daughter enough to get out of her life and stay out.

And now that he had seen her, he wasn't so sure he could return to Charlotte and live the life he had for the past five years. It was a life where he had tried so hard to forget her—but he never could. There wasn't a woman out there who could take her place in his life—and his heart.

So where did that leave him? Where did that leave *them?*

As far as she was concerned, there was no *them,* and a part of him felt that maybe he should accept that and move on, leave in a few days like he'd planned and be a spectator at the race in Daytona to cheer Bronson on to victory. But another part of him could not. It was the part that had heard the hurt and pain in Lisa's voice. It was hurt and pain the years hadn't erased and for her to believe that she was of no value to him, or possibly never had been, was unacceptable.

He turned when he heard his cell phone go off and quickly crossed the room to get it out of his jacket. "Yes?"

"Merry Christmas. I know the day is almost over, but I thought I'd check to make sure you'll still coming to Daytona next week."

A smile touched the corners of Myles's lips. "Bronson, Merry Christmas to you, too, and yes, I'll be there."

He heard the loud noise in the background. "Having a party, Bron?"

He heard his friend's chuckle over the loud music that was playing. "I decided to open the Race Track for a couple of friends. Wished you were here to party with us."

Any other time Myles would have wished he was there, too, but not this time. He was exactly where he wanted to be, right in the same town, breathing the same air as Lisa.

The Race Track Café was a popular hang-out in Charlotte that was owned by Bronson and several NASCAR race-car drivers. Myles found himself spending a lot of time there.

"Donovan sends his greetings," Bronson said. "He would come to the phone, but he is kind of indisposed at the moment."

Myles shook his head. For Donovan Steele, being indisposed meant he was cornered off somewhere with a woman. The man took his role as one of Charlotte's most sought-after bachelors very seriously. It was a top spot that Donovan shared with Bronson.

"Thanks. And tell Donovan that I might be missing the Christmas party, but I'll be at the New Year's party to celebrate your win in Daytona."

After talking to Bronson a few minutes longer they ended the call and his thoughts immediately went back Lisa. Once the picture-taking sessions at the reception had ended, she had avoided him, not giving them a chance to spend time together again. He wondered if she'd deliberately put distance between them because she knew her family would want her to.

He shook his head, realizing that wasn't the case. If he knew anything about Lisa it was the fact that she had never succumbed to any pressures her family placed on her. She had always been considered the rebel in the family, thinking for herself and not catering to what others wanted. That had been the main reason her parents had sought him out, pleading for him to do what they considered the right thing when it became apparent that she wouldn't.

Maybe he had hurt her too much and she could never forgive him?

He headed for the guest bedroom. Without a family to call his own Christmas would end for him just like the other Christmases that he had spent for the past five years. Alone.

LISA ENTERED HER APARTMENT, closed the door behind her and leaned against it. It might have been her imagination but she could swear she could detect Myles's scent. And when she closed her eyes she could still see the intensity of his eyes as they followed her around the room while greeting those she knew at the reception.

At any point and time she could glance up and meet his eyes and immediately she would feel sensations flow through her. Sensations that only Myles could evoke. He was still attracted to her, that much she could figure out from the way his eyes would roam over her, like a private and personal caress.

She kicked off her heels as she made her way to her bedroom. She was grateful that neither her parents nor her sisters had tried discussing Myles with her anymore. She was well aware that they had known she and Myles had arrived at the reception together, just like she knew they were aware she had caught a ride back to the church with Sheila's cousin Judy to get her car.

As much as she wanted to, she couldn't forget Myles's words that the two of them still had some talking to do. A part of her knew he intended to make good on that promise. And she wasn't looking forward to it.

MYLES SMILED AS HE entered Sybil's Delicatessen, and immediately the thought of dough, powdered sugar and honey made his stomach grumble. Sybil Porter had owned the pastry shop on the main street in Chiefland for as long as he could remember, and he considered her the best baker in the entire Southeast. While growing up it wasn't uncommon for him to stop by on his way to school or to the garage. One of the things that made Sybil special was that she had treated him with kindness.

The bell above the door had jingled as he walked in and the older woman turned in his direction and smiled. "I wondered when you would finally drop by. Once I heard you had returned to town I knew I might as well get the dough ready for those strawberry tarts you liked so much," she said.

Myles laughed. "You mean you made a batch of sticky fingers just for me?"

"Yep. I figured you deserved them. Not every day one of our own goes up against the likes of Grady McClellan and wins a NASCAR Sprint Cup Series race."

He lifted a brow. "When did you start keeping up with the races?"

"When I heard you had moved from being a mechanic for a NASCAR team to a race-car driver. Joe still comes in on occasion and he's proud as a peacock. Have you seen him?"

"Yes, I've seen him." What he didn't tell her was that upon arriving in Chiefland the first place he'd gone was out to Joe's place. The older man had since retired from working at Harris Auto and spent his days fishing on the lake behind his home. At seventy-five, Joe, the man who had taught him everything he knew about cars, was sharp as ever and just as ornery. But Joe had been the closest thing to a grandfather he'd had, especially after his own grandfather and father had gotten killed in a car accident trying to outrun the law. The Chiefland police had tried stopping them for speeding and, instead of pulling over to get a ticket, the two men thought they would give the cops a run for their money. Unfortunately, they hadn't planned on a huge semi truck unexpectedly pulling into their path while they'd been doing close to a hundred miles an hour. That had left Myles with no family. His mother had run off when he'd turned ten, fed up with her husband and father-in-law's drunkenness, and never looked back. When he turned sixteen he'd received word that she had died of breast cancer.

Myles slid onto one of the bar stools at the counter, about ready to order a tart and a cup of coffee when Sybil motioned to a customer sitting alone at one of the tables in the back. It was Lisa. She was reading the newspaper and hadn't noticed him enter.

"Wouldn't you prefer to join her?" Sybil asked, smiling from ear to ear.

He returned her smile as he got off the stool. "Yes, I would."

"I know what you want and will bring your order over to you."

"Thanks," Myles said, remembering that Sybil was one of the few people who thought he and Lisa made a good match.

He headed toward the table where Lisa was sitting and before he got within five feet, her scent filled his nostrils. It was as seductive as always and the fragrance stirred something deep and elementally male inside him. "Good morning, Lisa."

She jerked her head up. Her eyes widened in surprise and he saw that her grip on her cup of coffee faltered somewhat. "Myles," she said, putting down the cup. "I see you decided to stay in town another day."

"Yes," he said, taking the seat across from her. "I promised Ronald that I would hang around. He ordered some new furniture as a surprise for Sheila. It's going to arrive sometime tomorrow."

Lisa smiled. "That's wonderful. She'll be pleased."

Myles chuckled. "Not as pleased as Ronald since it's a bigger bed. A California king-size."

"I didn't know there was such a thing."

"Me, either. But it's bigger than a regular king."

There was silence as she sipped her coffee. Then he asked, "Are you up early to catch the after-Christmas sales?" It wasn't eight o'clock yet.

"No, I'm usually an early riser."

He, of all people, should know that. The couple of times they had managed to get away on private trips together, she was usually the first one awake in the mornings. One such trip had been to Cedar Keys. He would never forget that weekend, mainly because it had been their last getaway together.

Suddenly he wanted to be alone with her, away from the townspeople's prying eyes. Besides, they needed to talk. "How would you like to go riding with me?"

She lifted a brow. "Go riding where?"

"To Ocala. I have a huge fan there who owns a sports shop. I promised if I was ever in the area that I would make a pit stop to sign a bunch of T-shirts he sells."

She studied the contents of her coffee before looking back up at him. "I'm not sure that's a good idea, Myles."

"I disagree. Besides, like I said yesterday, we need to talk."

"Talking won't change what happened."

"No, it won't. But I refuse to leave town having you believe what you do." He knew she didn't have to ask what he was talking about. He was referring to the comments she had made yesterday. "Come with me, Lisa."

Silence surrounded them again and then Lisa set down her coffee cup. "All right, Myles. I'll go with you."

CHAPTER FIVE

IT WAS A BEAUTIFUL DAY and with the top down on Myles's convertible, Lisa enjoyed the feel of the wind on her face. She glanced over at Myles. As usual he looked the epitome of sexy. He wore a pair of jeans and a pullover jersey that said *Men of Steele.*

As if he felt her attention on him, he glanced over at her, taking his eyes off the road for only a quick second. She wasn't sure if it was her imagination or not, but his grip on the steering wheel appeared to tighten.

"Thanks for coming with me, Lisa."

She shrugged. "You don't have to thank me. I hadn't planned on doing much of anything today anyway. My sisters are the shopaholics in the family. They drove to Tallahassee before the crack of dawn to hit several of the malls."

There was silence again and then he said, "I want to set you straight on a comment you made yesterday about me not knowing if you were alive or dead.

That's so far from the truth it isn't funny. I talked to Ronald and Joe often and I always ask about you."

His statement surprised Lisa. "Why would you do that?"

He took an exit off the interstate. "Why wouldn't I do that?"

"I can think of several reasons. You left me behind because you didn't want me anymore."

Myles looked at her and the anger she'd seen in his eyes yesterday when she had made a similar statement was back. "I refuse to drive any further until we clear that up."

"Keep driving, Myles. There's nothing to clear up. Although I did hurt for the longest time, I understand why you did it."

"I don't think you do," he said, pulling into a fruit market off of Interstate 75. He parked the car in an isolated area of the parking lot and released the lever to push back his seat to stretch out his long legs. He then turned his body toward her.

"So tell me, Lisa, why do you think I left town that night?"

She rolled her eyes. "I know why you left town," she said, wondering why he was determined to rehash things. "You were contacted by a NASCAR team because they were interested in you being a mechanic for them."

"Yes, but that would not have affected our rela-

tionship. I still would hav
have sent for you when yo
matter what, I still wanted to ma

Now it was Lisa's time to be angr
but I don't recall you presenting that as
distinctively recall you saying you were lea
Charlotte and that we needed to end things."

"Yes, but that was only after your parents came
to see me."

Her eyes widened. "What?"

"I'm talking about you threatening to quit school in your junior year, telling your parents you were doing it to marry me, although I hadn't officially asked you yet. I had purchased the ring and intended to ask you Christmas night, but after your parents' visit I knew I couldn't mess up your life like that. You deserved better and—"

"What on earth are you talking about? I never threatened to quit school in my junior year."

Myles stared at her. "Are you saying your parents lied to me?"

"They did if they told you that."

Myles didn't say anything for the longest time and neither did Lisa as it became crystal clear just what her parents had done. And it didn't take a rocket scientist to figure out why.

"How could you have believed them?" Lisa asked in a soft voice.

ars she was
thinking the
years. "Why
ur parents and
d your future.
ings for you if

the longest time
ed you."

"I know, but ... tty convincing. I hadn't expected them to outright lie about something like that."

She knew that he truly hadn't. Her parents were members of Chiefland's upstanding community. They weren't supposed to lie. "Why didn't you ask me about it?"

"I did. I called you the next day and in a roundabout way I asked how your classes were going. You sounded stressed and said you were fed up and ready to quit."

She frowned, trying to recall that time and suddenly it did occur to her that she had spoken with him a couple of days before they had broken up. She had been studying for finals and she had told him that she was frustrated. "I remember you calling and saying that, Myles, but I hadn't meant it."

"Well, I didn't know that. I was thinking about

what your parents said and then hearing you confirm their words made me realize that I couldn't let you quit school just to be with me."

Lisa was silent for a brief moment and then asked softly, "You bought me a ring?" She had expected one, was hoping to get one, but what she'd gotten instead was his goodbye.

"Yes. I bought it four months before. In fact you almost came across it when you spent the night at my place and were going through my gear. You never looked in my gear for anything and I figured it was safe there."

She remembered that morning when she had sneaked into town from Gainesville and spent the night with him. She had been looking in his gear for more condoms. "So, you figured you were doing me a favor by leaving?"

MYLES WASN'T SURE SHE was asking a question or making a statement but decided to treat it as a question. "Yes. I loved you just that much, Lisa."

He watched as she wiped a tear from her eye and, knowing he wanted to hold her in his arms and could only do just so much with bucket seats, he released his seat belt, opened his car door and walked in front of the car to the other side. He then opened her door, leaned down and unbuckled her seat belt. "Come here for a minute."

Desire inched its way up his spine as he stood back to give her room to get out, appreciating the fit of her jeans and blouse. The moment she was out of the car he took her hand and pulled her into his arms, both wanting and needing to kiss her. He captured her mouth with his.

And she kissed him back.

The moment she did, years of denying himself the one and only woman he had ever loved came crashing down on him and he deepened the kiss. Every cell in his body seemed to light up, heat up, and send shivers through every single pore.

He tightened his arms around her, thinking the memories of their kiss didn't come close to doing justice to the real thing. And he also knew that he would never let her parents or anyone come between them again. No matter how many races he won, or how popular in life he became, he could only be complete with one woman by his side. The one he was holding in his arms. The one he had intended on asking to be his wife five years ago.

"I'm going to confront your parents about the lie they told me, Lisa," he murmured against her lips, glorying in the taste of her.

"We both are," she whispered, pulling in a deep breath.

He nodded. "And just so you'll know, so you won't have any doubt, I never stopped loving you."

And then he gathered her into his arms and held her. He released her when he realized they were getting unwanted attention.

He pulled back and looked at her. "Do you want to continue on to Ocala or turn around now?"

"I was looking forward to the drive with you. Now that we know what happened, we shouldn't let anyone ruin any more days for us. And just so you know, I never stopped loving you, either," she said.

Because he couldn't resist, he pulled her into his arms for another kiss.

IT WAS LATE AFTERNOON before they returned to Chiefland and drove straight to her parents' home. Lisa was glad she had suggested they wait before confronting her parents. Her time with him in Ocala had been priceless, definitely special. It was as if now that their true feelings were out there, she felt renewed inner joy, a sense of peace.

Although they had yet to discuss where they would go from there, she knew they would have a future together. Each time he had found the opportune time and private spot, he had kissed her, awakening more and more desires within her, making her feel wanted and loved.

"Looks like your parents have company."

His voice intruded into her thoughts and she noticed the cars parked in front of her parents' home.

"Just my sisters. It seems they are back from shopping."

She was glad they were there, since she intended to find out if they'd known what their parents had done and had hidden it from her. A part of her wanted to believe they hadn't known, but she couldn't be certain until she questioned them. As far as she was concerned, her entire family had a lot of explaining to do.

"WHAT IS HE DOING HERE?" George St. Claire asked in an angry tone the moment Lisa and Myles walked through the door. Everyone was gathered in the living room around the big-screen television George had gotten from his daughters for Christmas.

"Myles and I are here so we can talk. There seems to be some sort of misunderstanding as to why he left town, Dad." She glanced in the direction of her mother, saw the guilty look on her mother's face, and then said, "And Mom." She then turned to her sisters and the expressions on their faces let her know they didn't have a clue as to what she was talking about.

"There wasn't any misunderstanding. Your mom and I did what we felt needed to be done under the circumstances. You were making a mistake with him and it had gone on long enough."

"So you thought going to Myles and telling him a lie about my dropping out of college, blaming him as the reason for it and playing on his love for me to get him to leave Chiefland was the solution?"

The look on her father's face held no regret. "Yes, but it was only after your mom and I found that pregnancy kit by accident in your luggage when you came home from college."

Lisa felt Myles's surprised gaze on her and she turned toward him. She saw the questions in his eyes and knew what he wanted to know, especially since they had never made love without using some sort of protection. She shook her head before turning back to her parents.

"That pregnancy kit was not mine," she said, drawing in a shaky yet furious breath. "It belonged to a friend. There was never a time that I thought I was pregnant with Myles's child."

She didn't feel a need to go into any details and tell her parents that she had gotten a frantic call from Sheila one evening asking that she pick one up and drop it off at Ronald's place for her. Luckily it had been a false alarm. "Even if you thought it was mine, you should have asked me about it and not assumed anything. Not to mention the fact that you went through my luggage *by accident.*"

No one said anything for the longest moment and then Myles spoke, wrapping his arms around Lisa's waist and pulling her to him while he faced her parents. "I told the both of you how much I loved your daughter and that I intended to make something of myself for her. Lisa has always been the driving force behind my desire to succeed, mainly because she was one of the few people who believed in me. No man or woman can ask for more than that in the person they choose to be their lifelong mate."

He then tilted his head and met Lisa's gaze. "I love you just as much now as I did then, Lisa. If anything, I love you even more because you never stopped loving me—like I never stopped loving you. I still want a future with you if you want one with me."

Tears filled Lisa's eyes and at that moment she wondered what she had done to deserve such a wonderful man as Myles. They had dated for almost three years and her family, refusing to accept him, had gone so far as to deliberately break them up. Yet he still wanted her.

She shook her head and inhaled deeply before saying, "Yes, I still want a future with you, but I can't have one."

She glanced around the room and saw the surprised looks on the faces of her parents and sisters before turning to meet Myles's eyes. "And the reason I can't have one is because I don't deserve you, Myles."

She paused to wipe the tears from her eyes before continuing, "For years everyone thought I was too good for you. But the truth of the matter is that I'm not good enough for you. You asked me why I didn't pursue my dream of becoming a teacher. The reason is because once you left I couldn't refocus on passing the test to get my teaching certificate. I felt like a failure to lose you and to lose out on my dream as well. Evidently, I wasn't as smart as everyone thought."

And without saying anything else she turned and walked out of the house.

LISA SAT IN MYLES'S CAR waiting for him to come out of her parents' home. To her way of thinking it was taking him more time than necessary to do so. As far as she was concerned, there was nothing else left to be said.

The front door opened and Myles emerged. She could see her father standing in the doorway looking at her, but she turned her head away.

Miles opened the car door, slid beneath the steering wheel and glanced over at her. "You okay?" he asked in a soft, yet husky voice.

"Yes, I'm fine. Just take me home please." She wanted to be alone to sort out her parents' betrayal.

"Talk to me, Lisa."

She turned toward him as he pulled onto the road. "What do you want me to say?"

"That you love me."

She smiled sadly. "I love you."

He smiled. “Good, now we’re getting somewhere. Now tell me that you’re going to marry me.”

“I can’t.”

“Sure you can. I heard what you told your folks back there, but what you fail to realize is that our relationship doesn’t concern them anymore. It only concerns me and you and what we want. You are not a failure, and I think you’re one of the smartest women I know. And I want you, Lisa, and I love you, too.”

“Please, just let things be, Myles.”

He shook his head. “Sorry, I can’t do that. Once before I gave in where you’re concerned, but I won’t do it again. We were made for each other. You are mine and I am yours, and I feel sorry for anyone who hasn’t figured that out yet.”

He chuckled. “But it seems that you’re the one who hasn’t figured it out yet. I’ll give you some time if you need it—but not much. I’m leaving the day after tomorrow and heading to Daytona. I was going to ask you to come with me, but I think you and your family need time together to mend a few broken fences. I also think you need time to think about us, Lisa.”

He brought the car to a stop in front of her apartment building. A few moments later he walked her up to her apartment. When she invited him inside he shook his head, knowing what would happen once they were behind closed doors. “No, sweetheart. There’s still some doubt in your mind about us. You say you love me, yet you say you won’t spend the rest of your life with me as my wife. I refuse to make love to you again until that happens, until you’re absolutely sure of your place in my heart and my life.”

He leaned over and kissed her lips and pulled her into his arms. “I want you, but not this way. Only as my wife. The only race I want to win right now is the one to the altar with you by my side.”

He then released her, took a step back and walked back to his car.

CHAPTER SIX

THE NEXT DAY LISA WAS moping around the house still wearing her pjs at noon when the doorbell rang. She tossed down the magazine she was reading and raced to the door, hoping it was Myles.

She let out a disappointed sigh when she looked out the peephole and saw her parents and sisters. They had tried calling her last night and most of that morning, but she hadn't bothered answering the phone.

Deciding she would at least find out what they wanted, she opened the door. "Yes?"

"May we come in?" her father asked.

Instead of answering, she stepped aside to let all five individuals pass. She closed the door and turned to face them. She studied her father's features. He looked as if he hadn't slept most of the night. The last time she had seen him this way was that year he had pulled an all-nighter at the weather station when Hurricane Charley's fury had passed through town.

"We owe you an apology," her father said in a tired

yet sincere voice. "Your mom and I made a grave mistake in trying to dictate what man you should have in your life."

He paused a moment then said, "She and I take full responsibility for our actions. Your sisters knew nothing about it, so hold them blameless. Our excuse for our actions is that you're our baby girl and we were worried about you. Of the four, you're the only one who had a steady boyfriend and we could see how close the two of you were. When we saw that pregnancy kit we jumped to the wrong conclusions and we apologize for that as well. Can you find it in your heart to forgive us?"

When she didn't answer fast enough her father said, "Just so you'll know, we apologized to Myles last night after you had walked out of the house. He accepted our apology and has forgiven us. He also knows that if the two of you want to marry, he has my and your mother's blessings."

Lisa's gaze shifted from one family member to the other. She loved each one of them and she knew they loved her, but they had to realize that her business was hers and not theirs. "Will you all promise to let me live my life the way I want? And let any mistakes I make along the way be *my* mistakes?"

Her father smiled and nodded assuredly. "Yes, we promise."

Lisa crossed the room and walked into her

parents' open arms, and then she proceeded to get hugs from each of her sisters.

SUNNIE SURVEYED THE hundreds of people in the stands and shook her head. "Honestly, Lisa, how on earth do you expect to find Myles among all these people?"

Lisa had arrived in Daytona earlier that day with her sisters and parents. Tonight was the night of the New Year's Eve charity race, and although they knew Myles wasn't racing, his team was. His boss, Bronson Scott, was expected to place in the top five.

She had left her parents in their seats in the stands while she and her sisters made their way over to the Scott Motorsports pit box. She and Myles had spoken several times over the course of the past twenty-four hours, but she hadn't told him she planned to come to tonight's race. She intended to surprise him. Just like she planned on telling him that she intended to marry him…if the offer was still out there.

To keep her arrival a secret from Myles, she had contacted the headquarters of the Scott Motorsports in Charlotte. After explaining her dilemma, they told her they would give her phone number to Bronson and to wait for his call. In less than twenty minutes, Bronson Scott had contacted her.

He told her he was presently in Daytona and, after

obtaining the name of the hotel where she was staying, he indicated he would send a courier to deliver complimentary passes and would keep the news from Myles as a secret.

"And you sure this pass will get us behind the scenes to where Myles is?" Wendy asked as they continued their trek along the outskirts of the race track. The race would officially start in a few minutes and Lisa wanted to be as close to Myles as she could. This was his life, and as his wife, this would soon become her life as well.

"Yes, I'm sure. Bronson Scott gave me good directions," Lisa said as she continued walking. A few moments later she sighed in relief when she saw the sign indicating Scott Motorsports.

She recognized Myles immediately. His back was to her but she would recognize his good-looking tush anywhere. "Myles!"

He turned at the sound of her voice and the smile that suddenly appeared on his face would endear him to her for a lifetime. He quickly started walking toward her. She began running and he caught her into his arms and immediately captured her lips with his.

Myles ignored the whistles and catcalls and continued to kiss her and she kissed him back with all the love in her heart. Finally, he released her and, with a big grin on his face, asked, "Lisa, what are you doing here?"

She smiled back up at him. "I'm here for you. I want to tell you in person that I love you and if you still want me, I want to be your wife."

He let out a huge yell and lifted her off her feet and twirled her around. "Yes, I still want you, sweetheart, I'll always want you."

BRONSON SCOTT SMILED AS he witnessed Myles and the woman in a passionate embrace and figured she must be Lisa, the woman he had spoken to on the phone who was the love of Myles's life and the woman Myles had told him about so many times.

He looked past them to the three women standing on the sidelines and wondered about one in particular. Donovan Steele was standing beside him and Bronson whispered, "That woman in the jeans and purple top. Who is she?"

Donovan frowned at him. "A woman is the last thing that should be on your mind now, Bron. Just concentrate on the race, will you? We expect you to cross the finish line tonight with an impressive showing."

An arrogant smile touched the corners of Bronson's lips. "I will. Just make sure you have her name when I finish."

A few hours later, Bronson zoomed across the finish line grabbing a second place finish. Donovan was there when Bronson climbed out of his car. "Okay who is she, Steele?"

Donovan shook his head, grinning. "I talked to Myles. She is one of his soon-to-be-sisters-in-law. The three women you saw are triplets and the one you asked about is Sunnie St. Claire."

A huge smile touched Bronson's lips as he glanced around seeking out the woman again. "Thanks, Donovan. You've done your part. Now it's up to me to do mine."

EPILOGUE

TWO WEEKS LATER in her parents' lavishly decorated backyard, Lisa St. Claire and Myles Joseph became husband and wife. Myles had surprised her by placing on her finger the ring he had intended to give her years ago. Total happiness surrounded them and they fully intended to live happily ever after.

During the reception they walked hand in hand greeting their guests, including many drivers from the NASCAR Sprint Cup Series.

Moments later, Myles leaned down and whispered, "Let me know when you're ready to leave."

They had made plans to stay in a hotel in Orlando and would be leaving directly after the reception. Tomorrow morning they would catch a plane out of Orlando to spend four weeks in Key West.

Lisa smiled up at her husband. "I'm ready whenever you are." She then looked around. "Where're Ronald and Sheila?"

Myles chuckled. "They left a few minutes ago. I

understand they're still getting a kick out of breaking in their mega-bed."

He pulled Lisa closer into his arms. "Mmm, Ronald likes it so much that I'm thinking of getting us one. It comes highly recommended. But until then, a regular bed will have to do."

Lisa wrapped her arms around her husband, thinking he was so right. Until then, a regular bed would have to do.

When the photographer who had been hired to take pictures began snapping away, Lisa decided to give him a picture worth taking. She smoothed her palm over Myles's jaw and then on tiptoe she captured his lips with hers. This was a day she had thought would never happen. But it had. She had made it to the finish line, winning the race with the man she loved.

MARISA CARROLL

is the pen name of authors Carol Wagner and Marian Franz. The team has been writing bestselling books for almost twenty-five years. During that time they have published more than forty-five titles, most for the Harlequin Superromance line, and are the recipients of several industry awards, including a Lifetime Achievement Award from *Romantic Times BOOKreviews* and a RITA® Award nomination from Romance Writers of America. Their books have been featured on the *USA TODAY*, Waldenbooks and B. Dalton bestseller lists. The sisters live near each other in northwestern Ohio, surrounded by children, grandchildren, brothers, sisters, aunts, uncles, cousins and old and dear friends.

ALL THEY WANT FOR CHRISTMAS

Marisa Carroll

CHAPTER ONE

"THERE'S A STORE THAT'S still open," Annie Collier said, pointing out the front passenger-side window of the motor home at the lighted sign above the cinder-block building. "Ron's SuperMart. Pull in there, Daddy. We can ask if there's somewhere nearby we can stop for the night."

"Sweetie, we're only forty-five miles from Ann Arbor. We can make it fine. We don't need to get off the road."

"It's too icy to keep going. You heard the weather report. Two inches of ice by midnight. Do you know how much every additional millimeter of ice increases the odds of us having an accident?"

Trace Collier grinned over at his daughter. "No, but I bet you do." Annie was ten going on eleven, tall for her age, with strawberry-blond hair and her mother's hazel eyes. She was a genius, and not just in her father's eyes. She had an IQ that was almost off the charts and that's why they were chugging along the back roads of southern Michigan this Wednesday before Thanksgiving. He was enrolling her in a special program, so gifted children, like Annie, could study at the University of Michigan at Ann Arbor.

But they'd been routed off the Interstate soon after they crossed the Ohio state line into Michigan and now they were winding their way through the Irish Hills, an easy, scenic, hour's drive to their destination—if they hadn't been traveling in the middle of an early winter ice storm. Trace Collier had been driving stock cars professionally for eighteen years, half his life, but this behemoth forty-five-foot, diesel motor home was in a different league altogether. He wouldn't mind getting off the narrow, icy county highway before dark, himself.

"We've got reservations at the University Lodge," he reminded his daughter. "They've got an indoor pool and a great Thanksgiving buffet. Turkey, stuffing, all the trimmings." He'd made sure of that. He was the best dad he could be to his daughter, but a gourmet cook he was not. Annie frowned, opened her mouth to argue some more. "And pumpkin pie," he added quickly.

The moment the words left his mouth, the tail end of the big diesel motor home got loose and skidded toward the ditch at the side of the road. Annie gasped, and a startled yip came from behind him. This was followed by the sound of a small body sliding off the leather sofa and hitting the floor.

“Peanuts,” Annie squealed, twisting in her seat, her hand going to the clasp of her seat belt.

“Stay put,” Trace growled. The commanding tone of his voice elicited even more frantic yips from the salon area. Trace ignored the commotion, knowing Annie would obey his order. With one eye on the ice-coated road ahead and the other on the side mirror, he watched the rear wheels of the four-by-four he was towing leave the pavement. “Hang on, Annie.” He braced himself for the lurch of the big rig to the right. He resisted the urge to fight the wheel and stand on the brake. Instead he steered into the slide, eased off the accelerator and somehow got the pickup’s wheels back on the pavement. It was all over with in a matter of seconds, just the way a spinout happened on the race track, too.

He glanced over at his daughter, clutching the armrests of the leather captain’s seat that almost dwarfed her. Her face was so pale the smattering of freckles across her nose stood out in stark relief. “It’s okay, baby. We’re back on the road. Your mama was watchin’ over us again today. Even Peanuts isn’t hurt.” The curly-haired little poodle was standing on his hind legs beside Annie’s seat, whimpering to be taken into her arms, but he appeared unharmed, only shaken up. They all were.

“Let’s stop, Dad,” Annie whispered, cuddling the little dog that had been the last gift he and Beth had given her together. "It's too slippery. Pull into the store. Ask them if there's a place to stay. We're close to the speedway, aren't we? There should be campgrounds all around here."

They were close to the giant speedway complex where the NASCAR Sprint Cup Series cars raced twice each summer, but he'd never stayed in any of the campgrounds nearby, or even been in this part of the country at this time of year before. He and Beth always flew into the race venues a couple of days before the race and left the same way. He usually had a driver to drive the motor home to the race tracks. He'd never driven the coach himself until this year. He'd also be surprised if any of the area campgrounds were set up for winter camping. But the skid had shaken Annie badly, and sent an unwelcome jolt of adrenaline surging through his veins, as well. A pit stop was in order.

He steered the motor home into the nearly deserted gravel parking lot of the country grocery store and left it idling along the far edge in front of a windbreak of pine trees. Annie let Peanuts out to do his business while Trace checked the array of switches and lit panels that rivaled the cockpit display of a jetliner. Everything was running fine. Batteries at full charge, fuel tanks topped off, water tanks filled to the brim. If they had to, he and Annie and Peanuts could hold up in their home-away-from-home for three or four days without outside power sources or water supply.

Beth had loved the motor home. She'd loved being at one race track then onto the next during the NASCAR season. She'd always said living in the motor home was like playing house. A pretty expensive dollhouse, he'd always grumbled. And she'd always laughed. "Money is to spend," she would say, shaking her head. "And to do some good for others. You can't take it with you."

Two months later, at thirty-three, without a moment's illness or warning, she'd suffered a massive stroke. But the good Lord hadn't seen fit to take her immediately. She lingered on for almost two years, only a shadow of her laughing, loving self. She'd died just after Annie's eighth birthday, and he and his daughter had been fending for themselves ever since. A couple of months ago he'd sold their house in Concord, North Carolina, because he couldn't bear to live in it any longer, and when the NASCAR season ended, he and Annie had taken to the road, trying to outrun their loneliness and sorrow.

Some days he almost convinced himself it had worked. Almost.

"I'M NOT STAYING IN the truck. I've been walking on crutches since I was five. It's not that slippery out there."

Carrie Ferrell clamped her teeth tightly together to keep from ordering her fifteen-year-old son back into the vehicle. After all, Josh was right. He was an expert at getting around that way. Still, she couldn't help worrying that he might slip and fall on the ice and do yet more damage to his still healing ankle.

Six weeks ago Josh had undergone his eleventh surgery in nine years to repair the damage to his left foot and ankle he'd sustained in an ATV accident when he was five. The crushing injury had damaged the growth plates of his lower leg and ankle, necessitating numerous reconstructions in an attempt to give him the most flexibility and range of motion his foot and ankle could achieve.

He would never play professional sports, or run a record-breaking marathon, but Carrie had dedicated her life to giving her son the most normal childhood and the best chance at a successful adulthood she could manage. She didn't want to see all their hard work—and Josh's physical suffering—be for nothing because he insisted on following her into the grocery store.

But as her father so often told her, she couldn't wrap the boy in cotton balls and lock him in his bedroom until he was eighteen. She had to let him make his own mistakes, take his own risks. But not if it meant reinjuring the still healing ankle. She had invested too much of herself in his rehabilitation to let that happen. She turned around to order him back into the truck with Toby, their two-year-old golden retriever, only to find him a mere step behind her.

"Fastest man on crutches in the county," he said, giving her the devilish grin he'd inherited from his long-gone father. He was like Kyle in so many ways, the good ways, she always reminded herself. Not the cut-and-run, ne'er-do-well, that had walked out of both their lives with barely a backward glance.

"If you knock those pins out of alignment you'll be spending Thanksgiving in the orthopedic unit. Again," she said. Josh was a teenager. She might as well get used to this testing of limits. The obliging little towheaded kid who had endured months in traction and casts, and hours and hours in rehab, was a thing of the past. This scowling young man who was almost as tall as she was had somehow taken his place, seemingly overnight.

"Aye, aye, Captain Bligh," he said, lifting one crutch in a kind of salute.

"Be careful," Carrie yelped as Josh skated across a patch of ice on his good foot. She couldn't help it. She worried about him so much.

"Piece of cake. Or piece of pumpkin pie," Josh retorted, grinning harder because he'd managed to get a rise out of her. "Since that's what we came to get. Good thing Ron didn't close early like the hardware and the video stores."

"Hey, Carrie. Here to get your pie?" Ron Budde, the owner of the grocery was manning the register himself. Carrie wasn't surprised. It was like him to have sent his employees home early on a night like this, Thanksgiving eve or not.

"Yep. Can't have Thanksgiving without one of Ida May's pumpkin pecan pies." Ida May Cunningham had been running the bakery department of Ron's since Carrie was a little girl. She had customers come from all over the Irish Hills region, and Ohio and Indiana, too, just for her pies.

Ron lifted a white bakery box off the shelf behind the register. "Here it is. All ready to go."

Carrie fished in her purse for money and handed over a bill. Ron rang up her purchase and handed her the change as a man and a young girl walked up the frozen food aisle toward the checkout.

Carrie gave them a wave and a smile before she realized she'd greeted two complete strangers. But that's how it was in a town as small as Thunder Lake. Friendly waves and neighborly greetings were doled out to friends and strangers on an equal opportunity basis.

"Carrie, I was just telling this fellow about you," Ron explained. "He's looking for a place to park that big diesel unit outside for the night. Could you put him up?"

She looked at the stranger again. He was medium

height, medium build with brown hair cut close to his head and gray eyes etched with lines at the corners as though he spent a lot of time staring off into the distance. His face was square jawed and there were lines at the corners of his mouth that matched those around his eyes. He was tanned and fit, and the leather bomber jacket he wore over a chambray shirt and khaki slacks looked soft and worn with age, but it didn't take an expert to tell it had cost a pretty penny. Just like the rig parked outside. Carrie knew her recreational vehicles. That one ran to the high six figures, maybe even seven, not to mention the top-of-the-line crew cab it was towing.

"I'd appreciate someplace to pull in for the night," the stranger said. "We won't need a hookup, just space to get off the road and out of the storm." His accent was all softened consonants and long drawn out vowels. Southern as grits and biscuits. The man and his little girl were a long way from home.

Carrie had been ready to say no to his request. Thunder Lake Campground was closed for the season. She had a hard week's work ahead of her to finish getting ready for the steady parade of cars that would wind their way through the campground each evening of the holiday season to see the Lights Before Christmas display her dad had started twenty-odd years ago, and that had, year by year, grown to over half a million lights. She didn't have time to deal with late-season customers at the campground.

But something changed her mind before she could speak. Maybe it was because she glanced into their shopping basket and saw a plastic bag of salad greens, turkey TV dinners and a freezer-case pumpkin pie. Maybe it was the look of anxiety on the heart-shaped face of the little girl standing protectively close to her handsome father. Maybe it was the faint echo of sadness she saw in the man's gray eyes?

"Sure" she heard herself say. "We've got a spot for you. No one should be out in this kind of weather."

The smile that transformed the little girl's plain face was worth the inconvenience of getting them settled in for the night when she had a million things to do before she went to bed. "We're right on the lake about two miles down the road. Just follow the signs for the main entrance to the speedway, then make a left when you see the small one for Thunder Lake Campground."

"This time next week you wouldn't need directions," Ron said, beginning to ring up the man's pathetic attempt at creating a Thanksgiving meal from the freezer section. "You'd just have to get in line with the other cars. Carrie's family puts on one heck of a Christmas light show. Half a million lights. Folks come from all over to see it."

"A half-million lights?" the little girl asked. "That's one thousand six hundred sixty-seven strings if you are using the three-hundred-string commercial-grade lights. Are you?"

Carrie blinked. "Yes," she said. "Most of them are."

The girl nodded solemnly. "That's the most efficient use of your time putting them up and taking them down. Using smaller strings raises the time/energy expenditure ratio exponentially."

"Huh?" Josh said, tilting his head to stare at the coltish little girl who blushed and pulled her lower lip between her teeth as though to keep from saying more. "What'd she say?"

"We'll be right behind you," the man said, covering the silence that followed his daughter's words.

"We'll be expecting you." What was the child, some kind of genius? Carrie wondered. Force of habit had her stepping back so that Josh could go ahead of her and she could catch him if he stumbled and fell. The automatic door whooshed open, letting in a wave of cold, wet air.

"What a little geek," Josh said as the door closed behind them.

"Shh, they'll hear you." Sleet lashed against the side of the building, glazing the cinder blocks and the sides of her old pickup, stinging her face and gloveless hands. "Ugh," she said. "It's way too early in the season for this kind of weather. And on a holiday weekend, too, with everyone out on the roads."

"Mom, do you know who that was?" Josh said over his shoulder as he maneuvered his crutches expertly across the slippery gravel parking lot.

"Someone who needs a place to get out of the storm?" she said, watching her own footing so she didn't drop the pie. "Of course I didn't recognize him. Did you?"

"Yeah," Josh said, balancing on his good leg while he slid the crutches into the cab of the truck, prodding Toby into the center of the bench seat with the tips. "It took me a minute to figure it out. He hasn't been on TV much this season, but I'm pretty sure it was Trace Collier."

"Trace Collier? The NASCAR driver?" Carrie asked.

"Yep, I didn't recognize him right away. I mean, who expects to see one of those guys here in November? But it's him. I'm sure of it."

"What in heaven's name is he doing up here at this time of year? You must be mistaken." Carrie said, putting the pie box on the floor under her seat so that Toby didn't set one of his giant paws on it, or worse yet, inhale it in a single gulp. She hadn't asked the man's name. That hadn't been the wisest thing, but sometimes you had to act on your instincts, and hers had told her Trace Collier was trustworthy.

"Get over, dog," Josh said, using his arms to boost himself onto the passenger seat. "Yeah, it's him all right. He finished fifth at Homestead but way down in the points standings. Anyway, that rig in the parking lot is a dead giveaway. All the NASCAR drivers own them. They're on the road nine months out of the year, ya know."

Josh was a NASCAR fan, something else he'd inherited from his absent father. Carrie herself could name most of the high-profile drivers, and she had no objection to the business the busy summer race weekends brought to the area, and in particular to Thunder Lake Campground, but she couldn't call herself a fan, not like her ex-husband had been. Probably still was, for all Carrie knew. She hadn't seen or heard from Kyle Ferrell in seven years come next February. He'd left Carrie and Josh six months after he'd wrecked the ATV. Carrie could have forgiven him that folly if he hadn't taken their five-year-old son along for the ride that day.

Kyle had walked away from the wreck with scrapes and bruises and a broken collarbone. Josh had been trapped beneath the vehicle, his left leg crushed below the knee. He'd nearly died. That he'd survived the incident with only the lasting damage to his foot and ankle was a miracle that Carrie had prayed for night and day. The good Lord had answered her prayers to save her son, but with that priceless miracle achieved her luck ran out. Kyle took one look at the frail, fretful invalid that had replaced their rambunctious kindergartner and turned tail and ran—after cleaning out their savings account. From that day forward she and Josh had been on their own.

CHAPTER TWO

IT WAS STILL DARK WHEN Trace woke even though the clock said it was after seven. He might as well get up. He didn't like lying in bed by himself. He'd make a pot of coffee and wait for Annie to wake up. They'd have waffles for breakfast with strawberry topping and whipped cream on top.

He didn't have much fear of spoiling their Thanksgiving dinner with a big breakfast. Not when it was going to consist of frozen dinners and prebaked pie. He wondered if there was a restaurant anywhere nearby that would be open for the day? Probably not. He could still hear sleet chattering against the windows. They might have to stay longer than he expected. He shoved himself off the bed and headed into the bathroom before he started remembering the Thanksgiving dinners Beth had cooked for the three of them. Or the year he'd finished third in the Chase for the NASCAR Sprint Cup and they'd spent Thanksgiving in New York for Champions Week. She wouldn't want him to be always looking to the past. That hadn't been her way. She had wanted him to be strong and focused on the future, for Annie's sake. Even though she hadn't been able to articulate those thoughts after her stroke he could see it in her eyes, and he had given her his word he wouldn't dwell in the past.

So far, keeping that promise was the hardest thing he'd ever done.

He hurried through his shower, shaved and pulled on jeans and an old chamois shirt, faded from blue to gray with many washings. He slid open the pocket doors that separated the master suite from the small area behind the kitchen that could be closed off to form a second bedroom. He bent to pull the covers over Annie's shoulders as he passed her bunk bed, and brushed his hand over the silky softness of her hair.

So like her mother. He said a little prayer of thanks every day for this precious reminder of Beth and their love. The furnace kicked on, sending warm air flooding through the motor home as he slid the pocket door between Annie's room and the kitchen closed as quietly as possible.

Fifteen minutes later the smell of waffles and warming syrup filled the air and Annie appeared in the doorway looking both sleepy and hungry, her fine, straight hair tousled around her shoulders. She was wearing flannel pants, an oversize T-shirt sporting his sponsor's logo and fluffy slippers with googly monster eyes that had been a gag gift from Jake Winslow, his spotter, for her tenth birthday. Peanuts was cradled in her arms, squirming to be let down and taken outside.

"Happy Thanksgiving, Daddy," she said. "Something smells good."

"Waffles," he replied, waving her to the dinette. "Give me the dog. I'll put him out. It's still sleeting a little."

She handed over the poodle and slid into the padded banquette that seated six while Trace pushed the button that automatically lowered the outside steps and urged the reluctant poodle to head out into the cold gray of early morning.

But Peanuts was having none of the slippery, ice-coated concrete pad the motor home was parked on. With a muttered curse Trace picked him up and carried him down the steps, depositing the little dog on the white-coated grass at the edge of the concrete apron. "Hurry up," he ordered, crossing his arms to keep out the chill of the wet north wind. "I'll clean up after you later."

Carrie Ferrell hadn't pointed out a dog run when she'd directed him to the sheltered space that Trace now could see commanded an impressive view of the lake nestled at the bottom of the hill. He should have thought to ask, but it had been too miserable to stand out in the storm and talk, and she'd seemed impatient to be about her business so he'd kept the question to himself.

But he would have to ask her what to do about Peanuts when he got the chance since it looked like they were probably staying another night due to the weather. The thought caused him to glance in the direction he'd noticed lights shining through the trees the night before. Dawn was breaking, reluctantly, and he could make out a small fieldstone house with a steep, gabled roof, sheltered beneath huge oaks, twin fireplaces anchoring it at either end. Snow White's cottage—or the Seven Dwarfs' cottage anyway. Annie would love it. Especially now with a thin coating of ice giving every leaf and branch a fairy-dust glitter.

Fairy princesses, unicorns, Prince Charming on his white horse—his daughter loved all that stuff. Trace smiled. Despite the fact that Annie had the intellectual capacity to solve mathematical equations that stumped scholars three times her age, at heart she was all little girl.

He took another moment to look around, although the wind bit through his shirt and, at his feet, Peanuts whined to be picked up. Thunder Lake Campground was perched at the top of the hill, the lake at its base. Concrete pads, some with RVs still sitting on them, shaded by more big oaks and maples, marched down a terraced slope to a sandy, narrow beach. Wooden dock sections were piled along the shoreline, and picnic tables were stacked in neat rows nearby. Trace noted some of the houses surrounding the campground wouldn't have looked out of place among the minimansions that ringed Lake Norman, back in North Carolina. Carrie Ferrell may not live in the biggest house on the lake, but she sure had the best view.

He continued to ignore the cold wind and rounded the front of the motor home. Off in the distance, against the pale gray dawn he could just see the flagpoles that topped the grandstands of the big speedway. In summer, with the trees in full leaf, he doubted the race track would be visible from the campground, but the sound of forty-three racing V-8 engines certainly would carry this far.

He'd won twice at Michigan, both times at the August race, but the second time had been five years ago. Back before Beth's illness and death. Back when times were good and he didn't have to worry about whether or not he'd have a ride come Daytona.

Not like now, when he hadn't won a race for three seasons and his car owner was having money and sponsor troubles of his own. His life seemed as dreary and cheerless as the cold, stormy November day. On that thought, like a cue in a bad movie, the electricity went out. He knew the instant it happened, because the lights in the houses of early risers that ringed the gray waters of Thunder Lake went dark and Annie let out a yelp that he could hear from where he stood.

"Daddy. The electricity went out. I can't see a thing in here." Carrie Ferrell had insisted he hook up the motor to her utilities. She was charging him for the space, she pointed out. He might as well take advantage of the amenities.

Peanuts began to paw at his pant leg, whining to go inside. Trace bent to pick up the shivering little dog and, when he straightened, he saw a candle flare to life in one of the windows of Carrie Ferrell's house. For a moment he glimpsed her figure silhouetted by the candlelight. She was about his age, he guessed. Tall, not too skinny, nice figure, great eyes—green as spring leaves—he remembered from the grocery store. Her hair was brown, but that was about all he'd been able to tell about it, shoved up under a knit cap the way it had been last night. He wondered if it was long and straight, or shorter with a hint of a curl the way Beth's had been.

He paused, his hand on the doorknob. That was the most time and effort he'd spent speculating on a woman's appearance in a long, long time. Maybe his interest in the opposite sex wasn't completely atrophied. Was it possible? He let his mind conjure an image of his temporary landlady one last time. He liked what he saw and smiled. “I’ll be damned,” he said under his breath. “Maybe there’s hope.”

CHAPTER THREE

"THERE'S NO WAY I CAN cook a twelve-pound turkey over this sorry excuse of a fire," Carrie said to her son, shaking her head. "It'll never get done." The power had been out for three hours now. It was almost eleven o'clock. They wouldn't be having turkey and all the trimmings for Thanksgiving if the electricity didn't come back on soon.

Josh was huddled in front of the anemic fire in the kitchen fireplace—she never used the one in the living room at the other end of the house because it smoked, like well, a chimney—scowling at the meager flames. "What crappy weather. Why couldn't it do this sometime when we weren't on school vacation? And why an ice storm on Thanksgiving? Doesn't Mother Nature know it's the biggest travel day of the year? Can't even get in the car and drive somewhere to find an open restaurant for dinner," he muttered sarcastically, poking at the fire, causing a few more red coals to darken and die.

"Quit playing with the fire before it goes out completely," she said automatically. "What shall I fix us to eat? Peanut butter and jelly? We can probably heat some soup over this thing." So much for the money she'd spent on remodeling her kitchen last year—her brand-new all-electric kitchen.

"Wow. I can hardly wait." Josh huddled into his coat and stretched his leg out in front of him not quite able to hide the grimace of discomfort the movement caused. He'd insisted on helping her pull the couch in front of the fireplace. She had been afraid it had strained his healing ankle, and now her fears had been confirmed. She was about to risk a growling dismissal and ask him if he wanted her to bring a pillow to prop up his cast when she heard a knock at the back door.

"Goodness, who's out on a miserable day like this?" she wondered aloud.

"The turkey and stuffing fairy, I hope," Josh grumbled, rubbing Toby behind the ears. Toby laid his head on Josh's thigh and sighed with pleasure.

"Why, hello." Carrie opened the door to find Trace Collier and his daughter standing on the small porch outside the office that her dad had partitioned out of the utility room when he first opened the campground twenty-five years earlier.

"Is everything all right? Do you need anything?"

A short silence followed her questions. Trace Collier wasn't a big man, only a handful of inches taller than her five-and-a-half feet, broad across the shoulders and deliberate in his movements, and seemingly in his speech as well. “Happy Thanksgiving,” he said at last in that warm, Southern drawl that sent little shivers up and down her spine that weren’t caused by the cold air eddying into the room. The shiver surprised her just as much as it had when she’d experienced it the night before. She wasn’t used to being undermined by out-of-the-blue physical attractions to good-looking men; those days were long behind her. “We’d like to invite you to Thanksgiving dinner,” Trace said after another short pause. “We don’t have much to offer in the way of turkey and stuffing, but we do have heat and electricity back on in the motor home.”

“And a big-screen TV,” Annie piped up, standing very close to his side and smiling, a shy, sweet smile that transformed her earnest little face from plain to pretty.

“Why. I—” Carrie’s first instinct was to say no. She really wasn’t in the mood to make small talk with strangers.

“We don’t want you to feel obligated to spend the holiday with us,” he continued softly. “But the news reporter says the electricity’s not likely to come back on before evening at the earliest, probably not until tomorrow. The storm was a lot worse over toward Ann Arbor.”

"I was afraid that might be the case." She felt herself wavering. This was the first Thanksgiving she and Josh had spent without at least some members of their family gathered at the table. Her house was cold and empty feeling in more ways than the lack of electricity and the smell of turkey roasting in the oven.

"You're still welcome to use our kitchen to fix your dinner. It won't take us long to nuke our TV dinners when the time comes," he said, adopting a hangdog expression.

For a moment Carrie thought he was serious and opened her mouth to assure him that there was no way she would let him and his daughter eat TV dinners on Thanksgiving. Then she saw the glint of laughter in his dark gray eyes and felt her own lips smile in return.

"You're pulling my leg," she said.

He glanced down at her jean-clad legs. "Only a little," he said, and she could have sworn there was a hint of admiration in the look.

"Thank you," she said, and felt a little breathless all of a sudden. "But only if you let me do the cooking and share our turkey with us. It's far too big for just Josh and me."

For a moment Trace Collier looked as surprised as she was by her acceptance, then his mouth curved into a smile that was as slow and inviting as his North Carolina accent. "Great," he said. "You've got yourself a deal."

"SO WHAT DO YOU DO to keep busy around here in the winter?" Trace asked as he stirred a shot of smooth, aged whiskey into her mug of decaf coffee and followed it up with a dollop of whipped cream from an aerosol can. It was her second Irish coffee, and her last.

She took a sip and waited for the kick of the whiskey as it slid down her throat. She was beginning to feel very relaxed and a little tipsy. They'd had wine with dinner, a very nice white merlot Trace pulled from a temperature-controlled compartment next to the refrigerator. A motor home with its own wine cellar. She'd heard of units like this one, and even seen them breezing by on the road when the races were in town, but no one who rented space at Thunder Lake Campground sported a rig like this one.

"You're smiling," Trace said from his side of the leather banquette where they were sitting. He lifted his mug as she set hers down on the tabletop. "Want to let me in on the secret?"

"No secret," she said, waving her hand to encompass the dark polished wood and shining crystal and brushed nickel accents of the motor home. "I was just thinking I've never been in a house with a wine cabinet, let alone a recreational vehicle."

"In NASCAR we prefer the term motor home," he said, raising his eyebrows to stare down his nose.

"Well, out here in the boonies we call 'em RVs," she returned with a salute of her coffee mug.

"Want me to top that off?" he asked, reaching for the whiskey decanter again.

She covered the mug with her hand. "No way. Any more and I'm liable to slip on the ice going back to the house and fall on my a—backside," she finished hurriedly, glancing toward the small room where she could see Josh and Trace's little girl, Annie, sitting on a bunk bed playing a video game.

Josh had been on his best behavior all day, minding his manners, helping with the cooking and the cleanup afterward without being asked. She knew he'd been thrilled to watch football with Trace in the main salon, both of them ensconced in recliners while she and Annie cleaned veggies for a relish tray and decanted the canned cranberry relish she'd brought from the house onto a crystal dish Annie took from one of the overhead cupboards. After they'd eaten, her son had even condescended to play board games while the short, gray day faded into night and the sleet changed to rain and began to wash away the ice.

"You heard the weatherman," Trace said, nodding

toward the TV screen behind her. "The ice won't melt completely until tomorrow. I hope you don't mind Annie and I staying a day or so longer than we planned?"

"Of course not."

"There's not much chance of the power coming back on. You and Josh are welcome to stay the night."

There was nothing sexual or provocative in his tone, but the rush of warmth through her nerve endings it produced reminded her again of how very much aware she was of him as a man. "No, really. We'll be fine in the house."

He shook his head. "Okay, I won't force you to stay, but you're welcome if you change your mind." Perversely, Carrie found she was a little disappointed that he hadn't pushed any harder for her to say yes to his invitation. She really didn't want to roust Josh and Toby, or herself for that matter, out into the cold wet night. "You never answered my question," he reminded her. "What do you do to keep busy around here all winter?"

"I do taxes for a local accountant," she said. She sat up a little straighter. "I have an associate degree in accounting. It keeps me very well occupied from January to April fifteenth."

He snorted. "I bet it does. Steady work, right?"

She grinned. "Right. You'd be amazed how many

people are so afraid of the IRS they won't even file the short form on their own."

"I share their phobia," he said, and smiled that slow, lazy smile of his.

She raised her mug. "Hear, hear! Pays my heating bill and my insurance premiums."

"That's not all you do, is it?"

"No," she said, giving an airy wave in the general direction of the lake and the campground. "There's the Lights Before Christmas. Family tradition. I'm running it on my own this year since my dad's in Florida."

"What exactly is this Lights Before Christmas? You mentioned it last night, too, I seem to remember."

"My dad started it when I was a kid. For the first few years it was just some lights strung on the trees around the campsites. Then the diehards, the renters who leave their RVs here all year, got in the act and started decorating their trailers. About ten years ago, after he retired, my dad got really into it. He invited the local church groups and service clubs to come in and sell snacks and bazaar items in the pool house."

"You have a pool?"

"Yeah, and basketball and volleyball courts. They're in that grove of trees behind you. Can't see them now because the arborvitae Dad planted are too thick, but they're there. We'll have a couple thousand carloads of visitors coming through here over the next five weeks so the concessions are a real boost to the church collection plates."

He looked impressed at the number. "Do you charge admission?"

"Five dollars a carload. Naturally we don't charge the service groups anything. The admission fee covers the upkeep and electric bill." She smiled, and he felt himself smiling in return. "We give the local high school football team a donation and the guys help me put up the lights and direct traffic. We still make a nice little profit, though. And the renters have really gotten into it. There are some great displays down along the lake. You'll have to come back some night and check it out." He didn't say anything for a long moment and Carrie found herself feeling slightly anxious all of a sudden. Was he looking for the right words to politely decline her off-hand invitation? She was surprised to realize the brush-off would hurt.

"Would you consider letting Annie and me stay here for more than another night or two?" he asked, holding her gaze. In the overhead light his eyes were almost black. "I noticed this site has winterized hookups."

"All the sites on this level are winterized, actually. For a few snowbirds who come home for the holidays." She shut her mouth abruptly. She was rambling, again very unlike herself. He wanted to stay. Here at Thunder Lake. Josh would be over the moon to have a real live NASCAR driver living right next door.

"I've been thinking it over. Annie and I will be more comfortable in the motor home than in some furnished apartment in town. We've spent the last two winters rambling around a too big, empty house filled with loneliness and echoes of happier times. I sold it a few months ago. With all the other changes—leaving her school and her friends—I don't want Annie to be spending the holidays in some neutral-toned, department-store-furnished apartment complex filled with strangers. She's comfortable in the motor home and I like it here."

The statement elicited a smile from her. "You've only been here twenty-four hours. In the worst weather. You can't even see the lake for the rain and sleet."

"I know what I want," he said in that soft Southern drawl that she now realized contained a threading of carbon steel. "I want to stay here for Christmas if you'll have us."

"You're welcome to stay as long as you want," she heard herself say, and smiled again in return.

CHAPTER FOUR

"DID YOU HEAR THAT?" Annie Collier whispered from the top bunk where she'd been watching him play video games. "We're going to be staying here in the motor home instead of renting an apartment in Ann Arbor. I'll get to see all the lights and everything."

"Yeah, swell," Josh said. He was on the fifteenth level of Prowler, his favorite video game. He'd never gotten this far before. Before the little genius leaning over the edge of the bunk had gone into the program and tweaked it enough that he'd made it past the Demon's Gate that had tripped him up almost every time he played. Of course that was after she'd beaten him three games in a row without bypassing the Demon's Gate. He'd let her play doubles with him because it was better than having her talk and talk while he was concentrating. The kid was a genius, all right. She had every move of every game worked out so far in advance it was scary. And she made it all look easy.

Josh was barely making a B in algebra this semester

and she was on her way to study in advanced Honors classes at the university. He was going to have to buckle down the next year and a half just to make decent SAT scores and scholarships to make it to college at all, and she was already working toward a master's degree. How weird was that?

His ankle was aching and he reached down and scratched the cast absentmindedly. Of course he could play the crippled kid card and get some grant money that way. His school counselor had already looked into it for him. He didn't want to do that, though. He had his pride, after all.

"Josh, did you hear what my dad and your mom are talking about now?" Annie hissed, leaning a little farther down so that her hair swung in front of his face. It smelled like bubble-gum shampoo. He was about to tell her to buzz off when the scent of her hair reminded him she might be a genius but she was still just a little kid.

"Nah. You must have ears like a bat," he said, never taking his eyes off the screen. He was close to making it to level sixteen. He'd never gotten that far before.

"I have nice ears," she said. "I'm getting them pierced for Christmas. My dad said I could."

"Awesome," he said.

"You're spending the night," she said, ignoring his sarcasm. "I've never spent the night with a boy before."

That caught his attention. "Don't talk about spending the night with a boy when you don't have any idea what it means."

"I know all about sex," she said. "I can read."

"No sh—" He caught himself just in time. "You might read about it, but you still don't know what you're talking about."

"Regardless," she said, nodding solemnly, her face pink from being upside down so long. "You and your mom are staying here for the night. I just heard her say she'd changed her mind about going back to your house."

Josh stopped paying attention to the video game and focused on the adult voices coming from the salon. She was right. His mom had just agreed to spend the night in the motor home. "I'll be darned," he said under his breath, remembering to watch his language around the kid this time.

He turned and lifted the slatted blind that covered the window above the bunk. Their house and yard were dark and shadowed. The electricity hadn't come back on and probably wouldn't for the rest of the night. Well, that was okay with him. He wasn't in any mood to go out in the cold and the rain and drag himself upstairs to his even colder bedroom. He'd stay right where he was, thank you. In the luxurious motor home of a pretty famous NASCAR driver. The guys at school wouldn't believe it. He wished he had a cell phone so he could call a couple of them right now. But he didn't have one, although a cell phone was number one on his Christmas list.

"Did your dad die?" Annie asked.

"What?"

"Did your dad die? Is that why you and your mom live alone? My mom died. Three years ago, pretty soon. I miss her." She wasn't leaning over the bunk anymore so he couldn't see her face, but her voice was just a whisper, kind of lonely and lost sounding.

"My dad took off on us," Josh said, not adding any details. His mom never bad-mouthed his dad but she never talked about him unless Josh brought it up. He wasn't as smart as the kid in the upper bunk, but he had figured out a long time ago that a son who spent half his life on crutches wasn't what Kyle Ferrell had in mind when he signed up for the daddy gig. "I'm sorry about your mom dying," he added, reminding himself that other people had it worse than he did.

"Thank you." She was back, staring at him upside down, a frown pulling her eyebrows together. "Does your mom have boyfriends?"

"Nah," Josh said, already getting used to her just saying whatever popped into her overstuffed brain. Actually, he wondered why his mom didn't date. It wasn't like she was still in love with his long-gone dad. She was pretty and not too old. She'd only been twenty when he was born. And it wasn't that guys didn't hit on her. They did. A lot. She just didn't seem interested in them.

"My dad doesn't have girlfriends, either. Oh, they come around a lot. Real pretty ones. He's a NASCAR driver. They attract women," she stated matter-of-factly, as though she was forty instead of ten or eleven. "It's the uniform, Dad says. But he doesn't pay any attention to them. Not till tonight. Talking to your mom, that's the most I've heard him laugh for a long time."

"Yeah," Josh said thoughtfully. "My mom, too."

"They like each other."

"Yeah, I guess they do."

"I'm glad," Annie said. "I like it here."

"You'd get tired of driving back and forth to the university every day."

"No, I wouldn't. How much do you charge to stay here?"

"You'd have to ask my mom," Josh said. He was getting sleepy. Turkey would do that to you, he'd learned in science class. Make you sleepy.

"I will," she said. "I'll work up a cost analysis for my dad. Show him we could live here more cheaply than renting an apartment in Ann Arbor, even factoring in gasoline for the commute. Do you suppose your mom would rent us this space for the whole winter?"

"I don't know," Josh said, grinning. *Boy, was the*

kid strange. Cost analysis? Where did she come up with that stuff?

"We'll be staying for Christmas. We can decorate our motor home like you told me the other people who come here do. Have a little Christmas tree in the salon. It'll be fun."

"Decorating is a lot of work," Josh said, switching off the TV screen with the remote. "Believe me, I know."

"I think it will be fun," she replied stubbornly. "I want to stay here until it's time for my dad to go to Florida for SpeedWeeks. He can't miss Daytona even if he says he thinks he might retire."

"I hope he doesn't retire," Josh said, meaning it. "He's a good driver. Just had a run of bad luck."

'I know," Annie whispered. "Real bad luck."

He thought of her losing her mom and vowed to be nicer to the little geek. "Go to sleep," he said, not unkindly. "It's late."

"Listen," Annie whispered, sounding sleepy now, too. "They're still talking. And laughing." She giggled a little. A cute giggle, not geeky at all. "That's good. I like that, too."

Surprisingly enough, so did he.

CHAPTER FIVE

"HI," TRACE SAID, looking up at Carrie's very nice backside as she perched on a ladder beneath a crab-apple tree, strings of multicolored lights draped over her shoulder. The weather had turned warm again after Thanksgiving, melting the ice, giving the electric crews the chance to clean up downed branches and power lines and letting everyone else head for the malls to start their Christmas shopping. It had been clear and sunny all day. He could just see the flag at the top of the race track grandstand snapping in the breeze, backlit by the setting sun.

"Hi yourself," Carrie said, smiling down at him. "How did Annie's first day of orientation at the university go?"

"Fine. She's taking some tests, meeting with instructors, that kind of stuff. She won't start a full schedule of classes until after Christmas," he explained. "Can I help you with those lights?"

"Nope. Last string. And I do mean last string. This is it. No more."

He looked around the small yard that surrounded her little stone house. There were lights hanging from the gables and the gutters, ringing each window, draped over every bush and branch and shrub. "Your electric bill must be outrageous in December."

"We've got generators to run a lot of the lights, but it's worth the expense. You'll see."

She lifted her arms to drape the lights over a higher branch and he put his hand out to steady the ladder. "Sure you can't use some help?"

"Positive. I'm used to doing things for myself." She was stubborn that way, he'd learned over the past couple of days of living at Thunder Lake Campground. He hadn't yet given up offering to help her whenever he saw her tackling a job that was too big for her, but she had as yet to accept his offers. "There. Just right. Would you mind plugging the extension cord into the post over there so I can make sure they're all going to light?"

"Sure," he said. It wasn't much, as far as feeding his Sir Galahad habit, but it would have to do. "Looks like they're all burning."

She was leaning back on the ladder a bit to observe her handiwork and he liked what he saw, the soft, rounded, feminine shape of her through her jacket. He knew he was supposed to like his women model-skinny but he was old-fashioned that way. He liked his women curvy, not stick-thin.

"Great." She climbed down off the ladder and began to gather up the wooden spindles that had held the strings of heavy-duty Christmas lights. She piled them in a wheelbarrow that had seen a lot of use. "You said Annie's first day went well."

He looked at her closely, trying to gauge the emotion behind the pleasant tone of her voice. Was she one of those people who believed Annie should be in school with kids her own age, instead of being mixed in with college kids, even though she'd be bored to tears? "She seems to be okay. The boys mostly seemed to want to treat her like a little sister. The girls were kind enough. After the holidays, she'll be taking some kind of molecular theory or another class. Her math skills are off the chart."

"Is that what her major will be? Molecular biology? Or something equally esoteric?" She picked up the handles of the wheelbarrow and began walking toward what he now knew was the storage barn behind her house.

He fell into step beside her, not even offering to push the wheelbarrow this time. He was learning. "Her counselors want her to choose math and science majors. She's not so sure that's where she wants to go, though. She says she wants to be a vet."

"That's a good profession."

"For you or me, maybe," he said. "Annie's kind of a miracle. She's profoundly gifted. That's what the experts call it. She pegged the charts on every IQ test she's been given. She started reading highway signs when she was two. She could do long division before she was old enough for kindergarten. Her counselors think she should choose a profession to match her skills, something like aeronautics."

Annie stopped pushing the wheelbarrow and turned to look at him. Her nose was pink from the cold, her lips bright red, her eyes shining with intelligence. "She's not even eleven," she said. "I don't know if I could set my child on a life path at that age no matter how gifted he or she was."

"Are you one of those people who think Annie should study with children her own age?" he asked, wanting to learn her opinion.

She thought about it a moment. "Not necessarily. I think every child should be challenged to do their best, no matter where that best falls on the scale of life. But she's still a little girl. Attending advanced classes with older students is one thing, as long as she's allowed to be a little girl, too. But I don't believe that, at any age, she should be funneled into a discipline that might not be where she wants to spend the rest of her life."

"That's pretty much the way I feel about it," he said, relieved she shared his way of thinking. "I won't object to any of the classes the program mentor suggests unless Annie does. Or if I see her getting stressed and unhappy."

"She's a real perfectionist, isn't she," Carrie said. Annie had helped her bake cookies and put up mantel decorations over the past couple of days. She took every task very seriously, fussing over the measurements for sugar cookies, or the placement of Christmas baubles, with equal intensity.

He nodded. "It's a characteristic of a lot of really gifted people. Beth, my late wife, was always adamant that we not let her take herself too seriously, to keep her grounded in the everyday as well as the rarefied."

"Not an easy job, I imagine."

He gave a short nod. "I'm trying my best."

"You're doing a good job of it. She laughs a lot. Especially when she's with Josh, and that's a good thing for him, too."

"She has been laughing a lot lately," Trace agreed. "It's good to hear her giggle again. For a long time after Beth died she was too quiet." He was glad to have someone to discuss Annie with. Someone he trusted. And that thought surprised him almost as much as when he caught himself thinking about Carrie as a woman. He trusted her. After only a few days, he considered Carrie Ferrell a friend and a confidante.

"OKAY, IT'S SHOWTIME. Everyone ready to throw their switches?" Carrie released the transmit button on her walkie-talkie and waited.

"Station one, ready" came Josh's voice amid the static.

"Station two, check." That was the voice of her longtime neighbor and her father's good friend, Bryce Calvin, who was helping with the light display until Cork Ferrell returned from Florida the week before Christmas.

"Station three?" That was Trace and Annie's position down by the boathouse. When they threw their switch, the displays along the lakeshore and on the RVs still parked on their pads would light up.

"Station three ready to come online." Carrie smiled. Annie's excitement was detectable even over the static-filled walkie-talkie channel.

"Okay, Annie. Wait for my signal so we don't overload the circuit, okay?"

"Roger that."

"Let's light this candle," Josh growled, imperfectly hiding his own excitement. "There are cars already starting to back up on the highway."

"Okay. Here we go. Josh, throw the switch."

Carrie turned her head, holding her breath, as she did every year, and wondering if an undetected short, or a malfunctioning circuit breaker would wipe out days and weeks of work stringing the half-million lights the display encompassed.

The apple trees at the top of the hill blazed into light, multicolored with fiberoptic snowflakes hanging from the branches. She heard a smattering of applause from the small audience of volunteer workers readying the bazaar booths and food concessions that transformed the recreation building into a winter wonderland of delicious smells and pretty packages.

She toggled the switch. "You're up, Bryce."

"Gotcha." The trees and shrubs that lined the asphalt driveway from the road came online, twinkling red and green in the fading twilight of the late November afternoon, Christmas carols began playing from speakers hidden among the branches.

"Looking good," Josh transmitted.

"Very nice," Carrie agreed, and more applause seconded her compliment.

"Annie, Trace. You're good to go."

In response, the lights that covered the lake fence and boathouse in swags of royal-blue blazed into life, a rich background for the whimsically decorated RVs arrayed before them.

A couple of the renters had been very secretive about their designs for this season but some of the others were as much a tradition as the display itself. Dick Harmon and Roger Kellogg, brothers-in-law, had stuck with their long-held custom of decorating their side-by-side RVs in the colors of their alma maters, Ohio State and Michigan. The decorating had become so extravagant that they needed an auxiliary generator to power the display. Next to them the Petermans had gone with a Disney theme this season, and farther up the hill one of her newer renters had decorated his trailer with the number and color scheme of his favorite NASCAR driver.

Trace Collier's number and logo.

Wouldn't the owner be amazed to know the driver himself had thrown the switch to light his display?

The last to come on were the holographic images of Santa and his reindeer that were always positioned to seem as if they were flying up from the lakeshore to head off over the rooftops of the houses below her and perhaps end up on the top of the grandstand at the speedway. At least that's what Josh had thought when he was small and his grandfather had first put the flying Santa and reindeer into the display.

"Okay, Mom. You're up."

She pulled off her glove and threw the switch that illuminated the lights on her home. All white this year to match the trees along the driveway, with a crèche of life-size figures of the Holy Family and the Wise Men positioned beneath the Star of Bethlehem that Trace had helped place high on the kitchen chimney.

She had enjoyed having him around to help with the last-minute details of getting the huge light show ready for the public. She'd worried over how she would manage the heavy work with her dad gone and

Josh still in a cast, but they had finished on time, weathering the usual glitches, tangled light cords and final runs to the hardware for yet one more heavy-duty extension cord. Having a strong, hard-working man around the place had been a real help, she had to admit. Especially one as good-looking and easy to talk to as Trace Collier.

Carrie cut short her musings as the honking of several dozen car horns greeted the lighting of the final section of the display. People were anxious to hand over their money and tour the campground, carrying out their end of the Ferrell family tradition. Time to go to work. Time to stop thinking about how easy Trace Collier was to talk to. To be with. To confide in…

Bryce threw open the gate at the bottom of the hill and the first cars turned into the lane, following her neighbor's directions to turn off their headlights and to stay below the posted ten-mile-an-hour speed limit.

She watched from the shadows as a pair of figures came up from the lake. A medium-height, broad-shouldered man and a tall, coltish young girl at his side were silhouetted by the lights behind them. Since there was no one nearby she let her gaze linger on Trace. As they'd worked side by side the past couple of days she'd told him about her father's new girlfriend spiriting him away to Florida for the holidays, and how she wasn't certain she liked the woman all that much. She'd told him about Josh's father's desertion, something she seldom talked about to anyone, most certainly not the very few men she'd dated over the last half-dozen years. She'd learned the hard way nothing was guaranteed to send a man running for the hills faster than a recitation of that sad, old story.

But Trace hadn't turned tail and run away. He'd listened and he'd told her he admired her strength and the sacrifices she'd made to give Josh every opportunity to grow into a healthy and successful young man. And she'd believed him, because she knew he was fighting the same good fight for Annie.

If she was totally and completely honest with herself, which she usually was, she'd have to admit she'd even started to fall a little bit in love with him when he'd turned to her a few moments later with that slow-as-molasses smile she'd seen on TV and the sports page so many times, and said, "And excuse me for saying so, but I think your ex-husband is probably the dumbest man on two legs for taking off and leaving y'all the way he did."

CHAPTER SIX

"ARE THERE ALWAYS THIS many cars coming through here?" Trace asked as Carrie passed by on her way up the hill to the recreation building. It was Monday, early evening, and he and Annie were just getting back from Ann Arbor where she'd spent the day in orientation at the university and he'd killed time touring the campus and driving some of the back roads through the Irish Hills, waiting for her.

Carrie stopped walking and retraced her steps to where he was standing. Annie had decided their motor home was not going to be the only undecorated object at Thunder Lake Campground. They'd stopped at a hardware store on their way home and loaded up on lights and a small tabletop tree. Now he was putting the finishing touches on swags of snowflake lights that draped the unit from front license plate to the back bumper and everything in between.

"Yes, I'm afraid so," she said, looking slightly sheepish. "At least every evening. I'm sorry, I should have made that more clear when you asked to stay here for the holidays."

Trace waved off her apology as he plugged the last two strings of lights together and watched the snowflakes on them turn from opaque to iridescent. The strains of "Have Yourself A Merry Little Christmas" floated up the lane on the still night air. He'd always liked that song. But he couldn't carry a tune in a bucket so he didn't make the mistake of humming along to the music. "No problem. I just mean I didn't really grasp the full extent of the enterprise. This is really quite an undertaking."

"Uh-huh," she said, waving at Annie through the front window of the motor home as his daughter knelt on the passenger seat and gestured expansively at the small tree he'd jerry-rigged to the cockpit console, the spot Annie had deemed perfect for it. "I take it the pink and purple tree decorations were Annie's idea, not yours," Carrie said. It was too dark to read her expression accurately, but he could hear the smile in her voice.

"Yep," he drawled. "Every froufrou garland and string of lights on it were handpicked by my daughter. Good thing none of the other drivers are here to see it or I'd be laughed out of NASCAR."

"She'll remember this tree for the rest of her life," Carrie said. "And she'll remember that you let her decorate it all on her own. Isn't that worth a little embarrassment?"

"It sure is," he said, and smiled. Carrie smiled back. And out of the blue he wondered what it would be like to kiss those smiling lips. The image tightened his insides and threw him off balance. "Grab your coat and come outside," he hollered through the window to his daughter. With Annie in tow he wouldn't be having any more of those kind of inappropriate and unwelcome thoughts about his landlady.

Unwelcome? He took a moment to consider it. He'd had those kinds of fleeting thoughts about other women now and then since Beth died, but he'd never acted on them. But with Carrie he wanted to. Was that being disloyal to Beth's memory? He took a moment to consider that possibility, too, feeling the familiar tug of sadness around his heart. No, he decided finally. He wasn't being disloyal. He'd finally accepted the fact he wasn't buried beside his wife on that faraway knoll in North Carolina. He was here, living and breathing, and life went on. He needed to move on with it.

"Were you planning on going out for the evening?" Carrie asked, thankfully unable to read his mind.

"Nope, no plans to go anywhere." He heard the motor home door open and moments later Annie and Peanuts, on a leash since he liked to chase cars if he got a chance, appeared beside them. "But if I do want to head out some night, I'll just fall into line and wend my way down to the gate, just like I was following the pace car."

"That's as good a way as any to handle it. Hi Annie. How was class?"

"Okay. It was good to have something to do besides play video games. What do you think of my tree? Pink and purple are my favorite colors. I couldn't believe Dad let me buy pink and purple lights for our tree. We always have white lights. Always."

Carrie glanced at him and smiled as if to say, *See, I told you so,* and this time he thought about more than just kissing her. A lot more.

Luckily for him, because he was still staring at Carrie's lips, Josh came by in a golf cart a moment or two later. "I'm starving," the boy called out. "Who's up for a hot dog and a cup of hot chocolate?"

"I am," Annie said instantly. "I'm starving, too. Wait until I put Peanuts back inside."

"How about you?" Trace asked Carrie. "Can I buy you a hot dog and a cup of hot chocolate."

"There are twenty or thirty people in the rec hall," she said. "Someone will probably recognize you."

He shrugged. "It's not as if I'm the reigning NASCAR Sprint Cup Series champion," he said. "I'm not going to cause a riot or anything if someone does recognize me."

Annie scrambled into the front seat of the golf cart. “C’mon, Dad. I am so hungry I could eat Peanuts,” she called out, and giggled.

“We’ll walk,” Trace said, his mood suddenly darkening. He’d been avoiding thinking about his prospects for the upcoming season. He had a ride, sure, but for how much longer? Even a sponsor as loyal as EverStrong Steel wouldn’t stick with a driver in a terminal slump forever.

“You don’t have to go up there,” Carrie said, sensing his sudden depression. “I’ll make an excuse to the kids.”

“No,” he said. “I’m game. It’s just I’ve been avoiding thinking about next season until now.”

“Is that why you’re here and not in New York? It’s Champions Week. I’m not as big a NASCAR fan as Josh, but I know that much. It’s all over the TV.”

She stayed where she was as a steady stream of cars with darkened headlights and open windows, camera flashes going off like icy versions of summertime fireflies, idled past. She waited for him to respond.

“The drivers and owners who made the Chase are there. I’ll be thirty-second in driver’s points next season. No one’s going to miss me.”

“Sounds like sour grapes. But I know you well enough now not to believe that’s why you’re here and not there, staying at the Waldorf and getting interviewed on TV.”

"You're right. Mostly I'm here for Annie. But I'm also here because I'm not sure I want to get behind the wheel again next year or keep living like a gypsy nine months out of the year or drag Annie along with me from race track to race track, or, worse yet, leave her behind. I don't know what I want and I don't have much time left to make up my mind one way or the other."

"JOSH! JOSH! LOOK behind you. Quick! Look!"

"What?" She was tugging on the sleeve of his coat so hard he nearly lost his grip on the wheel of the golf cart. "What's going on?" His foot was cold where his toes stuck out of the cast, even though he'd covered it with the liner from an old pair of snowmobile boots. He wanted to get inside. And he was starving.

She jerked on his sleeve again. "Look." He glanced in the rearview mirror of the cart but couldn't see anything except the taillights of cars heading back down the hill and out onto the road, their trip through the display finished for another year. "He kissed her. I saw him. My dad just kissed your mom."

"No way." The words kind of arrowed through him, giving him goose bumps. His mom and Trace Collier, kissing. He hadn't exactly seen that coming. Laughing and talking over a cup of coffee, sure. But kissing? Weird.

"Way," Annie insisted, her pointy little face wreathed in smiles. "He put his arms around her and kissed her right on the mouth. I have excellent eyesight. I'm certain I interpreted their actions correctly."

"Well, it's not like my mom's a dog or anything, ya know. She's pretty cool looking for a mom. Guys have kissed her before." He congratulated himself that he'd kept his surprise out of his voice.

"Did you like it when it happened?" she asked in kind of a small voice, suddenly quiet, her eyes big and serious looking. "I've never seen my dad do anything like that with anyone but my mom. It makes me feel kind of funny inside." She took one more look over her shoulder, but Josh hadn't stopped the cart and they were turning into the parking lot around the recreation building so their parents were no longer in sight.

He turned his head so he could see her face. "When I was little I didn't like it either. I kept thinking my dad would come back, and I didn't want any boyfriends hanging around gumming up the works when he did. But a couple of years ago I figured out that was never going to happen and I quit giving her a hard time." He felt a guilty pang somewhere around his heart. Of course, by the time he'd quit acting like a little jerk his mom had pretty much given up dating. Well, he wasn't going to pull any of those kid tricks this time around. If his mom was going to hook up with Trace Collier, then he'd keep his mouth shut. He skirted the fence that surrounded the pool and pulled into an empty space by the Dumpster, about the only place he could find to park the cart, and turned the motor off.

"My mom's not coming back," Annie went on. "And sometimes, at night, I think about getting a stepmom. How it would be. I'd like it if Carrie and my dad—" She fell silent for a moment. "You know. If they were more than friends."

She sounded like she might start crying. The discussion was getting too heavy for Josh. "I like your dad, too," he said. "He's an all right guy. I like having him around. Even if it means I have to put up with you in the bargain." He reached out and pulled her knit cap down over her eyes, laughing when she squealed in surprise and feigned anger.

"Hey. Stop that."

"Hey," he said back. "If I didn't like you I wouldn't tease you." He tugged the hat back up and gave her a pat on the head.

"I like you, too. But don't do that kind of stuff again. I fight back, ya know."

"Yeah," he said. "Like you'd have a chance."

She made a grab for his ball cap and came within an inch of snatching it off his head.

He grabbed her hand. "Behave or I won't buy you a hot chocolate."

"You behave," she retorted. "You have to be nice to me. You're not my stepbrother yet."

Stepbrother? He thought about it for a moment as he fumbled for his crutches in the backseat of the cart. It had been just him and his mom for a long time. Was he ready to share her with another man? He looked out over the tops of the trees to where he knew the race track flags would be visible in the daylight, and he felt a grin start to curl his lips. Trace Collier, NASCAR driver for a stepdad. Not too shabby, he decided. Not too shabby at all.

"AND MOST OF ALL I don't know what to do about my feelings for you." Trace's words replayed in Carrie's mind. Then she remembered how he'd taken her in his arms, in front of half the county, and kissed her. Not a quick peck on the cheek, not a let's-be-friends kiss, but a full-blown, man-woman kiss that curled her toes and left her a little breathless and weak in the knees.

The emotional aftermath of the embrace still kept her wide-eyed and sleepless hours later. Carrie rolled over and punched the pillow. She pulled the covers up to her chin and stared at the shadows of tree branches on the ceiling. Her room was never quite dark during the holiday season, because once the displays were lit they were never turned off. Moisture seeping into light strings played havoc with the circuits so they stayed lit day and night.

Why had Trace complicated things by kissing her? She was just getting comfortable thinking of him as a friend, just letting daydreams of something more get a toehold in her thoughts and he had gone and pushed her over the edge into the deep, dark waters of full-blown fantasies.

Trace Collier, NASCAR Sprint Cup Series driver had kissed her. Plain Carrie Ferrell, who hadn't been kissed by any man for almost three years, had a NASCAR driver, and a very sexy one at that, a little infatuated with her.

What was she going to do? The man was still mourning his dead wife. He had a gifted child to raise, which was as difficult a job as her relationship with Josh. And he wouldn't stay. He wasn't meant for Thunder Lake, Michigan, even if he didn't know what he wanted to do with the rest of his life.

And she wasn't meant for the excitement and the endless travel and media scrutiny that were part and parcel of a NASCAR driver's lifestyle. She was rooted to this place and this land and she couldn't see herself or Josh living anywhere else.

She punched the pillow once more and shut her eyes, willing sleep to come. "It was only a kiss," she whispered into the darkness. "Only a kiss." It wouldn't go any further unless she wanted it to. Her eyes flew open again and the pattern of branches on the ceiling snapped back into focus. It wouldn't go any further unless she wanted it to. And, dear heaven, she did. She wanted it to go much, much further because, unlike him, she was past being infatuated. She was teetering on the edge of falling in love.

CHAPTER SEVEN

"NEW YORK HAS BEEN overrun with horses, ladies and gentlemen. Not the four-legged kind, mind you. But the under-the-hood horsepower of powerful NASCAR racing engines. Let's give a big round of applause to this year's NASCAR Sprint Cup Series champion—"

The back door opened and she hastily picked up the remote and hit the off button. It was Trace coming through the office into her kitchen and she didn't want him to catch her watching the late-afternoon talk-show host interviewing the new NASCAR champion. Not when all the other drivers were in New York and he wasn't.

"Hi," she said. "Are you off to fetch Annie?" It was her last week of classes before the university's Christmas break. Trace's daughter was settling in to her studies well and had made a few friends among her older classmates. She was even thinking of running for treasurer of the science club when the winter term started, she had declared at dinner the evening before.

They'd fallen into a routine over the past week, dinner at her house or in the motor home. Trace wasn't a gourmet cook, but he could grill a steak, and his motor home was equipped with a stove with an indoor grill, among its other luxury amenities. On days when there had been a lot of maintenance on the light display and she was too tired to cook, they ordered in pizza from the restaurant across the lake from the campground and ate it as a conga line of cars trailed by the kitchen window.

"Hi," Trace said, heading straight for the coffeepot and the cookie jar. She didn't consider herself highly domestic, but she did have a weakness for homemade cookies and baked them about once a week, summer or winter. Annie had a serious sweet tooth, so she was learning to bake cookies as well. "I'm on my way to the university right now. Anything I can pick up for you in town? It's colder than the devil out there today."

"No thanks. Got everything we need. Snow's coming," Carrie responded, wiping her hands on a towel before turning to face him. They didn't always have a white Christmas—most of their snow came after the New Year—but there was usually at least one snowfall in December to add authenticity to the light display. "Just a dusting, I hope. I love the 'White Christmas' look, but keeping the lanes clear is a headache if it snows a lot." She leaned her hips against the counter and smiled at the sight of him sitting at her kitchen table dunking oatmeal cookies into his coffee cup. He looked up and caught her staring.

"Sorry," he said, grinning and plainly not sorry at all. "You caught me at it. I have no table manners when it comes to homemade oatmeal cookies."

"Dunk away," she said, pouring herself a cup of coffee and joining him at the table. Josh wouldn't be home from school for another half hour. He rode with Bryce's grandson, a senior with his own car, to the big consolidated high school that served Thunder Lake and two other small neighboring villages, too stubborn and too cool to take advantage of the handicap-accessible bus the district provided.

"I'll give you the recipe before you leave. Annie's getting good at baking. She's helped me make the last two batches. She can keep you supplied when you're back out on the road." She said it deliberately to remind herself that her fantasies of the four of them becoming a family were every bit as unattainable as the darker, more private fantasies of Trace that invaded her dreams almost every night.

The grin left his face and his expression turned serious, highlighting the angle of his jaw, the fine lines at the corners of his eyes and mouth, transforming him, momentarily, into the silver-and-blue-suited warrior, portrayed on his hero cards. But the resemblance was fleeting, replaced by the reality of the troubled flesh-and-blood man sitting in her kitchen, eating her cookies.

"What if I told you I didn't want to leave Thunder Lake?" he asked her quietly.

"Why would you want to stay here? Out in the middle of nowhere?"

She regretted the words and the arch tone of her voice as soon as she spoke them. He'd caught her off guard and she didn't know how to respond. She was afraid to tell him the truth. That she wanted him and Annie to stay more than anything on earth. But she'd been hurt too many times in the past to open herself so completely to a man who for all intents and purposes was still a stranger to her in many ways.

He stood up abruptly and shrugged into his coat. "Take a walk with me."

It wasn't a command, precisely, but she knew she had hit a nerve with her remarks and now he was too restless to sit at her kitchen table eating cookies and talking of things that obviously weighed heavily on his heart and mind. She pulled her coat off the hook by the door and followed him outside. Trace shoved his hands in his pockets, silent, his jaw set, as they walked through the hedge and turned up the lane toward the top of the hill.

Trace turned his head toward her but didn't stop walking. "I'm thirty-six. That's one of the old guys in today's NASCAR. I have a good sponsor. I drive for a great owner but I've had three bad seasons in a row. Maybe it's time for me to step aside, let one of the young guns have my ride. Settle down. Raise my daughter. Put down roots."

They'd passed the recreation building and were deep into the trees at the top of the hill. "Look," Carrie said. "There are three deer at the edge of the woods. See them?" A buck and two does were standing just outside the tree line, grazing in the meadow, heads up, ears pricked as they sensed the humans nearby.

Trace nodded, narrowing his eyes. "Taking their chances coming out in the middle of the day, aren't they? Isn't it hunting season?"

"We don't allow hunters on the property," Carrie explained. "Only friends and family when there are too many deer to winter over without starving. That's a far more cruel way to die."

He nodded his understanding. "I didn't know you owned property this close to the race track."

"Dad rents this field out to race fans for the June and August races. He makes good money doing it. Enough to leave it fallow the rest of the year."

"You can see the grandstands from up here," Trace said. The deer had melted back into the woods and the only sounds beside the wind in the pine trees was the roar of an engine being tested in one of the race track garages, a low roar muted by distance and the low-hanging snow clouds overhead.

"Except for two weekends each summer we're about as far from NASCAR as you can get around here," Carrie prompted gently. She needed to know why he might want to stay here in Thunder Lake. She didn't want to let her dreams go any further if she wasn't a big part of the reason.

"Annie and I have no ties to North Carolina. Beth and I moved there because, you're right, that's the center of NASCAR's world. My parents have been divorced for years. My dad's in Phoenix, my mom's in Florida with my two sisters. Beth was an only child whose parents died shortly after we were married. Right now Annie and I are pretty much homeless. That makes Thunder Lake as good a place as any other to settle down."

Not exactly what she wanted to hear. "Homeless people don't own three-quarter-of-a-million-dollar motor homes."

His grin returned but with a rueful twist. "Okay, so we're not exactly homeless with a rig like that to vagabond around in, but you know what I mean. We're rootless and I don't want that for her."

Carrie shoved her hands into the pockets of her coat so he wouldn't see them tremble. "Ann Arbor would be a lot more convenient for both of you. There are some lovely neighborhoods—"

"This is a lovely neighborhood." He laid his hand on her arm, so she stopped to face him. It had started to snow in the past few minutes and big white flakes settled in his hair and onto the collar of his leather jacket. "You'd make a great neighbor." The words gave her a little pang. A good neighbor—was that all he wanted from her? He hadn't kissed her again since that first time, but now and then their hands would brush or he would catch her eye and wink—and she had been certain his feelings for her were keeping pace with her own.

"Good neighbors are hard to come by," she said, looking not in his eyes but at the top button of his shirt.

"That's not all I want from you," Trace said, his voice filled with warmth and the tantalizing hint of the South and, now, something more. Something elemental, something that spoke to her as a woman. "I'd like to think we're working our way toward being something more than good neighbors. Am I right?"

The motor at the race track had shut down, she realized. What she was hearing now was the sound of her own racing heartbeat. Could he hear it, too? She looked up into his gray eyes and saw the color of the lake and the sky before a summer storm, and more. She saw longing and need and hope that matched her own.

"I'd like you to stay, but only if you're sure. Don't

make me any promises you won't be able to keep. It's been a long season. A disappointing one. But it may not be your last." She took a deep breath and spoke from her heart. "I don't want to start to care for another man who doesn't want to stick around. Or, worse yet, one who does stay and doesn't want to be here. I won't do that to Josh. I won't do that to myself."

"Fair enough," he said. "I can promise you this. I won't offer anything I can't deliver. If I say I'm going to stay, then I'll stay. You're right, I haven't made up my mind yet about next season. But I owe it to my team, my owner, my sponsors to make that decision soon. Knowing you aren't indifferent will make it easier." He reached out and took her in his arms, bent his head and kissed her then, and it was even better than the first time.

TRACE RESTED HIS CHIN on the top of her head. Her hair smelled good, like coconut shampoo and cookie dough and clean cold air. He'd never counted on feeling this way again. The thawing of his heart and emotions had started on that stormy November night when he'd met Carrie at the grocery store and she'd offered sanctuary to him and Annie. It had kept on warming and thawing him from the inside out for the past two weeks.

He wasn't sure he loved her yet, but he knew he was just a few laps away from it.

But she was right about one thing. Could he give up racing? NASCAR had been his life for almost twenty years. Was he ready to turn his back on it all and walk away? Before he could consider further, his cell phone rang. Carrie stepped back out of his arms, her cheeks flushed, her eyes shining and bright with passion. He reached for her, wanting to keep her close, but she waved him off. "Answer your call. It might be Annie."

It wasn't Annie. It was his team owner. Damn, the man must be able to read his mind. He flipped open the phone and his eardrums were immediately assaulted with the grating voice of the one-time NASCAR Nationwide Series champion and owner of the No. 548 EverStrong Steel and the No. 526 Consolidated Investors Realty cars, Martin Cartwright. "Where the hell are you, Trace? The awards banquet's tomorrow night. Why aren't you in town?"

"I've been busy enrolling Annie in her classes at the university." Martin knew that as well as he did. They'd discussed it before he left Homestead after the final race of the season.

"I need you here to sweet-talk the sponsor, Trace. They're balking at kicking in another two million for next season. Fly in for the day. That's all I'm asking."

"I can't uproot Annie again, even for a couple of days and there's no one here I can leave her with." Trace shot Carrie an apologetic look, but she had turned her back and walked a few steps back down the hill to give him some privacy and she didn't see it.

"You need to be here, Trace. I've been networking my butt off since Homestead. I've got a couple of new associate sponsors on the hook, but they won't come on board if you aren't locked in with Ever-Strong for another season. Trace, this could be our chance to get out of the hole we're in. There'd be money for new engines. I had drinks with Malcolm Henninger's chief engineer the other night."

Trace's hand tightened on his cell phone. Malcolm Henninger's engines were the best in the business. With that kind of power under the hood he'd be a contender again. "I can't leave Annie, Martin. I'm sorry."

"Okay, okay. There's not much chance we'd get anything signed on the dotted line here, anyway. Too much partying going on to conduct serious business. But tell me you'll fly back to Mooresville for a couple days next week. Hell, you and Annie can bunk in with Donna and me. All I need is your word you're committed to another full season of racing and I'm good with that."

He might as well get it over with. He owed the man who had given him his first ride in a NASCAR Sprint Cup Series car that much. "That's the trouble, Martin," he said. "I can't say I am committed to next season."

CHAPTER EIGHT

SHE HAD LET HER IMAGINATION roam too freely once more, Carrie chided herself as she stared out over the gray, restless waters of the lake. He didn't feel comfortable asking her to take care of his daughter even for a day or two. Were his kisses only a dalliance and not a prelude to something more? She was confused all over again and she hated the feeling.

"Carrie, wait up."

For a cowardly moment she wanted to pretend she hadn't heard him. She wanted to keep on walking until she reached her own snug, warm house where she could be alone and get herself back under control before Josh got home. But she didn't let herself indulge in the black moment. She respected herself too much to behave that way. Okay, so it wasn't working out. It wasn't the first time. It probably wouldn't be the last.

But oh, how she wished it could be different. How she wished Trace Collier could be the one for her.

"Carrie. Wait."

She turned the second time he called her name. He was just a few yards behind her and it only took him another moment to catch up. "Sorry about the call," he said, falling into step beside her.

"Not a problem," she replied, her eyes on the road before her. She could do this if she didn't have to look at him.

"Yeah, it is a problem." He stopped her by laying a hand on her arm. "I'm going to have to go to Mooresville for a couple days next week. Could I impose on you to take Annie and Peanuts under your wing while I'm gone?"

She wondered if her ears were playing tricks on her. "I overhead you say you weren't going to—"

"New York, that's right. I'm not. But I do have to meet with my car owner, Carrie. I owe him that much. If I'm not going to be behind the wheel next season, I have to give him a chance to find a new driver."

"I can't imagine that would be too hard. There are only forty-three Cup cars, right? But there must be a lot more drivers who try to qualify and don't make those forty-three. And all of those who want a shot and haven't been noticed yet."

"Yeah," he said with a rueful grin. "But that doesn't mean you can just go out and scoop a qualified Cup driver up off the street. It's a team sport, Carrie. Most people don't realize that."

"From what I've seen on TV there are a few drivers who don't realize that, either."

He laughed. "That's what I like about you, Carrie. You say what's on your mind and the rest of the world be damned."

"It's not exactly my best character trait," she said. "But you have to learn to be assertive when you're a single mother dealing with a lot of doctors with God complexes." She tried to smile, too, and hoped she pulled it off. Lord, she didn't want to be just friends with this man, but it seemed to be where they were headed.

At least he trusted her enough to ask her to care for his daughter, but that knowledge was small consolation to her aching heart. "Of course I'll watch over Annie and Peanuts for you," she said automatically.

"Thanks. I won't be gone more than two, or three, days at most. I'll leave the day after classes end so you won't have to drive Annie back and forth to the university."

"Thank you. It's hard for me to get away this time of year."

"Yeah, I'm figuring that out." He reached out and wrapped his hands around her upper arms. "Look at me, Carrie," he said softly, but the steel beneath the softness in his voice brought her eyes up to meet his. "I need to explain," he began.

"No, you don't," she said forcing another smile. "You have commitments. You have to honor them."

"My word means a lot to me."

"Of course it does. You wouldn't be the man I've come to—" she almost betrayed herself by letting the *l* word slip out "—to know and admire these last two weeks."

"I was hoping it was more than admiration," he said leaning close. "I was hoping it was—"

"Friendship," she whispered. She'd meant for the word to come out strong and clear, but it sifted through her lips as softly as the snowflakes falling down from the sky. She lifted her mittened hands and placed her fingertips against his lips. She could feel the warmth of his skin even through the heavy wool. "Don't say something you'll regret later, Trace."

He sighed and laid his forehead against hers. "I want us to be more than friends, Carrie."

Her heart gave a painful little jerk then settled down again. "I have commitments, too, Trace. A lot of them. Important ones to me. I belong here. In this place. My roots go deep. I…I don't think I'd transplant to your world very well."

He lifted her chin with his fingers and kissed her on the lips. "I told you I wouldn't make you any promises I might not be able to keep. Martin Cartwright gave me my first Cup ride. If I can help him, I have to try."

"I don't want you to make promises to me that you'll regret in the spring. Let's just leave things the way they are now. We've been moving a little too fast for my comfort anyway." She stepped back out of his arms and cleared her throat of the little clot of tears that had lodged there. "You should go to North Carolina next week. Talk to your owner and your sponsor. Make up your mind about what you want to do with your life." She started walking, one foot in front of the other, proud her voice was so steady even though she was shaking like a leaf inside. "I'll still be here," she said, with a slight emphasis on the last word, "when you get back."

"I DON'T CARE WHAT happens back in Mooresville," Annie whispered. "I'm staying here."

"You don't have to whisper," Josh said. His ankle ached like the devil. It always did when he got a cast off it. He felt like a hunk of concrete was no longer weighing him down, that he could fly almost, and then he usually overdid it the first couple of days. This time was no exception. He was just a slow learner, he guessed. "Mom's up at the rec building talking Pastor Jackson down off the ceiling. He always gets all wound up if somebody blows a fuse up there when it's his church's turn to be in charge."

"My dad's been gone three days. That means there's a lot of negotiating going on. I know how these things work. Martin Cartwright is a sneaky guy. He's putting together an offer my dad won't be able to refuse." She was still whispering. She was the strangest little kid he'd ever met. There she was with some kind of Princess This or That Barbie doll in her hand, combing its long blond hair, her dog on her lap, talking about negotiations and multimillion dollar deals like a grown-up.

"Did you really think he'd give up being a NASCAR driver to live here in the boonies? Especially with a race track right over the hill to remind him of it every day?" Nobody would do that. But he had hoped Trace might make the sacrifice for him and his mom.

"I don't see why he can't have both," Annie said, looking up at him, her green-gold eyes, all squinted up. He could see the gears and wheels turning in that oversize brain of hers. "Racing on the weekends. Here the rest of the time. A lot of drivers do it."

"My mom's never lived anywhere but here," he said. "And we're really busy in the summer." He felt his stomach tighten with disappointment again. It had been doing that a lot the last week or so. "I guess we just wanted them to be together more than they wanted it."

"I still think they want to be a couple," Annie said stubbornly. "I just wish we'd figured out what was going on sooner. Maybe we could have done something to get them talking again before Daddy left."

"Yeah, lousy timing," Josh agreed. They were in the little sitting area of the motor home. He was setting up the video game unit for a game. She'd tweaked the Prowler program again so that they could coordinate their moves and they'd kicked butt every time they'd played since then. "I really thought your dad might be the guy. I don't think my mom was ever this happy. Not since my accident, anyway."

"Dad, too." Now she was braiding the doll's hair, frowning, the tip of her tongue between her teeth as she worked. "I…I really wanted us to be a family. That's what I asked Santa for."

"You still believe in Santa?" The words just burst out of him. He couldn't stop himself.

She looked up at him and sighed. "Well, not exactly, but it doesn't hurt to cover all your bases."

"Yeah, I guess you're right." He turned his gaze back to the knights and demons on the screen. "It's what I wanted for Christmas, too." And not just because Trace Collier was a NASCAR driver. He was a great guy. Sometimes Josh even forgot about the NASCAR part of it. Sure, he'd like to go to races, be an insider, maybe even get a job in NASCAR someday. But beyond that he wanted the same thing Annie did. For his mom to have someone to laugh with and talk to and love. He squirmed a little in his seat, even though he hadn't said the word out loud. He wanted to be a family just like Annie did. He wanted them to be a family, but right at the moment he didn't know how to make that happen.

Annie had no such problem, however. "We have to talk to her," she pronounced suddenly, bouncing up and down on the mattress so hard she jarred his ankle.

"Oof," he grunted. "Settle down. I'm going to end up back in that damned cast if you land on my ankle."

"Sorry," she said, instantly contrite. "Peanuts, be quiet."

Peanuts had started barking the moment she started bouncing. Now Josh's golden retriever, Toby, had gotten into the act. The motor home rang with their howls.

"Quiet!" Josh yelled. Both dogs were instantly silent.

"Wow," Annie breathed. "Wish they'd mind me like that. But animals are always more responsive to male voices. It's something about the resonance—"

"Annie, knock it off," he said in the same voice he'd used on the dogs, only not as loud. "How do you think you're going to get my mom to change her mind about leaving here? Even for just part of the time." He ignored the vision of night racing at Bristol that flashed before his eyes and turned his attention to the quirky prodigy sitting beside him.

"Why, we talk to her, of course," Annie said, as though it were the simplest thing in the world. "Adult to adult."

"MY DAD'S ON HIS way back?" Annie's voice rose to a squeal. "He'll be here for the fireworks over the lake?"

"I hope so," Carrie said, a smile curving the corners of her mouth at the little girl's excited reaction to her news. She wished she felt like smiling on the inside.

"I'm so glad. Dad didn't know anything about the fireworks when he left. It will be like a homecoming surprise. I love fireworks and if they shoot them off over the lake it should be even more spectacular. The water will reflect the light and the magnitude should be approximately—" She stopped talking abruptly and flashed a sheepish glance at Josh. "I forgot," she said. "The fireworks should be really bright," she finished in a rush.

"Josh, what have you been telling this child?" Carrie demanded.

"Nothing, just that if she wants to make some friends who aren't super geeks she has to save the geek talk for when she's on *Jeopardy.*"

"I'm getting better," Annie insisted. "I haven't quoted a single factor theorem today, right?"

Josh gave her a high five. "Right."

"What have you two been doing?" Carrie asked.

"Talking about you and Dad," Annie replied with devastating frankness. "We want to have a talk with you about him. Won't you sit down," she said, indicating a place at the kitchen table with touching dignity.

"There's nothing to talk about, Annie, honey," Carrie said, including her son in the endearment. "Your dad and I are friends, nothing more."

"We would like you to be," Annie insisted.

"I don't think that's possible."

Josh had propped himself in the doorway, hands crossed over his chest, not quite making eye contact. But Carrie knew her son too well to delude herself that his emotions weren't as heavily invested in this conversation as Annie's were. Her heart ached. She should have noticed that he had become as involved as she was with Trace Collier and his little girl. This time the end of one of her ill-fated love affairs would hurt him as well as her.

"Why not?" Annie demanded, folding her hands in front of her, looking up at Carrie with wide, too-knowing eyes.

"Because we come from two different worlds. And there's no way that I can see to make them into one."

"But lots of families travel with the series. I have friends who get to come to every race with their parents. Not just drivers' kids, either. But you wouldn't have to come to every race. I…I could even stay here," Annie raced on, stumbling over her words a little in her haste to have her say. "One of the professors and his wife lets kids like me stay with them. I…I could do that so the motor home wouldn't be so crowded."

"You don't have to offer to do that, Annie. I don't think your father wants you to live away from him, not for a long time yet. But you need to understand something. My life is here," Carrie said quietly, wiping her hand on a dish towel and holding it tightly to try to keep her emotions under control. "I have the campground to take care of. My accounting business. Josh's doctors are all here. His school. His friends."

Her son pushed away from the door and walked to the table, splaying his hands on the tabletop. He didn't look like a boy anymore, Carrie thought with a jolt of surprise. He had grown into a young man some moment when she wasn't looking. Josh leaned down and looked her straight in the eye. "Mom," he said. "We wouldn't be taking off for the ends of the earth if you and Trace got together. We'd only be gone on the weekends. And we wouldn't have to go to every race. Heck, twice a year the races would come to us. I may be just a kid but I know one thing. You can't always just love *someplace* because that's the easy way not to get hurt. Sometimes you have to take a real chance and let yourself love *someone*, too."

CHAPTER NINE

IT HAD BEEN A LONG DAY. Delays in Charlotte because of heavy rain before he even left the ground; backups over Chicago that kept his Detroit-bound flight circling over Lake Erie while stacked-up planes, low on fuel, landed beneath them; a change of baggage stations that kept him waiting for his suitcase for almost half an hour. By the time Trace got his truck out of long-term parking and back on the road all he wanted to do was floor the gas pedal and keep it there until he turned up the lane to Thunder Lake Campground.

The one-day trip to Mooresville that Martin had arm-twisted him into making had stretched out to three, filled with nonstop negotiations and strategy sessions. He'd done everything he could to secure the associate sponsors Martin needed to fully finance both race cars for the next season, because he owed his owner and friend that much and, because, admittedly, he was competitive by nature. He'd wined and dined and schmoozed until the wee hours of the night. He'd autographed die-cast models of his car, hats, coats, hero cards and coffee mugs for their employees until his hands cramped, and then he'd started over again because there were boxes and boxes of the same kind of merchandise sent in by loyal fans he'd neglected for far too long.

He'd plastered a friendly smile on his face, donned his helmet and uniform and driven assorted VPs and CEOs and their sullen teenage sons, giggling trophy wives and awestruck nephews around the Charlotte track in a car specially modified with a passenger seat to give them a taste of what it was like to be a NASCAR driver. And in the end, all the hard work had paid off. The associate sponsors were all on board, ponying up not insubstantial amounts of money to see their logo on his uniform and the back quarter-panels and deck—trunk lid to the rest of the world—of his race car.

And most important of all, EverStrong was ready to give him a contract to drive the Cartwright Motorsports EverStrong car for the next three seasons. All that was wanting was his signature on the dotted line.

Not so long ago that would have been the best thing that had ever happened to him. Now it was only one horn of a dilemma he had yet to solve. He had never been anything but a professional race-car driver. What would he do with himself if he left the sport? But more importantly, what would he do with himself if he did sign the contract extension he'd been offered and returned to the racing circuit as lost and lonely as he'd left it?

When he turned onto the road leading to Thunder Lake Campground he was met by a line of cars snaking their way into the gates. He heaved a sigh and pulled into line behind the last one. It seemed his long day of delays wasn't over yet. Ten minutes later he was through the gate and parked beside Bryce's pickup.

"Leave it here and walk up" had been the older man's advice when he rolled to a stop beside the outhouse-size building where Carrie's neighbor was sheltering from the cold while he collected fees. "Going to come to a dead stop around here soon as the fireworks start. You'll be stuck in the middle of it if you try to drive up to your motor home. Josh can bring you back down in the golf cart later to get your truck."

"Fireworks?"

"Winter Carnival in town," Bryce explained. "Didn't Carrie tell you it was this weekend?"

Once Bryce reminded him, Trace remembered seeing posters advertising the Thunder Lake Winter Carnival fireworks for tonight. He wondered where Carrie and Josh and Annie were watching them from. It was cold, but maybe they had walked down to the lakeshore, or farther up the hill to the meadow at the top. He kept walking, moving faster than the slow-moving line of cars beside him. He noticed a number of them had pulled off the asphalt lane into the gravel parking spots that fronted each campsite. There were at least a hundred cars in the camp area and twice that many people milling about, arranging blankets in the backs of pickups, visiting with friends and neighbors through open car windows.

He walked down to the lake where he'd spied a familiar figure perched on the rustic fence that separated the narrow sand beach from the grass. Josh was standing beside Annie, arms resting on the top rung. He wasn't using his crutches Trace noticed. That surely was a good sign that the latest surgery had been successful. But he hadn't spoken to Carrie at all in the three days he'd been gone, so he couldn't be sure.

"Hey, Ladybug, did you miss me?" he asked, coming up behind the youngsters, putting his hands on his daughter's narrow shoulders and giving her a hug.

"Daddy!" She swung her feet over the fence and threw her arms around him. "I missed you. I knew you'd be back for the fireworks though, because Josh and I tracked your flight on the Internet all the way from Charlotte."

"Hi, Josh," he said over the top of Annie's head. "How's the leg."

"Hi, Trace. Not too bad. Doc says I'll be able to do most everything I want when I get the new prosthesis for my shoe. Glad you made it back for the fireworks."

"Me, too," he said. He wanted to ask where Josh's mother was but didn't. He would miss the boy. He hadn't realized how much until just this moment. He would be losing more than just the promise of a future with Carrie when he and Annie left Thunder Lake. He would be losing the promise of a family.

"Daddy, guess what? Peanuts won third place in the dog-costume contest in town this afternoon. We dressed him up like *Pirates of the Caribbean.*"

"Peanuts in a pirate costume? I wish I could have seen that," he said truthfully.

"It was awesome," Annie assured him. "And he would have won first prize but he peed on the judge's shoe. That lost him points."

"I imagine it did," Trace said, trying hard not to laugh out loud at the mental image of the poodle's lapse of good manners.

"There were lots of other things to do today, too. Santa Claus was at the gazebo in the park. And Mrs. Claus was there with him. They gave rides on the fire truck and there were pony rides and a parade. And a chili contest with twenty-seven entries. But the five-alarm chili that won was somewhat lacking in Scoville units to truly qualify it as five-alarm. I would have rated it about a three and a half—"

"Geek talk," Josh said quietly.

"Oh, be quiet," Annie shot back, just like a feisty little sister should, Trace thought, and felt his gut tighten with regret and impending loss once more. "My dad knows what Scoville units are, even if you don't. I can talk to him any way I want. Can't I, Daddy?"

"Within reason," Trace said. "Where's Carrie?" he asked Josh.

"At the pool building. Reverend Jackson tripped a circuit breaker again so she's hanging out there till he settles back down. That man doesn't know a single thing about electricity except that it comes out of a plug in the wall."

"I think I'll walk up the hill and let her know I'm back," he said.

"But Daddy, the fireworks are going to start any minute. Josh says this is the best place of all to watch. They look like they're going to come down right on top of your head, right, Josh?"

"Yeah, they do. But there's a really good view from the apple orchard, too. Maybe your dad and my mom would rather watch from there," he said, giving her a nudge with his elbow.

"Oh, yeah. I forgot," Annie said, looking up at him. Her eyes were shining so brightly with longing and excitement he could read the emotions swirling through them even in the dark. "Why don't you watch the fireworks with Carrie. Then we can go back to her house and have cookies and cocoa when they're done. She and I made sugar cookies today. And decorated them, too. It was fun."

"I can't wait to taste them," Trace said. She hadn't asked him how the meetings with Martin and the Ever-Strong people had gone and he was glad, because he wasn't certain what his answer would be. They'd discuss it later, after the excitement of the long, busy day and the fireworks display had worn off. He owed her that much, because if he signed the contract it would affect her life as significantly as his own. Another hard choice. If he went back to racing he would be uprooting her again after he'd just gotten her settled into the new school. Could he do that? He wished he could talk it over with Carrie as he had so many things these past few weeks. He gave Annie one more quick hug. *Keep an eye on her,* he mouthed to Josh, then turned and headed up the hill to meet his fate.

"TRACE, IT'S GOOD TO see you're back. And just in time for the fireworks." Carrie was flushed and smiling and seemed genuinely happy to see him. His spirits rose a little, but only for a moment. She wouldn't be smiling any longer when he told her what he had to say.

"I came across the kids down by the lake. They said you were up here and that the orchard was as good a place to watch the fireworks as the shoreline was."

"Well, maybe not quite as good, but it's quieter, that's for sure. Want to join me?"

"Sure." She didn't seem nervous or upset about seeing him. He didn't know if that was a good sign or a bad one. She sure didn't look as torn up inside as he felt. She handed a plump gray-haired woman the tray of cups of hot chocolate she was carrying and reached for her coat.

The pool building consisted of one big room with a concrete floor and paneled walls and three sets of sliders opening onto poolside. At the far end there was a kitchen with a pass-through window and shower rooms. He suspected the kitchen doubled as a refreshment stand in the summer, but now it was filled with good smells and a half-dozen clones of the plump, gray-haired woman who had taken the tray, all of them watching every move he made.

They wove their way through the room past Christmas trees decorated with all manner of crafted ornaments, and tables piled high with knitted afghans and sweaters, colorful lap quilts and stuffed animals of every shape and size. Several people nodded and waved, and one or two of the men in the room called out a greeting, but no one came running up to him with something to sign. Trace realized Carrie's friends and neighbors were beginning to accept him as one of their own, not as a NASCAR driver who had fallen among them like an alien from a crash-landed spaceship. He could belong here if he wanted to. If Carrie wanted him to.

Outside the air was crisp and cold, the night clear, the moon and stars brilliant in the velvet darkness. Off over the lake, bottle rockets zoomed skyward and a mortar shell blasted off from the park where the fireworks were set up, announcing the beginning of the show.

"How was your trip?" Carrie asked as she led the way past idling cars up the hill to the orchard. Her hands were pushed deep into the pockets of her coat her expression hidden by the shadow of the soft-brimmed felt hat she'd shoved down over her brown curls.

"Hectic," he said. "And the flight back was a real pain."

She indicated a bench that he'd never noticed before and sat down, motioning him to do the same. "Did the negotiations go well?"

"I'm not sure how to respond to that." Christmas music came from a dozen different car radios tuned to an Ann Arbor station that was coordinating the music with the light show. The first of the big bursts of fireworks went off over their heads. Red and green sparks rained down over the water and a chorus of oohs and aahs carried up to them on the night air.

"We don't have to be coy about this, Trace. The answer's too important to me so I'm just going to ask you straight out." Carrie didn't look at him as she spoke but watched the spectacle of lights in the sky. "Did you decide to go back to racing, Trace?"

"They offered me a three-year contract," he admitted, watching her profile and not the fireworks. "I wanted to call and talk to you about it, but the meetings seemed to go on forever. The timing was never right."

"Don't apologize. I wouldn't have known what to say to you on the telephone, anyway," she responded in a noncommittal tone, and his insides tightened another notch or two. "Did you sign the contract?" she asked.

More explosions and starbursts of color. He ignored them and so did she as she turned to face him. He took off his glove and traced a finger down her cheek. He had imagined touching her a dozen times while they were apart. Her skin felt every bit as soft and velvet smooth as it had in his dreams. "I haven't signed it yet," he said, "but I'm going to." He'd known that all along, deep inside himself. "There are a hundred people that work for Cartwright Motorsports. I owe my owner, my sponsor, my team—"

She reached up and touched her fingers to his lips, silencing him. "I wouldn't have expected you to do anything less. But you didn't do it just because you felt obligated, am I right? You still want to race, don't you?"

"Yes," he said, admitting it to himself at last. "I still want to race. Carrie," he said, grasping both her hands in his. "I want to go out on top, not limp away and fade into oblivion. I wish I could, but that's just not the way I'm made. I told you I'd never make you a promise I couldn't keep—"

"And you haven't."

He was afraid she was slipping away from him, back into the shell she'd protected herself with when he first met her, the same defense mechanism he'd erected around his heart to keep hurt at bay for so long. "I don't want to leave here, Carrie. I don't want to leave you. There has to be some way we can make this work. Some way the two of us—the four of us—can be together."

She didn't answer him for a moment or two that seemed to drag on forever. "I told you when you left that I'm rooted to this place," she said at last. "That's still true."

She was going to turn him down. Going to tell him to go ahead and walk out of her life. He didn't want that. He didn't want to be alone anymore. He had to think of something to say that would change her mind.

"I'm falling in love with you, Carrie. I'm not going to just let you shut me out of your life because I have a job that's not nine-to-five. I want to be with you. I want the four of us to be a family. It just can't be here. Not yet. Not for a while." He pulled her into his arms and kissed her, and the fireworks that ignited when their lips met put the glittering explosions overhead to shame. "I love you," he said against her lips. "For now and forever."

"I'm falling in love with you, too," she said, and wrapped her arms around his neck, leaning her forehead against his. He could feel her smiling. "I'm not going to shut you out of my life because you go traveling from one NASCAR track to the next every weekend. I was told pretty plainly that I was being a fool to turn you down because you're a NASCAR driver and I'm a homebody who's so stuck in a rut she can't dig herself out. My son, a genius in his own way," she said, and the warmth in her voice began to melt the tension that had tied his insides in knots, "told me that I had to learn to take some risks in life. That I had to learn to love *somebody,* not just *someplace.* He was so very right. I do love you, Trace. I realized that the moment you left. I'm ready to go where you go. As long as we can all come back here when your racing days are done."

"Now that's a promise I won't have any trouble keeping," he said, sealing his pledge with a kiss.

"As for now, our exceptional children have it all figured out for us."

"They do?"

She smiled. "I'll explain it all to you later. Now it looks like it's time for the grand finale," she said, and he was pleased to hear she sounded as breathless from their kiss as he felt. Overhead the sky exploded with sound and color.

"Oh, no," he said. "It's not the grand finale. It's just the beginning." And he kissed her again just to prove his point.

JEAN BRASHEAR

Two-time RITA® Award finalist, *Romantic Times BOOKreviews* Series Storyteller of the Year and recipient of numerous other awards, Jean has always enjoyed the chance to learn something new while doing research for her books—but never has any subject swept her off her feet like NASCAR. Starting out as someone who wondered what could possibly be interesting about cars racing, she's become a die-hard fan, only too happy to tell anyone she meets how fascinating the world of NASCAR is. (For pictures of her NASCAR adventures, visit www.jeanbrashear.com.)

A FAMILY FOR CHRISTMAS

Jean Brashear

To Tina Colombo and Marsha Zinberg, with heartfelt
thanks for letting me be a part of the NASCAR fun.

To Patsy Meredith, John Hart and
Bob and Nancy Hart for making my Bristol trip
possible, and to the lovely people of east Tennessee
and all the terrific members of the NASCAR Nation
whom I met at the Bristol night race,
an experience I will never forget.

And, as always, to Ercel,
who never stops cheering me on,
however crazy the venture.

CHAPTER ONE

NASCAR HOTTIE! screamed the headline of the magazine Gib Cameron's aunt was flipping through in the checkout line. Champion Crew Chief Headed For Seychelles With Top Model Girlfriend.

Gib rolled his eyes. He'd stood next to the model for five minutes at a cocktail party during Champions Week in New York. And he hated being called a hottie. The gossipmongers had gotten one thing right, though—his team had won the NASCAR Sprint Cup Series championship three weeks ago, and he had two prior championship titles under his belt.

"Well, there's no question that you're more handsome than any of the drivers," remarked Rhetta Cameron. "But that girl needs some meat on her bones. Anyway, she doesn't seem your type."

It wasn't only his aunt who made remarks about his looks, and Gib squirmed every time they did. All that mattered was his ability to assemble the best team, to make sure his driver had the top car week after week after week. The fact that he got photographed so often was only an annoyance to him. The driver was the face of the team, the one who did all the public appearances, that sort of thing. What Gib looked like amounted to nothing—only how he performed mattered.

Anyway, did he have a type? Since he had no life outside the track, he wasn't sure about the answer to that question. That's what this trip home to Marysville, Tennessee, was all about: downtime. He hadn't been back since he left right out of high school to pursue his NASCAR dream.

Aunt Rhetta snapped the magazine shut and stuffed it back in the rack.

"Would you like to have that, Aunt Rhetta?" One thing about being both successful and a workaholic was that he didn't have much time to blow the money he made. Besides, squandering money wasn't Gib's style. A crew chief could have a far longer career than a driver if he wanted to, but Gib took nothing for granted. No one stayed at the top forever.

"No, honey." She patted his arm. "Having you here is all I need."

Which only made him feel more guilty. She and Uncle Buck had always been his favorite relatives, and though he called when he could, not once in the thirteen years since he'd left had he been back home to see them. He did make certain they had good tickets to the nearby NASCAR races each year and entertained them in what little free time he had. But now they'd lost Jack, their only son, to cancer, and this Christmas was their first without him. Although Gib was tired after the grueling season and he had a lot of work to do before Daytona in February, there was no way he could refuse when they'd asked him to come visit. His own folks had moved from Marysville to Florida years ago but would be on a cruise this Christmas, his gift to them.

So he was back in his hometown, the place he'd never wanted to see again.

Because of Cassie.

Cassie Wheeler was his first love, the girl he'd intended to marry. The one who'd promised to join him in Charlotte the second she graduated from high school one year behind him. The woman who'd moved away from Marysville at Christmas break her senior year instead.

And married someone else.

"I declare, I am so excited about going to the holiday light show!"

Gib yanked himself from his dark thoughts. Cassie was old news and had lost the power to hurt him years before. She might come home for Christmas, but even if she did, just seeing the sparkle in Aunt Rhetta's eyes was worth the risk of running into the girl who'd played him for a fool.

Aunt Rhetta had looked so fragile when he'd gotten out of his plane that he'd been afraid to hug her too hard. When she'd asked him to drive them over to the nearby speedway, tonight, his first night here, he hadn't had the heart to say no, even though he wanted to be near a race track even less than he wanted to be in Tennessee.

What he really craved was to fall into bed and sleep for a week.

But the holiday light show was an annual event that drew thousands to drive the track—a thrill in itself for a NASCAR fan—and view the wonders of a million and a half lights celebrating the season. There were also a carnival in the infield, photos with Santa and an ice rink outside the track. Admission fees went to benefit charities focusing on children, and one of the strongest credos of NASCAR was to give back. Every driver had a charitable foundation, and each team sought ways to give to others in need, especially children.

So how could Gib say no? Thus he found himself, a couple of hours later, taking his aunt and uncle on a spin around the light show, then parking the car and walking to the infield. What he hadn't counted on, since he had donned a ball cap and put up the hood of his coat, was getting recognized.

"Look—it's Gib Cameron!"

"Isn't that the crew chief of the No. 501 car?"

The rumble of voices grew louder, and soon he found himself surrounded by autograph-seeking fans, asking what felt like a million questions.

Gib wasn't a driver and did what he could to stay out of the limelight, but he knew that his actions would reflect on the team and its sponsors. NASCAR fans were notoriously brand loyal, and racing was a very expensive proposition. Sponsor money was crucial to everything they did, and being part of the championship team carried an extra responsibility.

So no matter what Gib wished he could be doing this night, he had to live up to the accessibility fans expected and just be grateful he wasn't a driver, or this would be ten times worse. He glanced over at his aunt and uncle. *I'm sorry,* he mouthed.

He needn't have. Both were beaming. Aunt Rhetta looked like a kid at Christmas.

"Did you know when you made the call for two tires and a splash at Phoenix that it would lock you into the points lead?"

Gib signed another T-shirt and glanced over at the speaker, a young girl of maybe thirteen or fourteen, he'd guess, wearing his team's cap with her blond ponytail sticking out the back. Pretty insightful question for a kid. "No," he admitted. "But we needed to get off pit road ahead of the No. 560 car."

"Is it true that all the teams in your shop get

victory bonuses, no matter which team wins?" Her eyes were blue and slightly tilted up at the corners. Somehow they seemed familiar.

He nodded. "I think it's a good policy."

"It seems odd to me. You're racing against the others in your shop."

He kept signing what other people stuck in front of him, but he found himself enjoying this conversation too much. "It's not an easy balance," he admitted. Tempers could fly in his very competitive business, and no one was more driven to win than him, but he couldn't lead a team if he couldn't control himself.

"So after a race, when your team loses and—"

"Molly!" A younger African-American boy skidded to a halt beside her. "Mom says we need to leave soon."

The girl named Molly looked exasperated. "Not yet, Andre," she whispered fiercely.

"You're gonna be in trouble," Andre said. "We were supposed to stay together."

"I know, but I just had to—" Her cheeks were fiery red. "Don't you know who this is?" she muttered.

Gib finished an autograph, then crouched down to the boy's level. "It's my fault," he said, extending his hand for a shake. "Hi, Andre. I'm Gib Cameron, crew chief of the No. 501 car. Your sister and I were just talking racing."

The boy took his hand but rolled his eyes. "That's practically all she ever talks about." Then his gaze widened. "The No. five-oh-one—wow! You're the champions!"

"We are," Gib agreed.

"That's really cool," Andre said. Then he frowned. "But I'm supposed to bring her back. Our mom's right over there." He pointed behind him.

"Well, I don't want to get Molly in trouble." Gib rose. "You suppose it would help if I explained?"

Molly's eyes were the wide ones now. "Would you?"

Gib glanced at his aunt and uncle. They nodded and smiled. "You go right ahead, son," his uncle Buck said. "We'll wait here."

"I won't be a second," he promised. "Andre, how about you lead us?" He glanced at Molly and winked.

"Sure!" Andre took off like a shot.

"Stay in sight—" Molly ordered, then sighed as the boy did exactly the opposite.

"So you follow racing," Gib began. "When did you start?"

She ducked her head shyly. "I can't remember when I didn't. I watched with my dad when I was little. I've seen nearly every one of your races." She smiled up at him. "I want to be in NASCAR someday."

"As a driver?" he asked. "There are more women in NASCAR every day."

"Drivers aren't the most important part of the team," she insisted. "They come and go. I'd like to own a team."

Gib's eyebrows flew upward. "That's quite a goal you've got there."

She slanted him a decidedly cocky look. "You don't believe I can?"

Gib laughed and clapped her on the shoulder. "I'd be a fool to bet against you, I'm beginning to think." They traded smiles. "So do you go to the races much?"

Those eyes that seemed so familiar darkened. "I've never been to one." She shrugged. "My mom can't afford it." Her features grew determined. "But I'm saving my money for the spring race. Mom doesn't like racing, but she won't let me go alone. If I can save enough for all of us to have tickets, I'm hoping I can change her mind." She glanced ahead. "Uh-oh."

"Young lady, did I or did I not tell everyone we had to stay together?"

That voice. Gib went very still.

"But Mom—" Molly protested. "This is—"

Even as Gib was turning to face the woman who'd spoken, something deep in his gut was telling him her identity before he ever took a look.

And when he did, his heart stumbled, even as the ashes of anger and hurt sparked to life again. The curly brown hair was shorter now, but the eyes—her daughter's eyes—still possessed the power to level him. To strike straight at his soul.

She stood there, holding the hands of a small Asian girl and an undernourished little boy. Her facc had lost all color. "Gib." Her voice was barely a whisper.

He wanted to hate her for breaking his heart. Wanted to make her explain why she had betrayed him.

But "Hello, Cassie" was all he could manage.

CHAPTER TWO

CASSIE WHEELER MAGUIRE was a schoolteacher, and a good one. She talked for a living, but not one word would come from her mouth except his name.

Gib. Dear mercy, but the lanky, somewhat shy boy who was so good with engines had grown into a heartthrob. She'd seen his pictures, of course. It was difficult to avoid them since Molly had followed his career like most girls idolized rock stars—but in person, he was even more handsome.

How on earth had he and Molly met? Of all the people in the world she didn't want her daughter within miles of, why had fate brought him here? After she'd been widowed, she'd moved back to Marysville, needing the familiar even though she had no family left. Gib never returned to Tennessee except for races. She'd checked that out before moving back. She'd given up so much to see that he could have the career he'd dreamed of, and he'd more than lived up to the steep goals he'd set for himself. He'd made it to the top, and she was happy for him, honestly.

She just didn't want him anywhere near Molly. She hadn't doubted the wisdom of her decision, the toughest one she'd ever made, not for years.

But now she wondered. Molly was literally glowing in his presence, and Cassie had seen, in those seconds before his identity had come crashing in on her, that he'd been good with her daughter. Hadn't patronized her but seemed truly interested in what Molly had to say.

Couldn't he see? More frightening, could Molly?

Her husband Tom's only condition for the marriage was that everyone believe that he was Molly's actual father, that Cassie would never tell anyone otherwise. At the time, it had seemed the right thing to do, for all of them. Gib had held such hopes, and a teenage marriage with a baby on the way would have destroyed all of them. She'd loved him to her marrow, and he'd sounded so thrilled every time he'd called from Charlotte that she couldn't bear to end those dreams. She didn't doubt that Gib would have returned to Marysville and gone back to work in the garage where he'd been employed all through high school, in order to support her and their child.

She'd loved him too much to put him in that position.

So she'd left Marysville and gone to live with relatives while she had the baby. She'd been supposed to give her up for adoption, but she'd known all along that she couldn't part with Gib's child, no matter what that demanded of her. When she'd met Tom, a decent guy whose family lived next door to her relatives, he'd fallen for her even though she was pregnant. They'd spent more and more time together, and one day he'd proposed marriage to her. Offered to raise her child as his own. Though she'd been heartbroken over Gib, she'd appreciated Tom's steady solidness…had eventually come to love him.

Just not like she'd loved Gib.

"Listen, it's not Molly's fault. We got to talking—" Gib began.

Exactly what Cassie couldn't let happen. Wrong decision or not, Gib's life was now lived in the fast lane. He traveled, dated gorgeous women, had a demanding career. His world was light-years from her own simple country existence. Anyway, he might not even want to know about Molly. Or might not believe her.

It wasn't like she hadn't lied to him before. *I'm sorry, Gib,* she'd said, though the words had literally nauseated her. *Our dreams are different. I've changed my mind. I won't be coming to Charlotte after all.* When she'd gotten off the phone, she'd cried until she'd gotten sick. Then she'd lain in her bed for days, too depressed to eat or sleep—until she'd realized that she might be harming her baby.

Their baby.

"Molly can be a bit headstrong," she admitted, which was like calling the Pacific a pond.

"Mommm—" Molly complained, her face a study in devastation to be denigrated in front of her hero.

Molly was her heart. Cassie found a shaky smile for her daughter. "Pot calling the kettle black?"

Molly's smile was her reward. "You said it, I didn't." Her smile was also her father's, and it tore Cassie up.

She had to get out of here. "Well, Gib, it's been nice to see you. We'd better be moving along." She nodded behind him. "You have more fans coming your way."

Gib's forehead creased at her dismissal. Just for a moment, their eyes met, and she could see questions she couldn't afford to answer.

She could also recognize that he was weary and troubled. A treacherous part of her wanted to reach out and take care of him.

"Cassie—" he began.

"I told you, Harley. That is Gib Cameron. Gib, over here—"

"Mr. Cameron, could I have your autograph?" A little boy held out a piece of paper.

"Bye, Gib," Cassie said. "It was—" Her voice cracked a little, and she prayed he hadn't heard it. "It was good to see you."

"Cass—" But he was rapidly swallowed up in a crowd.

"Mom, can't we wait?" Molly asked.

Cassie could see her daughter's heart breaking, but she had to hold firm or she would fall to the ground and weep herself. "Honey, it's way past the little ones' bedtime, and we all have school tomorrow."

Molly was a good child, if headstrong. Reluctantly, she followed. Cassie picked three-year-old Bobby up and held tight to six-year-old Lily's hand. "Andre, you hold on to Molly," she ordered. At eight, Andre took his role as eldest male in the house seriously, however much she wanted him to be free to be just a kid.

They were nearly to the car when Molly gasped. "Mom! I didn't get his autograph!"

"Oh, sweetheart, I'm so sorry."

"Can I go back in there?"

Cassie had never meant to hurt anyone all those years ago, and she didn't want to do so now. Though Bobby was asleep on her shoulder, and he was getting too heavy for her to carry while Lily was drooping, too, Cassie looked into the eyes of her firstborn and knew that she couldn't add one more black mark to her record, even though she was so exhausted she didn't know how she'd get through the evening and all the work she still had ahead of her.

“All right. Come on, gang.” She shifted Bobby upward on her shoulder and soothed Lily, who began to whine.

Somehow they made it across the huge parking lot and back through the tunnel.

But Gib was long gone.

GIB’S NIGHT WAS NOT the least bit restful. Instead, he lay awake, his mind awhirl with images of the young Cassie, so soft and sweet yet capable of deceit he’d never imagined. Those dreams were interwoven with ones of the woman he’d just encountered, still beautiful in his eyes but burdened in more ways than the four children she’d towed with her. Marysville was a small town, and Aunt Rhetta had filled in some of the details he was driven to know.

Cassie was a teacher, just as she’d always wanted to be. He would never have asked her to give that up. He’d had everything figured out, how their lives would proceed. All she’d had to do was join him in Charlotte as they’d planned.

He veered away from the bitterness that threatened. He was trying hard not to judge her, even though the very sight of her had been a knife to the heart and brought back everything he’d spent years burying: the rage, the ache, the emptiness. Most of all, the questions.

He would see her again, talk to her. Despite her obvious reluctance to be around him, he would force her to explain. He'd found out where she lived and, most importantly, that she was a widow, so there would be no husband to block him from seeing her. Asking her why she'd broken up with him.

Why does it matter? one part of him asked.

Gib shook his head. Because apparently he wasn't as over her as he'd thought. Hell.

Well, she might not want to see him, but he was going over there, anyway, at least once. He spent the remainder of the night analyzing. Strategizing. All things he was very, very good at.

As dawn rose, Gib wasn't rested, but somehow he still found himself full of energy. He hadn't gotten where he was by being timid. He was cautious with his money and, since Cassie, had been guarded with his heart. But in racing, he had never been afraid to take a chance.

Plus he had an ace in the hole. Molly. Clearly a diehard fan and gearhead in the making. What mother, even one less loving than Cassie, would deny her child a chance at a dream? There were all sorts of strings Gib could pull to give Molly a leg up, and if he had to use Cassie's daughter as an excuse to see Cassie again, he wouldn't hesitate.

He picked up his PDA and started making plans.

CASSIE WAS JUST BEGINNING dinner while supervising Andre's homework and placating a hungry

Bobby with slices of apple when she heard Lily call out from the living room. “Mommy, it’s that man.”

“What man, honey?” A shiver ran through her. *Please, no. No.*

“Mom! It’s him! It’s Gib Cameron at our front door!” Molly sounded as if she’d just sighted Elvis, only Elvis wouldn’t have thrilled her half as much.

Cassie checked the pots on the stove and made certain the handles were turned inward. “Andre, you work on that second math—” Her shoulders sank. Andre had dropped his pencil and raced for the front door.

“Man—” Bobby pointed. His mother had been a crack addict, and Bobby’s development had been slowed by that. He was also severely asthmatic. At three, his verbal skills were way behind, but she was making progress with him every day, she felt.

“Man,” she agreed. And sighed. “Shall we go join them?” She didn’t even want to think about how she looked after three hours’ sleep, wrangling with bills she couldn’t afford to pay and a long day with her fourth-graders. She’d changed into old, comfortable jeans and had drawn her hair up in a scrunchie. She hadn’t bothered with lipstick in a very long time.

Maybe, if she were lucky, she’d scare him off all by herself.

“Go see man,” Bobby ordered.

“Yes, sir.” She saluted, and Bobby grinned.

Then she squared her shoulders and marched them both through the doorway.

Only to see Gib loaded down with presents, surrounded by three very excited children. Bobby slipped from her grasp, squealing. Make that four.

"Mom, you won't believe what Gib brought me!"

"Mr. Cameron," Cassie corrected.

"I don't mind," Gib said.

Cassie glowered. Molly glowed. "Thanks, Gib. Look, Mom—a Sam Duncan jacket!"

Cassie's temper fired. She'd taught her children not to address adults by their first names. And how dare he barge in here like Santa Claus? What happened when he left? She could take care of her own children. She glared at him.

Gib simply smiled, if a slightly hard one.

She grasped for control. "Well, let me see," she said, and was quickly swallowed up in chattering children.

"Want to stay for dinner?" Andre asked. "My mom's the best cook in the world."

Cassie closed her eyes, but she couldn't block out the hopeful expressions of her children. "Mr. Cameron is very busy. I'm sure he doesn't have time." He couldn't possibly stay, and she couldn't bear to have him see how she lived. She'd once read an article about the huge house he owned on Lake Norman. Hers was a hovel, if a clean one, compared to it.

"Actually, a home-cooked meal sounds really good." Gib knelt beside her and took from her hand the race car Bobby was beaming over, demonstrating to the boy how to get it to make the throaty rumble of a racing engine.

She could feel his body heat. Could smell the scent of him that was permanently imprinted in her nostrils. She hadn't been with a man since Tom died—when would she find the time, even if she were interested?

But what she was feeling was not nearly so simple as desire. Gib's voice was older, but it was the same. His body had filled out, but she knew it from many, many hours of the teenage torture called making out. From one unforgettable night when they'd been each other's first.

But it wasn't even his body or his voice that drew her to him. It was Gib, simply Gib. She couldn't believe the hold was still there. They'd once been bound to each other in a manner that defied time. A part of Cassie, it seemed, still remembered vividly how it felt to belong to Gib Cameron.

"Mom?" said Molly, the reason why none of that could matter, and Cassie was jerked from her thoughts. This wasn't Gib's world, and he wouldn't stay. Even should he be able to forgive her if he found out. She couldn't risk Molly being hurt. Somehow she had to make him go before that happened.

Oh, how it burned that her children weren't going to have much of a Christmas on her budget. She loved them too much to take this evening away. Somehow, for their sakes, for the joy filling the room, she would make it through an hour or two of Gib's company, then close the door behind him as fast as she could. And she'd be grateful that he surely had to get back to his life soon.

"We're only having spaghetti, but you're welcome to stay," she said, far more brightly than she felt.

"Can I help?" he asked.

"No, thanks." Cassie rose on unsteady legs and re-entered her kitchen.

And battled the urge to race out the back door.

CHAPTER THREE

DINNER WITH FOUR KIDS left no room for adult conversation, and what Gib wanted to discuss with Cassie wasn't meant for young ears, anyhow. When he'd been issued the dinner invitation—however reluctantly on Cassie's part—he'd thought that once the kids were in bed, he and she could have it out.

But the more he observed her, the more his anger dimmed. She had a whole lot on her plate with four active children and a full-time job, yet she handled each child carefully and with all the love he'd known she would give the babies she was supposed to have with him.

She was thin. She looked exhausted.

Whatever she'd done to him, life had not treated his Cassie kindly. Certainly not the way he'd meant to treat her.

"This was great," he said, and meant it. "I don't get many home-cooked meals."

Cassie glanced at him from where she was helping the youngest, Bobby, with his food instead of eating her own. Bobby was awkward with his fork, though he seemed old enough to handle one better. No wonder she was so thin.

The boy's breathing seemed a little harsh, and he didn't say much, though he'd smiled really big at the race car and charged around the living room like the rest of them. Like it was Christmas already.

"It's simple food, nothing like you're used to, I'm sure." Spots of color stained her cheeks.

Gib had noticed that the presents beneath the scrawny Christmas tree were sparse. The house was small, the furniture threadbare and old, but everything was scrupulously clean and tidy, probably not an easy task with four active children to care for. Cassie kept averting her gaze and talking to the children but not him, as though his presence made her uncomfortable.

Damn it, this was wrong. He'd have provided better for her. Who was the guy who'd married her, that he'd left Cassie in such straits? And how had she wound up with all these kids, anyway—though that was less difficult to imagine. She'd always had a soft spot for an underdog and had a heart as big as North America.

"Molly," he said, making one of the snap decisions he was so good at. "Why don't you help me with the dishes."

"No," Cassie protested. "You're company."

And, he suspected, she was eager to get rid of him. But why?

"It's only fair," he noted. "You cooked." She wasn't getting out of talking to him that easily. He rose and began stacking dishes. Molly cast him yet another adoring glance, and Gib squirmed a little under the hero worship.

"Molly, is your homework done?" Cassie asked.

"Yes, ma'am. I didn't have much, and I finished it on the bus."

Cassie's mouth pursed in that expression he'd forgotten, the one that popped up whenever she was thwarted. Gib grinned. Miss Cassie Wheeler had been sweetness itself, but she'd also had one hard head. When she got her mind set on something, dissuading the sun from shining was easier than crossing her.

"Want man play," said Bobby. "Car."

"Yeah!" cheered Andre. "We could have a race." The set of smaller die-casts of all the Gannon Motorsports cars he'd been given had been a big hit, as well.

"Race!" crowed Lily. She'd been a tougher proposition, but she seemed very happy with her pink No. 501 car T-shirt and cap. She was still wearing both.

"It's nearly bath time, kids." Cassie's pronouncement was greeted with groans. She sighed. "Thirty minutes, and that's it. I have papers to grade."

The younger three kids raced from the room. "Bobby, you slow down, or I'll put you in the bath right now. Andre, you and Lily don't get him too excited."

"He's wheezing, isn't he, Mom?" Molly asked.

Cassie rose, nodding. "I'd better get him in bed. Might be time for the nebulizer."

Gib could see the weariness in her slow steps. "Your mom works too hard," he said to Molly once Cassie left the room.

"I try to help. We all do."

Man, he hadn't expected any of this. "What's wrong with Bobby?"

"He has asthma. When he starts that wheezing, it can get really bad. He can't help all his problems. He's behind for his age. His mother was addicted to crack." Molly's posture was defensive.

Gib focused on washing the dishes while Molly dried. No dishwasher, he'd noticed. "So your dad and mom had you, then adopted the others."

Molly shook her head. "No, it was just me until Daddy died. He always said I was all he needed. Mom became a foster mother a year or so afterward. Nobody wanted Lily and Andre and Bobby, so she adopted them."

"All at the same time?" Gib was amazed that she'd been allowed to, as a single parent.

"No," Molly explained. "Andre first—he was a

crack baby, too, but he recovered better than Bobby has. Lily was abused and was taken from her home two years ago. Bobby is new to us. He's not ours yet, but Mom's determined that he will be."

How did she do it? And Molly, too—she didn't seem to be at all resentful, yet she surely must bear some of the load as the eldest. Within Gib grew a determination to find a way to help them. Whatever Cassie had done to him in the past, she'd paid for her decisions.

"I admire her—and you, too," he said.

Molly shrugged, but a flush rose to her cheeks while her eyes glowed. "It's what family does, that's what Mom taught me."

Family. A pang went through Gib, a hunger he hadn't realized was there. He had a demanding job that he loved, and he had friends among the racing community and respect from his competitors.

But at the end of the day, he didn't even have a dog to come home to. With his travel schedule, a pet was impossible, as was a true home. The enormous house on Lake Norman was only a residence. He spent far more time in his motor home.

"Your mom always wanted a big family," he said. He'd believed she wanted one with him, but she'd changed her mind. He'd thought she'd changed inside, too, but tonight, he was far less certain.

"How did you know her?"

Wow. That was a loaded question. "We grew up together. We dated in high school." *We meant to spend our lives together,* he didn't add.

"Really?" Molly seemed overwhelmed. "Wow! My mom dated Gib Cameron. Unreal."

"Why do you say that?"

"Well, I mean…look at her." Molly gestured around the house. "And look at what you've done with your life." That she thought he'd done better was clear.

"Don't ever talk about your mother that way," he snapped. "What I've done with my life won't matter to anyone when I'm gone."

"But you're famous."

"Big deal. Your mom is making a difference with her life. No big house or all the fast cars in the world can measure up."

Molly's lip stuck out, and he was reminded that she was still very young. "Well, I'm not letting myself be trapped in Marysville like my mother, that's for sure. I'm getting out as soon as I can, just like you did."

Trapped in Marysville? Was that what Cassie was? She'd left once, when she'd abandoned him, so why had she come back? Still so many questions he had to ask.

"Bobby!" Cassie's anguished cry came from the living room.

Gib tossed the last pan onto the rack and raced from the kitchen. What he saw froze him to the spot.

Cassie was bent over the child, whose lips were blue and his breathing so labored that Gib could see the tendons in his neck straining and his chest heaving as he fought for breath. "Molly, gather up the kids. We've got to head for the emergency room. The county's EMS is too far away."

"We'll take my car," Gib said.

Cassie glanced up at him, startled, as if she'd forgotten he was there. "This isn't the first time. I don't need your help."

"You've got it, anyway." He grabbed for his coat. "I'll warm up the car and pull up in front of the door." He glanced over at Lily and Andre, who looked frightened. "Lily, you get a blanket for your brother. Andre, why don't you come with me." He picked up the boy and finished putting on his coat as he dashed from the house.

He wheeled the rental SUV in front of the door and leaped out as Cassie emerged with Bobby. Gib took the child from her while she clambered in, and kept an eye on Molly, who was buckling up the others. Then he settled Bobby in Cassie's lap and raced around the hood, whipping the car into the street with a skill his driver, Sam Duncan, might envy.

The ride to the hospital was silent except for the terrible rasp of Bobby's breathing. When Gib got to the emergency entrance, he leaped out and opened the passenger door. "I'll be back in a second, kids." He escorted Cassie inside and grabbed the first medical professional he saw, demanding immediate assistance. Once he'd seen Cassie and Bobby swept away, he returned to his vehicle.

"Everything's going to be fine," he soothed, though he could be sure of no such thing. He parked the car, then unloaded the kids and ushered them inside.

Minutes secmed like hours while they waited. Gib was surprised and impressed by the kids' composure. Molly was great with them, and he pitched in however he could, following her lead. What he knew about kids could fit in a teacup with room left over, but Molly was a pro as a big sister. She was really something, this girl.

Time dragged on. Lily fell asleep on his shoulder, and Andre curled up with his head on Molly's lap. "Why don't you try to rest," Gib urged Molly. "You can lean on me."

"I'm fine," she said, but as the minutes marched past, at last, she, too, succumbed and dozed against him.

It was an odd feeling, being surrounded by children who trusted you to take care of them. Gib was in charge of a lot of people and very accustomed to responsibility, but this was different.

It was kind of nice, really. But how on earth did

Cassie juggle this and so much more? Yes, he had to be mindful of the safety of his driver and pit crew when the track was hot, but they were adults and could take care of themselves. But these kids…Lily's soft breath on his neck, the warm weight of Molly at his side…

Gib was surprised by the lump in his throat. Humbled by what Cassie dealt with every single day. He still didn't understand why she'd betrayed their dreams, but it was reassuring to discover that the girl he'd loved hadn't changed in her basic nature, except for that one deeply painful choice.

Why, Cassie? He still wanted to understand.

Just then, she emerged—without Bobby. When she spotted him, an odd expression crossed her features.

If he'd thought her tired before, she was absolutely exhausted now. He wished he could stand, but he'd wake the children. He wanted to take her in his arms and swear everything would be fine.

But maybe it wouldn't. "How is he?" Gib whispered when she drew near.

She settled heavily into the chair beside him. "Better, but they want to keep him overnight." Pain washed her features. "I don't want to leave him. He'll be so frightened."

Gib might not have children, but he was quick to analyze a situation. There was one of her and two places she needed to be. Spending the night in the hospital was no place for the other three kids. "I'll take them home. You stay."

Surprise blossomed. "No. You can't—"

"Can't what? I'm in charge of a lot of people, Cassie. And I have to make decisions on the fly."

"You don't know anything about children."

"I know you can't be in two places at one time. Besides, Molly can help me. And I can call Aunt Rhetta, if Molly and I can't manage." He saw the indecision. "I'm not going to hurt your children, Cassie."

She glanced at him with those huge, beautiful blue eyes swamped with tears. "You don't have to do this, Gib."

He cupped her cheek and brushed away the tears with his thumb. Whatever had made her change her mind about him, all he could see now was his Cassie in trouble. She was in pain, and he'd never been able to stand that. "Let me help, honey," he said.

She dropped her head as if she couldn't put one foot in front of the other one more second.

Gib gathered her close with his one free arm, and for a precious moment, Cassie relaxed against him.

Then Lily stirred, and Cassie sprang back. "I'm sorry." She swiped at her eyes. "I didn't mean—"

Gib grasped her chin and turned her face toward him. "Do you have no one to help you? Cassie, you're carrying too heavy a load by yourself."

Her shoulders went rigid with pride. "I can handle everything just fine. This is an unusual circumstance."

Privately he doubted it, but he didn't argue. "Is there someone I should call about your class tomorrow?"

Her expression was bleak. "It's so hard to find a substitute, especially before the holidays. I'll call in the morning, if I have to, but maybe they'll let us go from here in time."

"Cassie, you can't seriously be thinking of going to work after the night you've had."

That stubborn face was oh, so familiar. "I don't need much sleep."

She needed about six months of it, best he could tell. But he also knew Cassie, and arguing would only stiffen her resistance. He didn't manage people for a living for nothing. "But Bobby won't be ready for day care, will he?" She wouldn't stay home for herself, but a child was another matter.

She shook her head, and her military posture crumpled.

"Look—" He was about to say that he'd keep the kids and she could sleep, but he stopped himself just in time. She'd already made the point that he didn't have any experience with children.

But he had an ace in the hole. "I'll call Aunt Rhetta as soon as I know she and Uncle Buck are up. After losing Jack, helping out with your kids would do her a world of good. She's great with kids—she was practically a mother to me, even though I had a perfectly good one. You stay here with Bobby and take your time. Tell me who to call in the morning, and then whenever he's discharged, I'll come get you."

"I can—" *Do it myself,* he would bet the farm she was about to say until she realized what he already had. She had no transportation without him. Reluctantly, she nodded. "All right. Thank you."

Gib smothered a grin. There was a decided reluctance in that thank-you. Cassie was a proud woman and she managed an unbelievable amount all on her own, but she wasn't a superwoman, however much she might try to be. "Can you be away from him long enough to stay with this bunch while I get the car? I don't want to scare them by leaving them alone when they're so sleepy."

Her smile was grateful and maybe a little relieved that a bachelor had thought of that. Hell, he might not be married, but kids were people, weren't they? Just smaller and more…tender. More easily damaged.

Cassie had set herself up to repair three scarred little souls, and these kids were very lucky she had. "You impress me, Cassie," he said.

"What?" She was startled. "Why?"

He chuckled and tucked a curl behind her ear.

"The amazing thing is that you don't even see it, do you?"

Lily whimpered and forced them to silence. Carefully, he handed her off to Cassie, then bent to Molly. "Molly, I have to get up," he murmured.

Molly stirred and blinked like an owl. Right now, she looked a lot younger. "What's going on? How's Bobby?" She rubbed her eyes and sat up. In her lap, Andre grumbled.

"Let your mom explain while I get the car." With long strides, Gib left the waiting room.

Feeling a little like he'd left something precious behind.

CHAPTER FOUR

THE NIGHT WAS SHORT and miserable, trying to tuck his six-foot-four frame into Cassie's small sofa, but Gib couldn't make himself sleep in her bed. Not that he wouldn't like to get to that, but he wanted her in it with him when he did.

Gib went still, realizing that he was clearly not over Cassie at all. When morning arrived, he was proud of Molly and himself, though in all honesty Molly deserved most of the credit, directing the younger children like a drill sergeant. Gib went through a dizzying whirl of tasks. Cooking breakfast wasn't bad—even if the kids seemed a little suspicious of his brand of egg-scrambling; assembling lunch boxes was scary; supervising toothbrushing was okay, but brushing Lily's hair and putting it into pigtails might have been the most daunting task he'd ever attempted. Winning a NASCAR Sprint Cup Series championship at the end of a grueling thirty-six races was a piece of cake compared to corralling slippery-clean hair on a wiggly little girl.

Somehow, though, he'd managed to get them all to school without having to call in Aunt Rhetta. He'd talked to Cassie, but Bobby wouldn't be released until the afternoon, so technically, Gib was a free man. Cassie had assured him she had a ride and would be home before the kids were, making it clear that his help was no longer needed.

He should have been happy. He could return to his aunt and uncle's house and catch up on lost sleep, or he could pull out his laptop and check in with the shop, tinker with some changes he hadn't had time to implement during the season. He headed back to his aunt's place, intending to do exactly that. He drank coffee and visited with his aunt and uncle, then pulled out his laptop.

But his renowned concentration and focus failed him utterly. Instead, Cassie's little house kept calling to him. Somehow, fish out of water that he was, he'd felt more at home there than any place he could remember.

"Aunt Rhetta, Uncle Buck, I have to go out for a while." They looked up from the double solitaire game they were playing on the kitchen table.

"You okay, son?" his uncle asked.

His aunt just studied him, then nodded in satisfaction, a small smile teasing the corners of her mouth. "You wouldn't be dropping by a certain little house, now would you?"

Aunt Rhetta wasn't related to his mother by blood, but she seemed to have the same scary ability to read his mind. "Whatever gave you that idea?"

Her eyes were concerned. "She broke your heart once, honey. You sure you want to let her back in?"

He glanced away. "I don't know. All I'm sure of is that Cassie needs help, but she'd never ask for it. She won't welcome me at the hospital, but I can't just sit around and do nothing. I saw some things at her house that need fixing, like a dripping faucet and a toilet that doesn't shut off completely. The stair rail is loose, and one of the back steps is warping. I still have the key, so I thought maybe, before she brings Bobby home, I could get a few of those things done."

"Need some help, son?" Uncle Buck asked.

"I wouldn't turn it down," Gib answered. "But it might be better if she's only mad at me and not you, too."

"Now where would be the fun in that?" His uncle's eyes twinkled. "Want to go, Rhetta?"

"I'd dearly love to," his aunt replied. "But a woman doesn't want another woman messing with her house. I'd better stay here."

"What about a man messing with her house?" Gib asked.

Aunt Rhetta shrugged. "Men can be excused. We don't expect them to be as smart."

Gib broke out laughing while his uncle rolled his eyes.

"Well, this dumb ol' country boy will miss you." Uncle Buck bent and kissed his wife.

Gib watched them with a curious ache in his chest. Those two had been married nearly forty years, had been through a lot of pain, yet the bond between them filled the room with warmth. Once he'd thought that would be him and Cassie.

He still had to find out why it wasn't.

CASSIE GOT HOME IN time to take a nap, but just to be safe, she put Bobby in bed with her, then conked out cold for two hours, not waking until the other children arrived. When she dragged herself from bed to face supervising homework and fixing dinner, plus doing the laundry she had to manage nearly every evening in addition to grading the papers she hadn't gotten to last night, she had a terrible struggle to fully awaken. When she filled the coffeepot with water, she noticed that the faucet was no longer dripping, but she didn't have time to ponder it.

Then she discovered that the toilet was shutting off every time and when she later went outside to put trash in the can, she realized the porch step had been fixed, along with the railing. A floorboard no longer squeaked, and the front door shut without slamming it.

Cassie knew immediately who'd worked all

these miracles—Gib had always been very gifted with his hands.

What she didn't know was what to do about it. How to feel.

I can't care about you again, Gib. Letting you go nearly killed me before.

Cassie poured a cup of coffee and stood staring out the kitchen window, trying to figure out how to hold her heart—and those of her children, who already thought Gib hung the moon—apart from a man whose basic nature was so good.

But whose lifestyle could never mesh with hers.

And who would never forgive her once he learned the truth.

She shook herself and went to the refrigerator. Thinking about supper was a big enough decision just then. She opened the door, mentally cataloging what would be left so that they would make it until payday—

And clapped one hand over her mouth to stifle her cry.

A roast, complete with potatoes and carrots and gravy, sat there, needing only to be reheated. Alongside it was a salad, already prepared, and an apple pie that looked to be homemade.

"What is it, Mom?" Molly crossed behind her and peered inside. "Oh. Wow. We haven't had a roast since—"

Since Tom died, Cassie mentally completed. *Oh,*

Gib, what are you doing to me? She couldn't possibly deny her children the benefits of a hearty meal, yet how did she deal with his generosity, knowing what she did?

When she heard the knock at the door and the shouts of glee, she didn't even have to look to know who'd arrived. Gib swept in like the force of nature he was, dispensing gifts yet again, these demonstrating that he'd paid attention to what the children were allowed to play with.

Her children literally glowed in his presence, and he seemed very happy to see them. He even took control of Bobby, holding the boy on his lap and managing to make Bobby feel an active part of things without moving around a lot or getting too excited.

And when he looked at her over their heads, his expression caused a lump to form in her throat and tears to spring to her eyes.

The boy she'd loved with all her heart had grown into a man to admire. A man to love.

But she couldn't. She had no right to.

Cassie turned away and went to warm up the bountiful meal Gib had provided, though she knew that each bite she took would be tainted by the bitter taste of lost chances.

CHAPTER FIVE

OVER THE NEXT FEW DAYS, Gib had no opportunity to have his discussion with Cassie, but somehow that didn't bother him too much. He was too busy with Cassie and her children to get impatient about a discussion that grew less and less important than spending time with her.

Not that he got much time, certainly none with Cassie alone. As a clueless kid, he'd never realized just what it took to mother a brood, especially as a single parent. Best he could tell, she slept four or five hours a night, max, and he worried about her. He tried to take up the slack when she'd let him; meanwhile, he found himself really enjoying the kids, each of them so different. It was a kick to bring them surprises, though after a dressing-down by Cassie, he quit choosing expensive toys, even though he could easily afford them.

Cassie couldn't, and it wasn't fair to raise their expectations when he wouldn't always be around, she pointed out. She was right, but the shop and the team seemed a distant universe at the moment.

Which should have worried the living daylights out of him—and did. His life wasn't here, and it couldn't be, as long as he was involved in racing.

But everyone from the team owner to the secretaries had been telling him he had to take time off or he would burn out, so that's what he was doing. Sort of.

Taking Molly to the speedway and giving her an insider's tour didn't count as working. Nor did letting Bobby watch a big version of the race car he slept with every night spin around the track. As for the session with Andre in a quarter midget on a local dirt track…that didn't count, either. He loved what he did for a living, but this…this was fun.

Only Lily turned up her nose at racing-related fun. She was crazy over horses, and a day spent at his uncle's place riding had her over the moon.

"You have to stop spoiling them," Cassie ordered one night, after all of them had finally—*finally*—gone to bed. It was Saturday, and she'd already graded papers while he entertained kids that afternoon, taking them skating at the ice rink that was part of the holiday festival.

Dinner was done, ditto the dishes and baths and bed, but Cassie was rearranging a kitchen cabinet. The woman could not sit still.

"Cass—" he began.

She peeked over her shoulder. "Are you leaving?"

Gib smiled. She looked about sixteen, still slim in her blue jeans and an old sweatshirt. "No," he replied and moved right up behind her.

Cassie froze. "Gib?" She started to turn, then gripped the counter instead.

And Gib did something he'd been dying to do for days. Carefully, ever so slowly, he drew aside the curls escaping from her topknot and placed his lips right at that spot that had once made her quake.

"Gib—" Her voice was strangled as she shivered. He smiled against her skin, kissed the side of her neck, then slid around to her throat.

Her head fell back, and a low sound emerged. Gib closed his arms around her waist and drew her back against him.

Cassie melted into him, and Gib took heart. He kissed his way behind her ear, around her cheek.

She whirled in his arms and pressed her mouth to his.

Sweet, ah, so sweet, he thought, even as his body heat climbed. She fit in his arms as perfectly as ever, as though the years between had never—

Cassie broke away. "No." She shook her head violently. "No, Gib, I can't." Her eyes were huge and wet and devastated.

"Why not?" But he knew. Cassie was not someone to have an affair with, not someone to be set on a shelf while his real life consumed him. She was a marrying kind of woman, one who would want his whole heart—and he had too many other responsibilities. He couldn't give her what she deserved.

Although he felt his heart tearing out of his chest, Gib forced himself to step back, to let her go. "You're right. It would never work." Watching her was killing him, though. Being this close and knowing that he couldn't have her, that he was already making a mess of the life she was struggling so hard to juggle—

He couldn't stand it. He, Gib Cameron, the guy who always had an answer, had none. Did he desert his team, give up everything he'd spent most of his life working for? Or did he ask her to become part of his life and settle for half the attention she deserved?

Maybe she'd been right to leave him the first time. Maybe she'd seen what he hadn't.

"I—" He shook his head. He saw no way out for them, so he seized upon the only thing that had made sense in his life: his work. "I have to go back to Charlotte for a few days. There's some PR that has to be done before the new season starts." That wasn't a lie, except in the timing. "I'll be back, though, for Christmas. You'll tell the kids?"

Her face was a study in emotions—sorrow, fury, relief, chagrin. "Don't come back, Gib. It will be too hard on them. I'll make your excuses. Just don't come back. We don't need you."

She hugged herself as she said it, and he knew it was a lie. Maybe she didn't need him, but she needed something. He would get out of here and gather his thoughts, away from the punch of her presence, the unbearable lure she couldn't help casting. He would figure out a way to help that would make up for some of what he couldn't give her.

"Cass—" *I'm sorry,* he started to say, but she wouldn't let him.

Instead, she turned her back and pulled out a stack of bowls from the cabinet, set them beside the plates. "Just go, Gib. Please." The line of her slender shoulders was so vulnerable, his resolve nearly broke.

He would love her until the day he died.

And if he truly loved her, he had to prove it.

He had to let her go.

CHAPTER SIX

"GIB?"

He missed the kids, missed his aunt and uncle.

Missed Cassie. How on earth had it come to this?

"Gib, where are you?" Ex-model Alexandra Craig waved one exquisitely manicured hand in front of his face.

"What?"

She frowned. "Are you all right? You haven't been yourself all night. You're getting funny looks from the sponsors. This is a Christmas party, after all. It's supposed to be a happy time."

Gib jerked his thoughts back to the present, the glittering ballroom. The Gannon Motorsports party was a premiere event, and everyone here, himself included, was decked out accordingly. "Sorry, just thinking. I'm fine."

One perfect eyebrow arched, and she smiled, reaching up to straighten his tie. "Mmm-hmm. Just dandy. That's why you've been scowling at the floor for the last hour."

Gib grinned. "Busted." She deserved better. They'd dated on and off for several months, and she'd put up with his crazy schedule when few women would. She was a class act, and he was acting like a jerk, mooning over the impossible.

Suddenly, he chuckled at the thought of how most people would compare the gorgeous blonde to a tiny house and a small brunette knee-deep in children.

"What?" Alex smiled back, and at the moment, a camera flashed, something he seldom noticed anymore.

"Nothing. I just—"

"Gib," she interrupted. "Something's wrong, and I can smell woman troubles all over it." She touched his face, and another flash erupted. Her smile was bittersweet. "Who is she? You've never once worried over me like that."

"I'm sorry."

"Don't be. I'm a big girl. You're the marrying type, Gib Cameron, and I always knew that."

"I am not," he protested.

"You are, and you always were. I knew this day would come. I just wanted to have the fun however long it lasted." She shrugged. "It's my loss that I'm not a white-picket-fence kind of girl. So—" She led him over to a table, perched on a chair and crossed one long, elegant leg over the other. "Sit down and tell Alexandra all about it."

Gib frowned. Shook his head. Sighed. "It doesn't matter. There's no way it can work."

Both eyebrows rose. "This, from the championship crew chief? Honey, now you've got me worried." She leaned forward. "Spill it, big boy."

Gib sank against his chair. "Her name is Cassie."

"WHERE'S MAN?" BOBBY asked for the thousandth time. "Gib." He held up his cherished race car.

"That's very good, sweetheart," Cassie said. "You remembered his name." She wasn't going to battle over a three-year-old calling him Mr. Cameron. She had no energy for battles these days, not when her nights were filled with memories of his touch, his smile, and her waking hours were spent trying to forget him.

"Mommy, I want to wear my pink shirt to school tomorrow," said Lily.

"You've worn it every day this week," chided Andre.

"I love it," she responded. "I love Gib."

"He doesn't love us," Andre responded. "He left."

"He does so!" Lily's eyes filled with tears. "Don't you say that! You're a big jerk!"

"Lily, you apologize to Andre this minute," Cassie ordered. Then she stared down Andre. "And you stop tormenting your sister."

"But—" Andre's expression was stricken. Lily

raced out of the room crying. Bobby clutched at Cassie for reassurance.

Cassie had the urge to cry herself.

Just then, Molly peered from her room, where she'd closeted herself after school daily since Gib left. She didn't have to say a word for Cassie to know that she might be older than the others, but she didn't understand Gib's sudden absence any better. Her hero had dumped them all, as far as Molly was concerned.

The situation wasn't Gib's fault, not really. She was the one who'd sent him away, however sensible a solution it was, and she owed Molly a better explanation than the one she'd given.

"Would you help me get them to bed, sweetheart?" Cassie asked.

Molly shrugged. "Sure." Not a single argument from her most strong-willed child. Cassie must look worse than she realized.

After what felt like hours, the younger three were bathed and in bed, and Cassie was waiting for Molly to finish her shower, then they would talk. As she waited, Cassie was too nervous to tackle the homework that needed grading, so she grabbed the newspaper she seldom had time to do more than skim. She dodged the sports section, even though there wouldn't be much on NASCAR this time of year, and rejected any thought of the front section, since she'd had all the bad news she could handle. She went for the lifestyle section, hoping for a nice bit of fluff. The front page didn't grab her, so she flipped the section open.

And her heart fell to her feet.

If she'd needed confirmation that she'd made the right decision about Gib, here it was. Gib in a suit, looking devastatingly handsome at some big function, a gorgeous, buxom blonde caressing his cheek.

And Gib gazing into the woman's eyes. Smiling.

Cassie snapped the section shut while her heart thudded and her stomach clenched with misery. *It doesn't matter,* she told herself. *He was never for me.* She blinked furiously to dispel the sting of tears.

Then she just had to look once again.

"Mom? Are you all right?"

Cassie folded the paper with a snap and buried that section beneath the others so Molly wouldn't see. "I'm fine, honey. Just fine."

"You miss him, too, don't you?"

Cassie considered asking who, but she wasn't in the habit of lying to her daughter.

Except, of course, about one very basic issue.

"A little." At Molly's skeptical glance, Cassie amended, "Okay, more than a little, but it doesn't matter, Molly. Gib has a very different life, one in which we don't fit. He travels all the time, and he's chosen not to have a family, which is his right." Talking forcefully to convince her daughter as much as herself, she continued. "He and I were close when we were young, but we were just kids. People grow apart." She locked eyes with her daughter. "He'll always be special to me, but our worlds don't mesh, and that's okay. But never doubt that he cares about you, about all of you. He was sorry to have to leave."

"I don't understand why he couldn't stay for Christmas. He likes it here, and Mom, he's lonely, I can tell." Molly's eyes glistened. "I don't like to think about him being alone at Christmas."

Cassie could too readily remember the longing she'd seen when he was buried in children. The happiness that shone from his face when he was answering questions or horsing around or simply sitting on the floor watching them play.

She should have remembered that when she told him not to come back. But how could she risk her children getting any closer to him? The heartbreak would only worsen.

"He's a grown man, honey, and he has a whole life in Charlotte. I'm sure he has lots of friends. He'll be fine." The reassurances rang hollow in her ears.

Molly's jaw got that stubborn jut that was pure Gib Cameron, and the sight of it made Cassie want to laugh and cry both. "I think you're wrong, Mom. We should call him. Invite him to spend Christmas with us."

"He has his aunt and uncle, sweetheart."

"They could come, too." Once Molly got an idea in her head, she was immovable.

Cassie tried a feint. "I don't know how to reach him, and anyway, Molly, drop it. He's gone, and that's that." The crushed look on Molly's face made Cassie want to take it all back, but she didn't dare. Prolonging her daughter's hopes would only hurt her more. "I'm sorry, sweetie. Sometimes life just isn't fair. Now, you need to get to bed. Next-to-last day of school tomorrow, and we've got Lily's program tomorrow night. Gonna be a long day, so get some sleep, you hear?"

Molly's hug was halfhearted, but Cassie understood and didn't press.

After all, she had less than half a heart left, herself.

CHAPTER SEVEN

"YO, GIB! PHONE," CALLED his car chief, Randy Holcomb. This close to Christmas, much of the staff was taking time off, but Randy was nearly as obsessed with the team as Gib himself, plus he had visions of someday replacing Gib.

Not yet, buddy, Gib thought, but aloud, he only said, "Who is it?"

"Some girl named Molly."

Gib stood up so fast his chair nearly toppled. He grabbed the phone. "Molly? Is everything all right?"

"We need you to come home, Gib."

Home. The word was sweet as honey, but Marysville couldn't be his home. His home was here. Had to be. "What's wrong? Is it Bobby?"

"Everyone's fine, except—"

His heart hit the ground with a dull thud. "Except who? Is your mom okay? Is it you? What about Lily and Andre?"

"Nobody's sick, it's just that—" Her voice quivered

a little. “Nothing’s happy since you left. Why did you go?” Her tone was more hurt child than preteen.

“Oh, Mol.” He sighed. How to explain? “It’s a long story.”

“Could you come back, just for Christmas? You don’t work on a holiday, do you?”

Actually, he worked most every day, but at the moment, he couldn’t quite remember why as longing swamped him, thinking about spending Christmas with Cassie’s little family. Having even one more hour with Cassie herself. “Molly, it’s just that—” He exhaled in frustration. He couldn’t tell her that Cassie had sent him away. That was Cassie’s secret to reveal.

“We love you, Gib. Mom does, too.”

Gib’s heart thumped like it might leap from his chest. “She said that?”

“Not exactly,” Molly admitted. “But I can tell. She’s sad, Gib, in a way I’ve never seen her. We all are. We miss you.”

Gib closed his eyes against the yearning. “Honey, I wish I could, but—”

“Lily’s program is tonight. You could still get here.”

Lily had recited her lines to Gib a hundred times, so proud to have a speaking part in the holiday show. Molly wasn’t pulling any punches in her effort to convince him, and Gib was filled with reluctant admiration. She was some kid.

And she was right. He could get there easily in his plane. Cassie couldn't control who attended the show, and he would remain out of sight, anyway, but he'd see Lily play her part, and later he could write her and tell her what a great job she did.

He longed to do so much more—sit with the family, cheer Lily loudly, but, well…just glimpsing them all would be better than nothing. *Sure thing, Gib. It's gonna break your heart and you know it.*

But so be it. For the only time he could remember, there was somewhere he wanted to be more than the shop.

"You're going to make a good team owner, Mol. I dare anyone to try to stop you, with those persuasive skills."

"You'll come?" The thrill in her voice warmed him to his toes.

"I'll be there," he promised. "But don't say anything to your mom."

"Mum's the word," Molly replied. "Thank goodness the phone bill won't show up until next month. I'm not supposed to make long-distance calls."

Gib grinned. "I'll cover this one, don't you worry."

"Cool! Bye, Gib. See you tonight!" The sunny girl was back.

"Bye, Molly." Gib hung up, sporting his first smile in days.

THE EXCITEMENT IN HER children was palpable. Cassie could barely stop them squirming, waiting for Lily to appear. Then there was Molly, who kept glancing toward the back, as though she expected someone.

Cassie wished Gib would surprise them by showing up, too, but it wasn't going to happen. She would have to buck up and explain to Molly that she was at fault for Gib leaving and never coming back.

If only he hadn't kissed her. Being with him had been hard enough, the constant reminders of the boy she'd loved mingled with a man she was coming to admire more every day. Discovering that the heat and hunger were more alive than ever had thrilled her, shocked her—then slapped her with a dose of cold reality. She was a hairsbreadth from falling for him, and the blow when he'd have to end it would be more than she could bear. She couldn't risk it.

Suddenly Bobby squealed from her lap, "Man!"

Cassie's heart stuttered. *No.* It couldn't be. Terrified, she nearly didn't turn to look in the direction Bobby was pointing.

But she couldn't help herself, and as she did, she caught Molly's expression, furtive and glowing at the same time. "What have you done?" she asked her daughter.

Molly's defiant jaw was once again in evidence, but Cassie spared no time to argue because she'd just caught sight of Gib, ducking behind a pillar in the back. "Oh, Molly…" Yet, as she groaned, her heart leaped.

"Are you mad, Mom?" Molly hovered between headstrong teen and little girl. "He needs us, and we need him."

Cassie closed her eyes. *But we can't afford to.* Yet the plea in her daughter's eyes, the delight on Bobby's face—

Then Andre caught a glimpse of Gib and took off like a rocket.

"Andre!" Cassie rose, but Andre had scooted down the row and slithered so quickly through the crowd taking their seats that she was helpless to stop him. All she could do was try to keep her eyes on him and pray Gib was, too. "Go ahead, Molly. But don't lose your brother."

Molly's eyes lit. "Yes!" She popped from her chair and charged after Andre.

"Gib," Bobby crowed, his wide grin everything that Cassie wanted to let herself feel as she watched Gib lift Andre into his arms and hug Molly to his side, both kids chattering a mile a minute.

She loved him, she might as well admit it. She would never get him out of her heart, but there was so much separating them.

Including a secret that might part them for good.

She was jolted from her thoughts as Bobby literally launched himself from her lap. Gib managed to catch him without dropping Andre. "Cassie, I—" His face was troubled.

She shook her head. "I'm pretty sure I can guess who got you here." She cast a glance at Molly, who blushed but kept her head high.

Then the lights dimmed, and there was no time to talk. Somehow Molly arranged it so that Gib sat beside Cassie, holding Andre in his lap, while Molly cuddled Bobby.

Everything in Cassie struggled to focus on Lily's play.

Instead of the strong, sexy, beloved man beside her.

THE EVENING WAS CHAOS. Lily had managed every line perfectly, and Gib had cheered louder than anyone in the family. He'd cajoled Cassie into letting him take them all for ice cream to celebrate after, then suffered with her through the after-effects of the sugar rush as they wrestled three squirmy, beyond-exhausted children to bed.

He couldn't believe how much he loved it. How much he'd missed them all.

Now Molly was taking herself off to bed after kissing his cheek and assuring her mother that she didn't need tucking in because she was far too old for that. Cassie seemed both sad and relieved.

They were alone, at last, and he would have to face the music.

"I know I didn't stay away—" he began.

"I saw the picture," she said at the same moment.

"What?" they said in unison.

"You first," Gib offered. "What picture?"

Color stained Cassie's cheeks. "Your gorgeous blond girlfriend." She looked anywhere but at him.

"What girlfriend?" Though he thought he knew.

"Hello? Slinky red dress? Big boobs?"

"Oh. That's just Alex."

Her eyebrows rose. "Just Alex? She's a model, Gib. No man calls her *just Alex* unless he's got too many other women on the string to care."

"We've dated." He shrugged. "That's all. She's a friend." He leaned forward, trying to see her averted face. "And I don't have a string of other women."

"It doesn't matter. That photo only highlights how different our lives are. How little we have in common. Which is good," she said brightly. "Since you'll disappear again soon." She rose and walked to the kitchen.

He followed, grabbed her shoulders and turned her to face him. "I'm not the one who disappeared, Cassie. You knew where I was, and you understood why. You participated in the decision. You promised you'd join me in Charlotte, and I worked like hell to create a life for us there—but you never showed.

You vanished, then turned up later with a husband. And all you could say was that you wanted something different. That we were too different." All the old hurts and bewilderment resurfaced. He loomed over her. "I loved you with everything in me, and you walked out, Cassie. I want to know why."

Cassie stared up at him, not afraid, not angry, not fighting back. Instead, her blue eyes were swimming with unshed tears, and she looked devastated. She pressed one hand to trembling lips as the tears spilled over. "Gib—" Her voice caught, and she struggled to master her feelings. "Let's sit down."

Her tone was starting to frighten him. "No, tell me right here. Right now."

She was as pale as water, and her whole frame quivered. He grasped her arms, afraid for her.

"No." She wrenched away. "I can't. You won't want to comfort me when you know."

He'd always had a second sense that told him when a driver was in trouble, when a race was going bad, but never in his life had he felt a dread like this. "Tell me, Cassie." His voice came out harsher than he'd intended. "Please," he amended.

Her back was to him, and he thought he'd never seen her so vulnerable. "You can't be afraid of me." The very thought horrified him. "Cassie, I would never—"

She held up a hand, then slowly turned. "No, but you'd have every right—" Her voice broke.

"Honey, you're scaring me. Maybe we should wait." What on earth could be causing her such distress?

"No." She shook her head violently. "We've waited too long. I've waited too long." She lifted her head and faced him like a prisoner staring down the firing squad. "I never meant to hurt you, Gib, you have to know that. I did it for you."

"Did what?" The sick feeling spread.

"Molly."

"Molly?" he echoed dully. "What?"

"She's your daughter, Gib. I got pregnant from that one night, and I couldn't tell you. If you'd known, you would have come back here and given up your dream, and I knew what that dream meant to you. I left town to have the baby, and my parents wanted me to give her up, but I couldn't." Tears flooded again. "I'd lost you. I couldn't lose our child, too."

Most of her words were a dull gong, a racing river drowning out his ability to absorb more than *Molly* and *daughter,* at first. Then they were quickly swept away by fury at the realization of all he'd lost. "Daughter?" That bright, beautiful child with all the moxie to defy her mother and bring him back? She was his? "I have to—" He wanted to see Molly, to hold her, to somehow fill the sudden void of years of missing a baby, a toddler, a little girl looking up to him with that smile he only now realized was his own.

He rushed to the door, only to have Cassie grab his arm. “No, you can’t. Gib, please. She doesn’t know.”

He turned back to her, the woman who’d replaced the girl he’d once loved. Had he ever truly known her, if she’d been capable of this deceit? The Cassie he’d loved would never have done this to him, never have slid this knife between his ribs. “Haven’t you robbed me of enough time already?” He could see the slap of his words, and he knew that if he stayed, he’d say things he’d regret, terrible, hurtful things. Fragments of what she’d said echoed. *I couldn’t ask that of you. I couldn’t give up your child.*

Gib was known in the racing world for his cool head, for never getting rattled, but he was as rattled now as he could remember being only once in his life—the day he’d gotten a short, soul-killing phone call from the woman in front of him, telling him that everything between them had amounted to nothing.

He had to get out of there now. “I can’t talk about this. I have to go.” He strode to the front door, and Cassie followed him.

“I don’t expect you to forgive me, Gib.” Her voice was so small, so dead. “But please don’t punish the kids. Is it possible you could—” He heard her struggle to continue. “Would you please just come by a time or two until Christmas is over?”

Gib exerted every last ounce of control he'd ever possessed to respond without lashing out at her. "I don't know if I can ever forgive you for what you've taken from me." He was breathing as hard as if he'd run a marathon. "You have to let me think."

She nodded but didn't speak.

He opened the screen and paused. "We're not done yet, Cassie."

"Please, Gib, promise me you won't tell Molly. Not yet." She straightened and lifted her downcast head. "We should tell her together."

He closed his eyes, then gave her a curt nod.

And left. His life in ruins.

CHAPTER EIGHT

CASSIE SAT ON THE SOFA all night, unable to sleep, going over and over in her mind the decisions she'd made, ticking off on her fingers all the times she could have turned from this path, could have chosen differently. The occasions on which Gib had missed important parts of Molly's life he would never get back.

Finally, about three in the morning, dry-eyed and hollow, she sat on the floor with her boxes of photos and began assembling a pale substitute that was all she had to offer him. As she went through box after box, the ache in her heart threatened to consume her whole body. Each picture that usually made her smile was accompanied with a sharp dart of pain that Gib would only know Molly's history secondhand. That another man had done all that he would have so loved doing for his little girl.

Gib might have had grand ambitions, and her decision might have paved the way for him to accomplish them, but she had always known that Gib loved children, that he'd wanted a family with her. Where he was now, what he was feeling, all of that tortured her, even as she imagined it torturing him.

He had every right to be angry. She'd believed she was doing the best thing for him, and a little piece of her was angry, as well, that he wasn't grateful.

But she was old enough, experienced enough with human nature now to understand that she should have given him a chance to make his own decision. She was almost positive that she'd been right, that he would have forsaken his NASCAR dreams, but the extraordinary successes he'd crafted showed that Gib didn't give up on anything easily. That he tackled the impossible and somehow managed to make it work.

But could he have done that so many years ago?

She didn't see how a family could thrive under the pressures of a NASCAR season, year after year, but there were racing families that continued through generations, so obviously they'd figured out how.

Oh, Gib. I am so sorry. She mourned for him, for Molly and for herself. Tom had been a good man, but what would it have been like to experience the last thirteen years with the one love of her life?

Her heart was hollow, and it was Christmastime. Her children deserved better, and somehow she had to summon the strength to make the season one they would remember with joy, not the same ache that crowded her chest.

Cassie clutched a stack of photos to her chest and prayed for the strength to conquer the despair of a woman who has lost something precious.

Knowing she had no one but herself to blame.

GIB COULDN'T SLEEP, AGAIN, and dawn found him sitting in his aunt's dark kitchen, staring at nothing. Going over and over in his mind, like the drip of acid eating into stone, all that had been stolen from him. Bitterness carved gouges in his heart. She had no right. She should never have—

Light flared, and he jolted. Blinked like an owl.

"Gib, honey, what's wrong?" Aunt Rhetta asked. "What are you doing up?" She got a better look. "What's happened? Is it Cassie? Her children? Somebody hurt or—" His aunt's fingers crept to her throat. Ever since Jack died, she was quick to assume the worst.

"No," he reassured her. "Well, yes, but—" He shook his head. "Never mind."

Her hand came to rest on his shoulder, and he suddenly longed to lean into her embrace and give in to the sorrow that was turning his world dark as he thought of all he had missed of his daughter's life.

"Gib, talk to me. I can see you're hurting."

Gib's jaw worked, and it was a minute before he could speak. "Molly's mine," he managed.

"What?" His aunt drew back. Then she exhaled

sharply. "Oh, my." Then, of all things, she chuckled. "How on earth did I not see it? She has your mouth. Your hair."

Gib rose so fast his chair squeaked on the linoleum. "How can you smile?" Suddenly, pure rage shattered the shell of misery that had entombed him. He slammed his fist on the table. "Cassie lied to me. She betrayed me. I had a child. A bright, beautiful little girl whose first steps were into another man's arms. Whose first words called someone else daddy. I didn't get to teach her to ride a bike or how to swim or—" All the hours he'd been locked in silence vanished, and he could not sit still one more second. He began to pace.

Aunt Rhetta let him rage, even when he woke up Uncle Buck. Both of them stood by as he slammed a fist into his palm, when he cursed Cassie for screwing up his life, robbing him of his child, wrecking his dreams. Gib had not lost his temper like this in years. Emotion was the enemy when you were the leader of a championship-caliber team, and he was careful to keep a tight rein on his.

Finally, he ran out of steam. Abruptly he was so exhausted he could barely stand. "Here," his aunt said, pulling out a chair and pouring a cup of coffee for him. "What you really need is sleep, but first I'm giving you a piece of my mind, and I want you wide awake to hear it."

Gib recoiled. "What? Haven't you been listening to a word I've said? Cassie betrayed me. She ruined my life."

His aunt and uncle sat, flanking him, each with a cup of coffee, as well.

"She was seventeen, Gib," Aunt Rhetta pointed out. "Not all that much older than Molly is now. Think about Molly trying to make that kind of decision alone."

"Cassie didn't have to make it alone!"

"You're right, she didn't. But do you remember how you were back then? Oh, sure, you loved Cassie the way a boy loves a girl, but every soul in this town knew that racing had a grip on you that nothing could displace. You made your dreams clear to every last one of us from the time you were seven, and you never once lost sight of them. You think Cassie didn't know it, too? Didn't wonder, maybe, somewhere deep inside, if you didn't want it just a little bit more than her?"

"I did not," he countered hotly. "She was my world."

"And you were hers. Loving you the way she did and knowing what your dreams meant to you, understanding that you were the kind of boy who would have come back home and done right by her whether you wanted to or not, can you imagine how hard that decision must have been for her?" When he started to protest, she held up a hand. “Cassie’s parents were divorced. They got married when her mama got pregnant. Don’t you imagine her worst fear was that you would do the right thing by her, and your relationship would suffer because both of you had been denied your dreams?”

Gib fell silent.

“Can you honestly say you would be where you are now in your career if Cassie had told you back then?”

“That wasn’t her only chance. Molly’s twelve years old!” he roared. “I’ve missed everything important in her life!”

“The past is over, son.” His uncle finally spoke. “What matters is what you do from here. You’re still Molly’s dad, and she needs you.”

“She doesn’t even know.” Gib looked up, his jaw hardening. “That has to change. Right away. Molly has to be part of my life.”

“Exactly how do you plan to manage that?” his aunt asked. “You’re on the road from February through November.”

Gib raked his fingers through his hair, then scrubbed at his face. He’d never been so exhausted. “I don’t know.”

“What will you do about Cassie?”

His shoulders sank. “I don’t know that, either.”

“Can you at least understand that she meant no

harm? That she was trying to save your dreams—at the expense of her own, I might add?"

"She shouldn't—" Gib subsided. Hadn't he learned to win by putting defeats aside and focusing on the future, not the past?

And didn't he indeed believe, now that the boil had been lanced, in the goodness of Cassie's heart?

I'd lost you. I couldn't lose our child, too. The anguish on her face rose before him. Finally, he was able to see beyond his own hurt, to remember that sweet young girl whose own life had been anything but sunny, yet who had brought golden light into his. To picture how alone she must have felt. To hear now what he hadn't caught in that long-ago, fateful phone call: the tremble in her voice as she fought to convince him that she hadn't really loved him.

Gib slumped in his chair. The woman he'd rediscovered had the heart of a lion, and she'd possessed that at seventeen, too. He was humbled by her sacrifice, however much it had cost him, as well. Maybe it was only now, when he was so burned-out from years of being driven, that he could see the price he'd paid to earn fame and fortune.

He had money, yes, and a big house and a career many envied.

But he was alone. He always would be, if he didn't make some changes. Rearrange his priorities.

He had some thinking to do, but not when he was

this tired. He rose wearily, kissed his aunt's cheek and squeezed his uncle's shoulder. "Thank you both. I—" He shook his head. "I'm sorry I haven't been back to see you. Sorry I forgot how important family is."

His aunt stood and cupped his cheek, smiling softly. "You were a good boy, Gib, and you're a better man. You'll do the right thing."

"If I can figure out what that is," he said.

"You go on to sleep, now. Let your mind sort it out while you rest up. Things will seem clearer then."

"I hope you're right." Gib hugged her, then walked over and hugged his uncle. "I love you both."

Their eyes were glistening as he trudged out of the room.

GIB ONLY SLEPT FOUR hours, but when he awoke, he knew exactly what he wanted: all of it—the family, the career and, most of all, Cassie.

Wanting too little had never been his problem, he thought wryly as he showered and dressed. He didn't have all the answers to the puzzle pieces that didn't seem to fit together.

He did, though, have an inkling. First on his agenda was a call to his team owner, Rich Gannon.

Then an extended shopping trip.

CHAPTER NINE

THE PHONE RANG, BUT Cassie was deep into making sugar cookies with the kids, and Molly was closer. "I'll get it!"

The phone was becoming Molly's boon companion, and Cassie knew that her daughter's fondest wish was for a cell phone of her own. One more cxpense Cassie had no idea how she'd manage.

Molly's whole face glowed. She glanced at her mother, then away quickly, whispering.

Cassie frowned, but just then, Andre decided to get a little slaphappy with the vanilla he was measuring, so her attention fractured. "Here, sweetie. Vanilla is great, but too much will spoil the flavor."

Molly hung up and returned to her part of the task, keeping Bobby too busy to stick his fingers into the bowl.

"Who was that?" Cassie asked.

Molly shrugged. "Just a friend."

This secretiveness was new. And unwelcome. Still, this was the most fun any of them had had since Gib thundered out, and Cassie was loath to risk upsetting it. She and Molly could speak later, when the little ones were in bed.

Just then, the doorbell rang. "I'll get it!" Lily cried.

"No, I'd better," said Molly.

Lily's bottom lip stuck out.

"On second thought, you come with me," Molly offered. When she passed by Cassie, the glow was back, but handling Bobby and Andre was all Cassie could manage just then.

"Gib!" Lily squealed.

Andre leaped off his stool and Bobby launched himself from the counter. Cassie barely caught him in time, and he wriggled like an eel in her grasp. In self-defense, she released him to follow the others.

For herself, well, the cookies still needed attention. She rationalized that staying in the kitchen was her only option, even though she was perfectly aware that she was dodging the moment when she'd have to face the man she'd wronged so grievously.

The high, excited voices of her children contrasted with the deep, calming tones of the man who had become too important to all of them. Yet again, Cassie worried over how they would manage when he inevitably left.

Then she heard the front door open, followed by the sudden silence as her children's voices moved outdoors. She turned to see what was going on.

Gib stood in the door frame, big and gorgeous and beloved.

"They've gone outside to play for a bit," he said. "So we can talk."

Cassie's breath caught. She grabbed for a dish towel and wiped her hands. "I'm, uh, making cookies."

"Smells great," he said, and began to walk toward her. She couldn't read his expression, though his movements were steady and graceful. Unhurried yet intent.

"Gib, I'm sorry," she blurted. "I was wrong, I see that now. I just didn't know what to do, and I couldn't bear for you to give up—"

He held up one hand just as the other one clasped her waist and pulled her close. "I'm sorry, too," he said.

And kissed her. Kissed her so passionately, yet tinged with sorrow and apology and something that felt like hope.

"Gib?"

"Just let me hold you for a second, all right?" He folded her into his embrace, and she nestled against his broad chest, her head sinking into that spot right by his shoulder where she'd always fit so perfectly.

Her eyes closed, and she wrapped her arms around him, too. For a very long moment they simply stood together, swaying slightly, and Cassie knew, for the first time in thirteen years, what it felt like to be safe and cherished.

Then Gib began to talk, but she didn't move her head from its refuge. She listened to his voice rumble in his chest and slowly registered his words.

"You gave me my dream, Cassie, and I don't know how to thank you for that."

Of all the things she'd expected him to say, this was not one. Tears prickled as she heard the words she'd longed to hear all those years ago, the rationale for her whole life to this point.

"I am sick at heart about Molly—"

She tensed, but he ran one hand up her back, soothing her.

"—but I understand why you did it. And I'm more sick that I accepted what you said so easily and didn't fight you on it. How stupid could I be not to suspect that there was more behind the sudden change?"

She lifted her face then. "I didn't give you much chance. And you have no idea how many times I practiced that speech."

He cupped her cheek and kissed her lightly. "That's another thing that kills me, thinking about how alone you must have felt. I should have been with you, Cass. I should have gone through all that with you." His face was a study in conflict. "Was he…was Tom kind to you?" His throat worked. "Did you…did you love him? Did he love you the way you deserved?" His eyes were pure misery.

"He was a good man, Gib. The only condition he put on raising Molly was that she believe she was his own. That's why I could never tell you." She ducked her head. "He loved me. It's my own shame that I could never love him as much. I cared for him, but I—he wasn't you."

Gib squeezed her hard, until she could barely breathe, but she didn't protest. How many times had she craved exactly this, Gib here, wanting her as desperately as she wanted him?

"I can't stand to think of him with you, lying in your bed, having the right to touch you, to hold you when you cried, to—" His voice cracked. "To raise my daughter and be there for her every day." A shudder ran through him. "But at the same time, I owe him. I don't know how to feel about that."

"I'm so sorry, Gib." Her shoulders curved inward with her shame.

"No." He shook her gently. "Don't you apologize again. You were just a girl, and you did it out of love. I am an ungrateful jerk that my first reaction was anger. You don't deserve it. You deserve so much more, and I want to give it to you."

She froze. "What are you saying?"

He glanced toward the living room where four sets of eyes were plastered to the window. "Those little monkeys." He grinned as he turned back to her. "They're waiting."

"For what?"

He knelt in front of her. "For this."

Out of his pocket, he drew a small velvet box, and Cassie's heart stuttered. "Gib?"

"We've lost a lot of years, Cassie, and I don't want to lose one day more." He opened the box, and a lovely round diamond in an old-fashioned setting, all curlicues and tiny rosettes with smaller diamonds in them, sparkled out at her.

"Oh, Gib." She put her hand to her throat. How well he knew her, even after all this time. "It's beautiful."

A sound broke into her concentration, a chant of "Go Mom, go Mom, go Mom" coming from the front porch. She glanced over to see Molly holding Bobby up, and the other two children jumping up and down.

Gib laughed, but quickly sobered. "Will you marry me, Cassie? Will you let me love your family and make them mine?"

"But—Molly?"

"We'll tell her together. I don't think she'll mind that she's mine, do you?" He rose to his feet, but she still didn't make a move toward the ring.

"She'll be in heaven. But what about your job?"

"My job is not more important than you. Not even close."

"You can't give it up, Gib." Her mind was racing.

"I don't want to be away from my family so much of the year. I've talked to my team owner, and he's willing to kick me upstairs. Make me competition director, so I don't have to travel as much."

"Is that what you want? I couldn't bear being the cause of you giving up your dream now any more than I could then."

"You are my dream, Cassie. You always were. I love racing, and I'll be honest that walking away would once have been unthinkable—but now there's you." He nodded toward the window, where anxious faces greeted them. "You and my new crew." He grinned. "So are you going to put us all out of our misery?" He took the ring from the box and held it out.

She could barely speak. "I have an idea."

"If it's not saying yes, I don't want to hear it." His eyes gave away a vulnerability that surprised her. "Don't you want to marry me, sweetheart?"

"Too much," she answered.

"Then say yes."

Oh, how she wanted to. How she longed to cast away all caution about where they'd live and what he should do and all the realities that got in the way of romance.

"On one condition."

He looked wary. "Which is?"

"Don't leave your job yet. Let us try an experiment."

"What kind of experiment?"

"Travel can be very educational, and you forget that I'm a teacher. Let us come with you, and I'll homeschool the kids. They can learn so much in a year traveling all over America, and Molly would be in heaven, being that close to racing."

"You would do that?" He seemed stunned.

"There's very little I wouldn't do for you, Gib."

"You've already proved that, but it's my turn to make the sacrifices."

"I think you've already done that, as well. You've been alone for a long time."

"I have missed you more than you can imagine." His eyes darkened. "All I know is whatever it takes for us to be together, that's what I'm going to do."

"Oh, Gib." She cast a glance at the window, where uncertainty shadowed her children's faces. "They know what you're proposing?"

He smiled. "They're all for it." He sobered. "I love them already, Cassie, all of them, not just Molly. And not only because they're yours." He held up the ring. "Will you give me the best present ever? Will you be mine and give me a family for Christmas?"

Tears rolled down her cheeks as she nodded. "I love you, Gib." She held out her hand.

He slipped the ring on it. "I love you, too."

She launched herself into his arms, and he wrapped her close, twirling her and laughing, then kissing her as she'd never been kissed.

The front door burst open, and they were quickly surrounded by cheering children soon climbing all over Gib and talking a mile a minute.

Cassie nestled into his side and glanced up to see the love she'd waited a lifetime for. The sheer joy on Molly's face told her their news would be a shock, but a welcome one, indeed.

Gib held up a hand to quiet the mob. They obeyed instantly, but not one of them stopped touching him. His gaze scanned the group, and he smiled.

"I can't wait to take you to our new home," he said.

"And show us your trophies?" Molly asked.

"Sure thing," he promised. His eyes locked on Cassie's. "But I'll tell you right now that not a single one of them will ever compare to this. Today," he said, bending to kiss Cassie as his new family cheered. "I've won the only prize that really matters."